Sailing the
Apocalypse

ALSO BY SCOTT B. WILLIAMS

Fiction
The Pulse
Refuge
The Darkness After

Nonfiction
On Island Time
Paddling the Pascagoula
Exploring Coastal Mississippi
Bug Out
Bug Out Vehicles and Shelters
Getting Out Alive:
The Prepper's Workbook

ISBN-13: 978-1505997798
Cover photograph: Wharram Tiki 46 at anchor © Scott B. Williams
Cover and interior design: Scott B. Williams
Illustration: catamaran under sail © Sam H. Barker,
shbarker.cgd@gmail.com
Editors: Betsy Barker, Jasmine Calvert
Proofreader: Michelle Cleveland

Sailing the
Apocalypse

a misadventure at sea

Scott B. Williams

For James and Hanneke,

One

TERRY BAILEY WAS BY far the most interesting man my mom ever married, although I couldn't be sure that my own dad was not in some way interesting because I only met him once and knew practically nothing about him. Of course, I didn't know Janie's dad either, since she's almost five years older than I am and he was long gone before I came along. Mom always said he was her first major mistake and that Janie was the *only* good thing that came of that relationship. Even after that, Mom had a run of bad luck when it came to picking husbands, but somehow I knew that she would stay with Terry Bailey. They had already been together almost two years, and that was a lot longer than her marriage to Janie's father and my dad combined.

Before Terry came into her life and swept us all up in his crazy dream, we briefly had a step-dad named Wayne

SAILING THE APOCALYPSE

Delaney, who we mutually concluded was a selfish bastard who would have much preferred to have just Mom without either of us kids attached as part of the package. He positively *hated* kids, but even so, he was so good-looking, according to Mom anyway, that he lasted almost a year before she found out he was still sneaking over to see his ex-wife on the side. Without a word, she packed us all up one morning when he was away at work to move us five hundred miles from Richmond, Indiana to our grandma's house smack in the middle of nowhere in north Mississippi. In the tiny town of Calloway City, with a population of only eight hundred people, and absolutely *nothing* fun to do, Janie and I were certain our lives were over. We just knew that death by boredom would release us from our misery in a matter of weeks.

That was a bit over two years ago, when I was just ten. It was only about a month after we got here that my mom met Terry Bailey, Janie's eighth-grade history teacher, and from that day forward, we didn't have time to be bored. Terry turned our lives upside down; introducing us to ideas we had never given any thought to. He challenged everything I had learned about the world prior to meeting him, and at first I hated him because he made Mom get rid of our TV. Terry *despised* television.

"Look around you, Robbie! They're like a bunch of zombies!" he said. "Everyone you see is tuned into the tube while they sit around getting fat like a herd of cows ready to be slaughtered. That TV is the cowboy, rounding them up and moving them out, keeping them in line and telling them what to do, how to do it, what to want, what to wear, how to act, and what to say. People don't think for themselves anymore! The first thing you've gotta do if you want to really *live*, is blow up that idiot box and go outside and face reality!"

Mom didn't let him blow it up, but she did let him talk her into giving it to one of our cousins after Grandma passed away. I hated her for that at first, but it wasn't long before I realized I wouldn't have time to watch TV anyway. Terry said we were building a boat—a freakin' huge forty-six-foot sailing boat called a *catamaran*—and we were going to leave before the whole country imploded around us and sail to some island somewhere where he said we were going to live like natives and go spearfishing and climb coconut trees. And when we got tired of that place, the wind would blow us wherever we wanted to go next. It *did* sound kind of fun to me, at least if I didn't ever have to go to school again, like he promised, but I didn't really believe it was going to happen. Nothing I got excited about ever did.

At first, I thought the only reason Terry married my mom was because she inherited Grandma's house and there was an old barn out back where my grandpa used to have his cabinetmaking shop. Terry said that barn was big enough to build a boat inside, and it was just what he was looking for. He sure couldn't have built it at his place. Terry was living in an apartment by the school when they met, his study area cluttered with boat plans, piles of books about boatbuilding and sailing and even more books about the islands that he talked about all the time. His walls were practically papered in nautical charts and pictures of tropical lagoons and beaches.

"This country's screwed, I tell you, Robbie. I'll be surprised if it lasts long enough for us to finish the boat. That's why we've got to hurry. That's why we've got to stay *focused.* You want to live to be a teenager someday, don't you? Then help me mark off these hull panels. If we work fast enough and don't take any days off, we might get out of here before the Poop Hits the Fan!"

When he talked about this to Mom, he said "shit" instead of "poop." It conjured a funny image in my mind: somebody throwing big handfuls of turds into the blades of a moving fan and pieces of crap flying out everywhere…hitting *everybody!* I couldn't help but grin every time I heard him say it.

But to Terry it was no joke. He said our only hope was to leave. He was always pointing out stuff to back up his reasoning. We would go to Memphis sometimes on Saturdays to buy hardware for the boat, and he would stop by the bookstore near the interstate, always making a beeline for the outdoors and sports section to see if there were new books on sailing or survival.

"See what I mean, Robbie?" he would say, pulling books off the shelf and handing them to me. "Why do you think they're writing all these survival books all of a sudden?

There's a new one every week: books on living off the grid, surviving an economic collapse, terror attack, Ebola pandemic, zombie uprising... Books on bugging out, bugging in, disaster prepping, how to live after The End of the World as We Know It... Books on survival medicine, storing food, building bomb shelters, life after oil, solar flares, EMP attacks, the Mayan Apocalypse that got postponed... You name it, Robbie, and there's a book. Some people *know* it's about to go down, but look around you, Robbie. We're the only ones in this section. They're buying books about vegan smoothie diets and magazines with reality show stars on the cover. They come in here to drink six-dollar frappés and sit there using the free Wi-Fi to surf the Internet on their two thousand dollar MacBooks! You think this can go on forever? Let's get out of here Robbie; we've got a boat to build."

Even though it was the same every time we went, Terry never missed a chance to stop at that bookstore so he could remind us. Then, on the two-and-a-half hour drive back to Calloway City, he ranted about how stupid it was to drive anywhere and threatened to make Mom sell her car.

"We can get everything we need for the boat delivered to the house by UPS and FedEx. This is insane. Look at these idiots! Eighty miles an hour, and for what? To get home in time to watch the latest *Two and a Half Men* reruns while they eat their supersized burger combo from the drive-through and take iPhone pictures of their cats to put on Facebook? We make this run one time too many, Robbie, and none of us

11

will survive to sail anywhere; we'll end up as roadkill snuffed out by a hit-and-run teenaged texter."

Terry hated driving almost as much as he hated TV. He didn't own a car himself. When he was still living in the apartment, before Mom married him, he either walked to his job at the school or rode a beat-up old mountain bike. He said we would all be riding bikes once we moved aboard the boat, and everybody else would anyway once the oil dried up or got shut off by a Third World War that he said would start in the Middle East. He said we'd have plenty of room on deck to carry bikes and they would be our transportation on land whenever we stopped in the various ports he said we would visit en route to the islands he was dead set on reaching.

I had my doubts we would ever be sailing anywhere when we started building the boat. I had never even seen the ocean and the only beach I had ever been to was at a park on the shore of Lake Michigan when we lived in Indiana. Calloway City was a long way from the Gulf Coast, but Terry said we would launch the boat in the Tennessee-Tombigbee Waterway about a hundred miles to the east and float down the river to Mobile, Alabama. He said once we reached the Gulf of Mexico the world would be our oyster and the wind would take us anywhere we wanted to go. It seemed far-fetched, even to a ten-year-old, but Terry had a way of making his dream contagious. It sure swept my mom away, but I think at the time she just thought it was going to be like a long vacation of swimming and lying on the beach in the sun.

The dream first became tangible when a delivery truck from the local building supply came one day and unloaded over a hundred sheets of plywood in front of the shop at Terry's direction. I had a hard time visualizing that pile of flat wooden panels being transformed into a boat, but Terry said plywood was one of the best boatbuilding materials available, especially for a catamaran, which had to be lightweight, according to him. It didn't look lightweight to me though, considering that the truck driver had to use a forklift to set the bundles on the ground. The plywood was rough-looking too, just ordinary construction-grade material like they used for building houses. Terry said it would be ridiculous to spend the money on fancy marine plywood for a boat like this, because we were going to cover all the wood with fiberglass and epoxy resin anyway. Terry had all kinds of stories about the various boats he had built and the places he had been. I didn't have any reason to doubt that he was telling the truth, because I didn't know enough about either boats or other places to know the difference. What I did know is that he had a near religious belief in the qualities of epoxy resin—that messy, expensive goop that we had to mix together to coat every piece of wood that went into the boat so that water couldn't penetrate it and cause it to rot. The epoxy was also the glue that we used to assemble the parts, every joint requiring carefully-mixed batches of the stuff that had to be spread quickly before the chemical reaction caused by adding

13

the hardener caused it to get too hot and set up before it could be used. Mixing epoxy was one of the first boatbuilding jobs I learned, and I became the main mixer for big operations that required a lot of it in a hurry.

"There're aren't many things in this world you can truly believe in, Robbie. But I assure you, you can *believe* in epoxy resin. Out there on the salt, when there's a gale blowing and the waves are as tall as those trees, epoxy resin is the only thing that's going to hold this vessel together—the only thing preventing you from becoming shark bait. You make sure you get the mix right and you don't have anything to worry about it."

I looked up wide-eyed at the trees he was referring to. They must have been fifty feet tall. Could waves really get that big? I was careful when I pumped out the resin and hardener for every batch. Two counts of resin to every one count of hardener. Mix it thoroughly with a stirring stick to ensure that it will react and cure properly once applied to the parts that were temporarily clamped together overnight. After we began the building, I saw that he was right. The epoxy was amazing. Once it cured there was no way to separate the parts. The wood pieces would break before the glue joint failed.

I also learned how to use power tools, and this was the most exciting part of it for me. Terry trusted me with saws and routers that could take off a finger, and belt sanders that he said would grind the meat right to the bone if you got your hand in one. I was scared but at the same time using

14

such powerful tools made me feel grown-up and important. I couldn't cut a very straight line with a power saw, but then neither could Terry. He said it didn't matter anyway, because once again, epoxy was the key to *everything* on this boat and sloppy carpentry work would be hidden by it anyway. Then the whole thing would be painted.

"We're not building a *yacht,* to show off to the idiots at some fancy marina. No sir, Robbie, this vessel is our *ship.* A ship that will take us anywhere we want to go as long as she's sound and sturdy. Mother Ocean doesn't give a damn if she's pretty or not."

Mom and Janie were involved in the building right from the beginning too, although Janie said there was "no way in hell" she was going to live on a boat and threatened to run away if we actually did it. I knew she would change her mind though; she just had to try and get her way first because she was used to it. And besides, Mom said she was going through that rebellious teenage-girl phase, whatever that meant. Janie's main interest was boys, and several times during the course of the construction one of her temporary boyfriends would hang around pretending to be interested in helping us with the project. Terry said kids these days didn't know how to work because none of them had to. He said what they were good at was playing video games and texting, and that most of them could type forty words a minute on an iPhone with their thumbs. He said these redneck high school boys following Janie home didn't know one end of a sailboat from the other, and could care less, but they made a show of it, hoping to get in her pants before we left. Boatbuilding and sailing weren't exactly extra-curricular activities in Calloway City anyway, but aside from girls, most of the high school boys were obsessed with one other thing, and that was *deer hunting.*

"Give them a scoped .308 rifle and put them in a heated tree-stand and they might be able to shoot a yearling buck over a baited field," Terry said, "but most of them won't survive what's coming, Robbie. Hard times are going to call for hard men, and the survivors are going to be the few that can track a deer through the swamp and kill it with a sharp stick. People are going to get so hungry after a while that they'll take to eating each other, because other people, especially the fat ones, are going to be the only food they can catch."

"You mean like *cannibals?*" I asked.

"Yes, *eaters,*" Terry said, "just like in a Sci-fi novel I read where all modern technology fails and people go medieval. "There'll be lots of *eaters* in this country after the doo-doo hits the big ventilator blades. They'll be the ones too stupid to survive any other way and they'll eat each other until they're all gone. Get the stew pot ready, Billy-Bob! Go chop some more firewood, Leroy! Lookie-here, Cletus, we caught a nice fat little 10-year-old porker today!" He lunged at me, pretending to drag me away.

I recoiled in horror, even though I wasn't fat. Sometimes

Terry scared me with the picture he painted of the future. Of course that was his point, to make us all want to go with him, but I wasn't sure I wanted to live in the world he described, especially if we didn't get the boat built fast enough to get out first.

Janie was always telling me Terry was full of shit. She thought the world was going to end too, but she said that it would blow up so fast we wouldn't feel a thing—probably from an asteroid strike or a bunch of nuclear bombs. That's why all she wanted to do right now was get high and chill with her friends, because what was the point of doing anything else? But Terry got her on board with the boat project by telling her tales of the islands, where wild ganja grew twelve feet tall in the jungle, free for the taking. He told her this when Mom wasn't around of course, and because he didn't care if she smoked or not, Janie begrudgingly began to like him. As the boat took shape, she slowly came around to the idea that we really *might* be leaving.

I found out that building a boat is not something you can do in a hurry. Even with all four of us working on it almost every day after school, as well as every weekend and all summer, it was a year before the two forty-six-foot-long hulls were built. Then it was another year before they were ready to be moved out of the barn, which was too small for the final assembly into a catamaran and the fitting of the two masts. During the last six months, we worked on it pretty much all the time. Terry resigned from his teaching job at the school and he and Mom took us out of class, saying to anyone who asked that they were home-schooling us.

I didn't know what was true and what he made up when it came to Terry's past before he arrived in Calloway City to teach school. He claimed to have first moved to Mississippi to teach graduate-level Anthropology at Ole Miss, just up the road about an hour away in Oxford. He said that before that, he had been a university professor in California for a while after he came back to the States from a 10-year stint of living in the jungles of Irian Jaya, studying a tribe of Stone Age savages. He had so many stories that he told in such great detail, it was hard to doubt him, but on the other hand I didn't see how any one person could have so many fantastic adventures and know so much stuff about so many different things. He was either the biggest liar or the most adventurous real-life person I could imagine, or more likely, some combination of the two.

I don't know exactly where he got the money to build the boat either. Even before he quit his job, it wasn't like he was making much as a history teacher at Calloway Jr. High, and Mom sure didn't have any money. Janie's father hadn't paid her child-support in over ten years, and my dad never paid a dime and we had no idea where he was. Mom made ends meet by working as a receptionist in a dentist's office back in Richmond before we moved here, and in Calloway City she answered the phones and made appointments for a local attorney.

But Terry didn't have a car to put gas in like Mom did, and he knew how to squeeze every penny out of a dollar when he bought stuff. He said it didn't cost near as much to build an ocean-going sailing ship if you didn't mind doing the hard work and didn't have to have all the shiny yacht fittings factory boats came with. He ranted about how the local good old boys around Calloway City spent twenty thousand dollars or more for their overpowered bass boats with fancy metal-flake paint jobs.

"They put a one hundred and fifty-horse outboard on the back of an eighteen-foot boat to go bass fishing in a lake less than three miles long! They don't care what it costs, because all that matters is whether or not they can pay the note every month and still fill up the cooler with beer when they go out. That's another reason this country's going down the drain, Robbie—*credit*! They give it to anybody stupid enough to sign a note and dumb enough to work nine to five the rest of their lives to pay it off. But our boat isn't some flashy toy to show off at the local lake, Robbie. It's our transportation, our escape pod, and our permanent *home*—all for less than the cost of a new Ford pickup that can pull one of those atrocities up the local boat ramp."

Terry said the main thing we had to buy was the plywood and the epoxy, because for that there was no substitute. But most everything else could be scrounged here and there or made from scraps, rejects or salvaged junk. He scored big on getting all the solid timber we needed for the boat when he mentioned what he was doing to Mr. L.C. Pickens down at the hardware store. Mr. L.C. had an old barn that was falling down that he wanted gone because he was about to plant all his farmland in pine timber—the new cash crop throughout Mississippi. Terry said it was crazy that no one was farming real crops like cotton anymore and blamed it all on the big corporations that made farming an industry and put the little guy out of business.

"Besides, Robbie, people are too lazy to farm these days. Farming means *work*. Outside work. Hot. Cold. Daylight to dark work, *every* day. They don't want to live like that anymore and anyway, they don't know how. Only the old folks do and they are a dying breed. Instead, everyone who owns a little land plants pine trees. The government gives them the seedlings, they stick them in the ground in rows and twenty years later their kids cut them all down and sell the paper wood to buy dope."

But Terry didn't complain about Mr. L.C. wanting his dilapidated barn torn down.

"Look at that, Robbie. This timber is as good as the day it was cut. That's longleaf yellow pine—one of the finest shipbuilding timbers in the world. You can't even buy this stuff anymore because they logged it all out when they settled this part of the country. See those big square timbers there?"

He was pointing to the beams that spanned the lower part of the barn and supported the floor of the loft. All I saw was ugly, gray wood, weather-beaten and full of rusty, bent nails.

"Those timbers were hand-hewn by slave labor, you can bet on it. See the marks left by the axe and adze? Everything around here was built by slaves, and not that long ago either. Back then you would have seen nothing but snow-white fields of cotton stretching from here to the Mississippi River!"

"How is this gonna be part of our boat?" I was almost afraid to ask. I knew that whatever he had in mind, it was going to be hard work, and I was right. We spent a week taking that barn apart board-by-board, hammering out or pulling all those rusty nails and stacking the lumber in a pile so that Mr. L.C. could load it on his trailer and bring it to our barn behind the house. It was one of the hardest jobs of the whole project, but Terry said we had better timber than money could buy, and best of all, it was free. And that meant we had saved enough money on wood to buy cruising stores and supplies for an entire year!

"This will be all our structural framing, Robbie; the crossbeams tying the two hulls together, the framing inside the boat, the decks between the hulls; and most importantly, the two masts. Terry said our catamaran was going to be rigged as a schooner. But that didn't mean much to me back when all I could see was a pile of old boards with nail holes in them. I knew nothing of ships or the sea, much less schooners, but I learned a lot in a hurry. Terry talked about it non-stop while we worked, over meals and during most other breaks. He was truly obsessed with the idea, and was the first person I had ever encountered in my scant years who was so passionate about anything.

His obsessive passion paid off eventually. Once the connecting beams were made and the two hulls were joined together, for the first time since we'd begun, what we were building *did* look like a boat, or at least a big raft or something that *might* float. Not that it was pretty or anything—Terry's work was sloppy—with big runs of solidified epoxy standing out on practically every vertical surface, and rough-cut, ill-fitting joiner work visible anywhere he hadn't buried it from sight in epoxy and paint. The railings on the outside edges of the decks were made of galvanized plumber's pipe, and several blue plastic tarps stretched between them and were supported in the middle by two-by-fours serving as makeshift awnings while we worked. He had ordered a bunch of used sails from somewhere online and then recut and trimmed them to the size he wanted using an old antique sewing machine he found at a yard sale. The finished result was not going to be mistaken for a yacht; that was for sure. Even I could see the difference from looking at the pictures in Terry's books.

It wasn't like the people in Calloway City knew the difference either, but nevertheless they didn't like it. To them our boat was just an eyesore—an ugly contraption built by those "crazy people" over on Winfield Avenue. The eighty-something-year-old lady in the neighboring house complained the most: "They're disturbing the peace. They're out there running power tools at all hours of the night! They even work on the damned thing on Sunday!" She said this wasn't a shipyard… and who did Terry think he was, Noah? And on and on….

Terry didn't care what they said. They thought he was crazy, and he thought they were all idiots. Now that the boat was nearing completion, he told me the same thing every day: "There's only two kinds of people in the world, Robbie: *sea people* and *shore bastards*! Now which one do you want to be? If we don't hurry up and get this boat launched, you won't get a chance to decide!"

Two

MOVING A FORTY-SIX-foot catamaran over a hundred miles to the water seemed to me as daunting a task as building it. But just like the construction phase of the project, Terry wasn't worried about things like that.

"Moving it's the easy part, Robbie. What I dread is dealing with all the bureaucrats we have to get permission from before we can launch. It doesn't matter that we built it all with our own hands and our own money. Now we've got to pay the government for permission to keep it! That's what's wrong with this country, Robbie. They would tax every breath you take if they could figure out how to do it!

"Look at these houses right here on this street. The people that live in them think they own them, what a joke! You can't own anything in this country, Robbie, especially not a house or piece of land. You rent it from the government for however much they decide to charge you every year in property taxes to let you use it. Get behind on your payment and they auction it off to the highest bidder. Don't mow your grass and they send a crew to do it for you and hit you with a bill in the mail. Leave an old car parked in your driveway too long and they'll tow it away. That's why we're moving aboard a boat, Robbie. Who wants to pay all that money to live on a piece of dirt and be told how to do it?

"But now they're going to tax the crap out of us just to give us a registration number! That's how the government operates, Robbie. They love numbers. Everything is a number to them, including you and me. Without both a hull identification number and a state registration number painted on the topsides, some game warden or water cop will write us up. Then you've got to pay the fine and *still* pay the taxes and registration. If you don't pay, they send men with guns to take you to jail!

"They'll want to know every penny we spent on the materials that went into the construction, and then they'll make up a number for what they figure the whole thing's worth and hand us a tax bill for that. What's worse, if we don't go now, they may not even let us leave."

Terry was especially worried about the latter possibility. He said the government was getting bigger, turning into a monster that required even more taxes to keep it fed and that gave it more and more power to tell people what they could and couldn't do. He said it was all under the guise of making

26

us safe, but it was really about control. He said that up until now, we had it pretty good compared to some places, but that it wouldn't be long before the rules and regulations would get as bad as some European countries already were.

"In France, they make all the decisions as to whether your boat is seaworthy or not, and then tell you how far you can sail it from shore, if at all. Wanna go farther? Then you gotta buy everything on their list of "safety" equipment and have your vessel inspected by the bureaucrats who make the decisions. Then there are the all the taxes and the insurance requirements on top of that. In the U.K., you can't even sell a boat you built yourself until after you've owned it for five years. It's coming over here too, Robbie. I'll give it six months to a year before they sign bills like that into law. There are plenty of people who would love to see it happen; tax-hungry, rule-loving *shore bastards* like I said. They're afraid of real freedom and don't want anyone else to have it either. That's why we've got to get down the river to Mobile and out to international waters ASAP! We're going to be citizens of the *world*, Robbie, not just Americans. That's what living on a boat is all about! Things aren't the way you like them in one country, you set sail for a new horizon and try someplace else. The people who started this country did exactly that, it's just that their descendants seem to have forgotten."

Terry always had the same sense of urgency from the day he came into our lives. First it was to get the boat built. Now that it was built, it was to get it in the water. Then it was to escape the taxmen and lawmakers who he was sure were out to squash his dreams before he even set sail. I began to wonder if his urgency would end even after we made our escape, if we ever did. It seemed to me that Terry was always going to be worried about something, and he could rattle on for hours about all the reasons why life as we knew it couldn't go on much longer.

"Anybody who thinks it can is insane, Robbie. The whole country is broke. All the jobs have been outsourced to China, and we're fighting wars all over the world, especially where there's oil. And even where there is oil, it won't last forever. Not with every Banana Republic on the planet burning it up at the rate they are, driving cars and living in air-conditioned buildings just like the fat-assed Americans they want to emulate. It's all going to collapse, Robbie, and the only ones left will be driven into the sea. That's why we're getting a head start. We're going to beat them to the best places, and we're going to have the right boat to do it, too."

Terry raved on and on about the virtues of the catamaran he had finally chosen to build, claiming decades of careful research and hard-won experience guided him in his decision:

"There's no better boat in the world we could pick to sail the troubled waters of the apocalypse, Robbie. A James Wharram catamaran is the ultimate in seaworthiness and simplicity, and she'll take us places other boats her size couldn't dream of going. They've been building these things all over the world for fifty years. They've been built in jungles, deserts, warehouses, backyards and even piece-by-piece in city apartments. They've been sailed from Culatra to Fatu Hiva. You'll find them anchored everywhere from the Rio Dulce to the Great Barrier Reef. You can refit and rebuild them anywhere too. You don't even need a boatyard to haul one of these cats out for a bottom job, Robbie. Hook up the sheet winch to a palm tree and drag her right up on the beach. Need a new mast? Cut a straight tree or glue one up with epoxy and two by fours and plane it round by hand. The beauty of these designs is that they don't need hardware, just wood parts and rope lashings for the most part. You can get what you need *anywhere!*"

It was true that the whole thing was held together by rope. I didn't know enough to know this wasn't the norm in boat and ship building, so I didn't say anything. I had seen enough rafts in cartoons and books to know *they* were lashed together, so it didn't seem all that unusual at the time that the four main beams of our catamaran were literally *tied* to the hulls instead of bolted or joined with fiberglass and resin as one unit. Besides, the ropes looked strong and there were a lot of wraps of it at every connection. And when it was time to move the whole thing to the water, all we had to do was untie them and take it apart. Otherwise, transporting a twenty-four-foot-wide catamaran down the highway would have been practically impossible, according to Terry.

At first he considered having them moved one at a time by an eighteen-wheeler, but after calling several trucking companies for prices he ranted and cussed about how outrageous their quotes were and said we'd do it ourselves. Terry talked to Mr. L.C. again at the hardware store and armed himself with names and addresses. Then he took us on a drive in Mom's car to visit several farmers in the nearby countryside. What Terry was looking for was a trailer he could rent, along with a truck to pull it, if possible. He soon found out that was *not* possible. Every farmer he talked to insisted on doing the driving, reluctant to let an ex-school teacher take off with his equipment to move some homemade contraption of a ship halfway across the state. He finally reached an agreement with an unemployed former trucker named Hal Jenkins, who had a well-worn twenty-year-old Ford F350 pickup and a forty-foot flatbed car hauler. When he came over to the barn to look at what Terry was asking him to move, Mr. Jenkins scratched his head and spat tobacco juice on the ground, then walked around the two massive hulls a couple times before committing to anything.

"I'll do it for eight hundred dollars for the first hull, and six for the second one if the first one goes smooth enough. That's as low as I can go 'cause it takes a lot of diesel to pull something that big that far. But it's up to you to figure out how we're going to get 'em on the trailer and back off again at the other end," he added. "I ain't got no insurance neither, 'cept for liability. Can't afford it. So if something happens getting them boats on or off the trailer or along the way, that's on you and I ain't responsible."

Terry muttered something under his breath about *fourteen hundred effin' dollars*, and then looked at Mr. Jenkins' truck again before finally agreeing to the man's price. He told me later, after Mr. Jenkins left that it was highway robbery, but not as bad as what the trucking companies were trying to take him for.

"How are we supposed to get the hulls all the way up on that trailer?" I asked. "Don't we need one of those big crane machines like they use to build stuff to pick them up?"

"Nope. You've still got a lot to learn, Robbie. Getting a truck crane out here would cost even more than this opportunistic farmer is taking us for. We don't need a crane; we just need a little mechanical advantage. You'll see."

That afternoon and the next morning we worked on building a sturdy lifting framework consisting of four vertical poles connected at the top by heavy beams and braced at the bottom on either side. We erected this framework over the starboard hull first; (Terry refused to let me call them left or right; saying I had to use the correct nautical terminology if I was ever going to be his navigator). The lifting frame was assembled with big galvanized bolts that we had to tighten with wrenches while standing on two tall stepladders that had belonged to my grandfather. Terry designed it so we could take it all back apart and load it on the truck for the move, as we would need it at the other end to get the hull back off the trailer. It seemed like a lot of trouble to me when a crane could have probably done it in a few minutes, but Terry

31

wouldn't hear of it. When the bolts were tight, he showed me how we would lift each hull, one at a time. He took several turns of heavy rope around the center of each top beam that spanned across the width of the structure, over the starboard hull, then used the rope to lash a big pulley-like device he called a chain hoist under each one, directly over the decks. Then he had me crawl under the hull at each lift point, passing a wide nylon strap under the keel so he could hook each end of it together at the top for connection to the hook on the chain hoist.

"It's a force multiplier, Robbie. The mechanical advantage the chain hoists provide will allow us to manually lift the hull high enough so that Jenkins can back his trailer under it. Then we'll let it down easy and strap it in place, and it's good to go."

It still seemed like an awful lot of work to me, but I had already resigned myself to a life of hard work now that Terry was in control. I would be his number one deck slave, with Janie and Mom a close second and third. Terry called Mr. Jenkins, and when he arrived with his long trailer, we lifted the hull as high as it would go using the chain hoists. Terry was furious to discover that he had miscalculated the height needed as Mr. Jenkins slowly inched the trailer backwards, lining it up with the forty-six-foot-long hull that hung precariously from our wooden lifting contraption. It seemed the beams were high enough, but he hadn't taken into consideration that he would lose a couple of feet of vertical travel at the top because of the space needed for the hooks under the chain hoists and the bails at the top. There was no way to lift the hull high enough for the trailer to back under the keel without rebuilding the wooden lift frame at least two feet higher.

Mr. Jenkins told Terry that his mistake had cost him half a day, and that if he still wanted to get this hull loaded before tomorrow, he would stay and help rebuild the lift, but only if Terry paid him another two hundred dollars for his time. He said it was the same two hundred he had agreed to knock off for the second hull if things went smoothly, which they already didn't.

Terry pitched a fit but forked over the two hundred, telling me later that Hal Jenkins had probably never made that much money in one day in his entire life. By the time we unbolted all the connecting beams and braces and lengthened the vertical posts by screwing stacked two-by-six boards to each side of each of the four posts, four hours had passed and it was two o'clock in the afternoon. We lifted the starboard hull again with the chain hoists, and Mr. Jenkins slowly backed his trailer beneath the hull, ignoring Terry's frantic shouts and hand signals. The man knew what he was doing, and it was clear that he didn't need any help, even though Terry didn't want to admit it.

Our catamaran hulls were shaped like very deep "V"s on the bottom, which Terry said was a distinct characteristic of all James Wharram catamarans. This knife-like "V" would allow them to slice through the waves, and according to Terry, sail into the wind. That was all well and good when the boat was in the water, but Terry said the shape made the hulls a real pain in the butt to move around on land. I already knew he was right about that because I had to help him build the elaborate cradles that supported them and held them upright and secure as we were working on them. Without the crossbeams tying them together, the individual hulls would fall right over on their side if left to stand on their own. This was true on the ground, and now on Mr. Jenkins' trailer. So once the trailer was under the first hull, we had to first strap down these building cradles that it had been supported in, securing them to the bed of the trailer so the hull could be lowered into them. This took another hour of farting around, trying to get them lined up and level and then figuring out how to keep them secure. When it was all done, Terry had probably used two hundred feet of half-inch nylon line in addition to the big nylon webbing straps he'd used to lift the hull. Mr. Jenkins pulled the trailer forward and drove the hull out from under our lifting frame, which we then spent another hour disassembling and securing, piece by piece to the trailer. By this time it was four in the afternoon and Mr. Jenkins said it was too late to leave because he didn't want to be pulling a load like that at night on two-lane highways where deer jumped out at every turn. He insisted on waiting until tomorrow, and wanted even more money for his trouble.

Terry went ballistic at this and refused to negotiate, telling

Mr. Jenkins we would unload the hull and find somebody else to move it before we paid another dime. Mr. Jenkins gave in, unhitching his trailer and blocking up the tongue so he could drive home in his truck, and then left, promising to be back at dawn in the morning.

"He said when he agreed to do it that it was up to us to get it on the trailer and back off again," I said, defending Mr. Jenkins after he drove away and Terry continued cussing him up and down.

"That's beside the point, Robbie. He quoted me a price for *moving* the boat with his truck and trailer. He wasn't charging by the hour, he was charging us for a completed job. Just because it took us longer to get the boat on the trailer doesn't give him an excuse to try and charge us what he would earn for driving his rig all day."

"But it's our fault he couldn't drive today, wasn't it?"

"It doesn't matter. Here's the thing, Robbie. Without us needing this boat moved, he didn't *have* a job. He'd be sitting out there on his porch in the country watching chickens peck and drinking beer. And when he's done with this, that's what he'll be right back to. We presented an opportunity for him, and a good one too, but he turned it into an opportunity to try and screw us out of even more money. If we don't get to the sea soon, Robbie, we won't have a dime left to even buy groceries. Like I told you, the *shore bastards* are going to do everything in their power to keep us here just like them. Now go get some sleep. Tomorrow's going to be a long day!"

SAILING THE APOCALYPSE

* * *

Mr. Jenkins arrived at daybreak just as he'd promised. It only took a few minutes to hook the trailer up to his truck, and we were off. Part of the deal Terry made with him was that the two of us would get to ride in the truck with him, so that when he got to the launch site way over on the east side of the state near a town called Iuka, we would be there to reassemble the wooden lift and offload the first hull. Terry didn't want to buy the gas to follow him over in Mom's car, so I was stuck in the unfortunate position of having to ride in the middle of the truck's only seat, right between the two of them. It was going to be a long day: at least three hours over there, probably four to do all the work of getting the hull off and disassembling the lift again, and another three to get back.

Terry started his ranting as soon as we pulled out on the road. I don't think Mr. Jenkins knew what he was talking about half the time, and he only replied to direct questions that Terry wouldn't let him avoid.

"I don't know nuthin' about that," Mr. Jenkins said. "I ain't got no reason to go to them other countries. Hell, I don't even like going across the line to Alabama or Tennessee."

"You're staying here at your own peril, Hal. This country's finished. Why do you think we spent the last two years working every spare minute building this ship? We're barely going to get out in time as it is. You might have a chance for a few years, living out in the sticks like you do, but sooner or later they'll burn all these little towns like Calloway City too."

"We'll see about that! I don't know who you figure'll burn 'em. Any outsiders come around here tryin' to start trouble, they'll find out us country folks has got something for 'em they may not like."

"That's delusional thinking, Hal. I hear that kind of talk all the time. People think they can hole up in the woods with their guns and ammunition and fend off the savage hordes. You can't see what's really coming, can you Hal? I'm talking about a major meltdown. It won't be the good guys against the zombies. Everybody you know will turn against you when they get hungry enough. I'm talking about a total collapse, Hal. It's all coming apart at the seams and nobody can stop it or put it back together again."

"So you figure you're gonna get away from it on that contraption you built there? Whatcha gonna do when a hurricane comes? Don't you know it's hurricane season right now? Hell, Katrina tore up every boat on the Gulf Coast! They had eighty-foot shrimp boats sittin' in the middle of Interstate 10! I know because I hauled debris outta there for six months under contract for FEMA. Ain't no tellin' how many people drowned. They still ain't found all the bodies, and probably never will."

"While it is still technically hurricane season, statistically the greatest threat of tropical cyclone activity in the Gulf of

SAILING THE APOCALYPSE

Mexico is from mid-July through September. That's why we've waited until the middle of October to launch. The odds of a storm are slim, and we'll reach the tropics before the first hint of winter frost. But hurricanes are the least of my concerns, Hal. A good sailor can avoid hurricanes—that's easy. We won't be caught in hurricane zones during the peak season. We'll soon be south of the cyclone belt anyway, sticking close to the equator. There are plenty of safe places to wait out tropical cyclone season; you just have to know where they are. What it takes is research and experience."

"Well, I hope you know what you're doing. Me, I wouldn't sail out of sight of land on anything smaller than a Destroyer, much less some homemade plywood boat. That Gulf ain't nuthin' to mess around with, I'll tell you that! I got too many friends that's worked out there on the rigs. You ought to hear the stories they tell about the weather they've seen out there."

"The Gulf of Mexico isn't even the ocean," Terry countered. It's like a pond compared to where we're going. Yes sir, the blue Pacific is the place to be! Do you know there are still hundreds of uninhabited tropical islands out there, Hal? Islands so isolated that the nearest other land to them is a thousand miles away? Those islands are scattered across the Pacific like stars in the Milky Way. All we've got to do is decide which ones we want to see and set our course. The wind will take us there for nothing."

This conversation went on for the entire trip across north Mississippi. Terry wouldn't shut up about all the things he said we were going to do, while Mr. Jenkins remained convinced we were crazy to even think like that. Neither one of them gave the other credit for having any sense at all, and I didn't dare get into the discussion, even though I was *literally* in the middle of it, stuck there for three hours on that dirty truck seat. I couldn't wait to get out and get away from both of them, even if just for a few minutes to run to the men's room when Mr. Jenkins stopped to fill up the truck with diesel.

Our destination for dropping off the first hull, and later assembling and launching the boat, was a place called Bay Springs Lake, near the tiny town of Iuka, not far from the Alabama state line. Terry said the lake was a man-made impoundment created when the U.S. Army Corps of Engineers built the Tennessee-Tombigbee Waterway. It was a big lake, with lots of fingers and coves and there were several boat ramps and campgrounds that Terry pointed out on the map as we got closer. He told Hal where to turn and we followed a hilly, winding road for miles through a forest of mixed pines and hardwoods until we finally came to the park entrance, where there was a gate and a ticket office with a ranger on duty. Terry muttered something about more highway robbery as Mr. Jenkins eased the truck and trailer forward, the huge starboard hull of our catamaran looming high over the ranger station roof.

Nobody else had a boat anywhere near the size of ours here, and I saw several fishermen with those expensive bass boats Terry always complained about stop and stare, their mouths agape and their heads shaking as they tried to figure out what our boat was. The ranger on duty was so baffled by what he saw that instead of collecting the entry fee through the drive-up window, he opened the door and stepped outside, taking in the length of the trailer and the monster hull before turning back to Mr. Jenkins.

"What is that thing?" he asked.

"It ain't mine, that's for damned sure," Mr. Jenkins said. "This feller here just hired me to move it over here. Let him tell you about it."

Terry was already out of the truck and had walked around back of the tailgate and stepped over the trailer tongue to greet the ranger. I was right behind him, anxious to find out what was going to happen next.

"I'm here to launch my boat," Terry said, in a matter of fact tone.

"Boat! That thing looks more like a ship! How do you think you're going to launch something like that in here? You'll never float it off the trailer. It looks to me like the waterline is six feet above the ground, the way you got it loaded up there. Our boat ramps are designed for fishing boats. They're not nearly deep enough or steep enough for something like that."

"This is not the whole boat, this is just half of it," Terry said. "It's a catamaran, you see. This is the starboard hull. We have to unload it first near the water, then go back to

Calloway City and bring the other one tomorrow. Then we'll put the whole thing together with the crossbeams and decks that go between them, and it'll be a simple matter to slide it down the ramp on skids and rollers."

"Half of it? How big *is* it then? Why are you launching it here? A boat like that belongs in the Gulf."

"It's forty-six feet long and twenty-four feet wide. And yes sir, we *are* going to the Gulf. This lake connects to it; that was the whole point of the Corps of Engineers building the Tenn-Tom, wasn't it? We want to launch here because I don't want to have to transport it a single mile over land that's not absolutely necessary, and this is the closest navigable water to Calloway City."

"Well, I can't let you take it off the trailer and just leave it. It's against the regulations. There's a parking lot at the boat ramp, but the spaces are for trucks with regular boat trailers. That thing's longer than a truck and trailer combined."

"We only need to leave it one night," Terry argued. "We'll be back tomorrow at the same time with the second hull. It won't take long to put it together, then we'll have it out of your parking lot and into the lake."

The ranger kept saying no and Terry kept insisting that he call someone higher up to get the matter cleared up. He said he was a tax-paying citizen of this country and this lake was built with federal funds. He said he had the right to use it just as much as anyone else with a boat, and that they couldn't discriminate just because his boat was bigger and required some assembly before launching. Mr. Jenkins just stood there watching the whole thing without saying a word, looking at whichever one of them was talking at the moment, and turning aside every few minutes to spit a stream of tobacco juice into the grass beyond the edge of the pavement. Finally, the ranger relented and went inside to use the phone.

"See what I mean about bureaucracy in this country, Robbie? They've got so many rules the underlings like him they hire to enforce them don't even know what's allowed and what isn't. They're like androids programmed to do a simple task. Throw a curve in there by asking something that's not on their cheat sheet, and it nearly causes a melt-down when they try to figure out what to do!"

The hold-up at the gate ended up killing an hour. Finally a ranger with more authority drove down to the entrance station and looked over the boat and listened to Terry explain all over again what it was exactly that we were doing. After asking lots of questions and looking over the trailer and boat carefully, this older ranger finally agreed to let us unload the hull. He made us follow him in his truck down the road to the boat ramp parking lot, where he showed us where to set it off. Terry was furious at the delay, and after the ranger left, said we'd be lucky to get it off and get the lift broken down again before it got too dark to see. Mr. Jenkins was grumbling too, complaining about how he wasn't going to get home in time for supper and then he'd have to get up at five o'clock again in the morning to move the other hull.

Finally, we were done just as the evening twilight faded. The starboard hull of our catamaran was sitting upright in the cradles, on the pavement off to one side of the boat ramp. With the bow pointed toward the edge of the lake, it looked like it was ready to slide into the glassy water that reflected the almost-full moon rising over the pines on the other side of the cove.

"Just one more to go, Robbie! Look how she shines in the moonlight! Before you know it, we'll be anchored out on nights like this every night, away from all these melon farmers and their idiotic rules. Home from now on is going to be wherever the boat is!"

Three

TERRY WOKE ME UP the next morning pounding on my door at 5 a.m. Mr. Jenkins would be here soon, he said. We were too tired when we got in the night before to assemble the lift frame over the port hull, so we had to do that this morning before we could load it onto the trailer. Terry had everybody in the family running around in a frenzy before Mr. Jenkins backed into the driveway. Mom and Janie were staying behind, spending another day packing up the last few things in the house that we would need. After we moved the port side hull over to the lakeshore today, we would still need to make one more trip with Mr. Jenkins' truck and trailer tomorrow to carry the crossbeams, the deck structures, and all the miscellaneous parts like the two masts, rudders and assorted gear that was part of the ship. Terry had negotiated with Mr. Jenkins until he agreed to make that last trip for four hundred dollars—half of what he charged for each trip with a hull in tow. I guess Terry had been right. Mr. Jenkins didn't have much of anything else to do after moving the hulls for us, and even after buying diesel he would be able to put another three hundred dollars in his pocket for this last trip.

"It will be the most he's ever made in three days in his life. But now we're down two grand just to get the ship to the water! Do you know how long we could live on two grand in Kiribati, Robbie? At least a year, maybe two when I get the rest of you up to speed on spearfishing and coconut palm climbing. That's why we have to get out of U.S. waters fast, Robbie! Those idiot yachties that tie up in marinas every night go through that much in a week or two here, and they've taught every business owner on the coast to overcharge anyone they see coming in a boat."

I didn't know about any of that, but I knew two grand was a lot of money, at least that's what Mom said, considering she didn't make that much in a whole month at her job. I still didn't know where Terry got all the money he spent on the boat. Even though he cut every corner he could when we built it, it still took a lot, and he had to have some left, even though he claimed people like Mr. Jenkins were breaking him. I know my Mom didn't have any money saved up, but she did get three thousand dollars when she sold her Toyota Camry to my cousins she gave our TV to back when this all started. She didn't really want to sell her car, but Terry said she had to, because where we were going we'd never need a car again.

Mom also owned the house that Grandma left her, and while it wasn't worth a lot in Calloway City, it was worth a whole lot more than her old car. Terry wanted her to sell it, but she flat out refused. He said we'd never need a house again either, and she argued that you just never had any way of knowing about those kinds of things. She said she could buy another car someday if she needed one, but she wasn't about to give up that house because her mother had left it to her, and it was where she grew up. Besides, my cousins needed a bigger place to live, and she had promised them first dibs when we were ready to move out. She agreed to rent it to them for three hundred dollars a month.

"Three hundred dollars a month! They can't live in a homeless shelter for that kind of money! They ought to be paying at least eight!" Terry said.

"It's Calloway City, Dear. This isn't Memphis or Jackson. Besides, you said we didn't need much money to live on the boat. You said we would catch fish, and that the wind was free, and that anchoring anywhere we wanted was free, and we wouldn't have to pay taxes, or buy car tags or insurance. You said that a dollar was worth ten times as much in some of those island countries as it is here, and that there wasn't anything to buy there anyway. If all that's true, then three hundred dollars a month ought to help a lot!" Mom said.

"It will but it's the principal of it. They ought to be paying more! And if you sold the house, we would be set for life, living on the boat. When this country goes up in flames,

47

that three hundred a month is gonna be gone with it!"

But Mom wouldn't budge when it came to the house. She refused to sell it no matter what argument Terry presented. So eventually he quit bringing it up, because the important thing to him was that we *were* leaving. That was his number one priority through all of this anyway.

A lot of our essential belongings like pots and pans and stuff for the tiny kitchen in the boat that Terry said we had to call the "galley" were already packed in the hulls before we started moving them. The galley was in the starboard hull, the one that was already at the lake, and the "head," which was the silly boat name for a toilet, was in the port hull that we were moving today. Terry made us get rid of all kinds of stuff we wanted to keep, saying there was no way everything we had in the house was going to fit and we didn't need it where we were going anyway. I didn't think we had a lot, because we had already gotten rid of half our stuff when we moved south from Indiana. But Terry said we had to make room for the important things, like navigation charts and guidebooks, as well as spare parts and tools. He said we didn't need any winter clothes and that once we got to the Gulf we could throw our shoes overboard too. Janie said that would be a cold day in hell but Terry said where we were going cold would be a distant memory.

At least we got to take our bicycles, which was a big deal for me because I had just gotten a new bike the Christmas before last and I sure wasn't about to leave it at home. Janie complained about getting screwed out of the chance to have her own car like all her friends did. She had gotten her license when she turned sixteen and she drove Mom's car some, but what she really wanted was to have her own like a normal teenager. Terry told her she wouldn't have been able to drive it long anyway even if she had one because the oil would likely run out before she hit twenty-five, and it was a waste of time to learn a useless skill. He said she would be an expert sailor and navigator in no time at all though, but Janie said she could care less about driving some stupid, slow sailboat.

* * *

Moving the second hull certainly went smoother and took less time than the first, mainly because we didn't have to hassle with the park rangers at the lake this time. What we did have by now though, was a small crowd of people watching, trying to figure out what we were doing. Most of them were fishermen coming and going at the boat ramp, and old folks from the RV campground nearby. I heard all kinds of speculation as these onlookers muttered among themselves, some of them snickering and making jokes about our workmanship and others calling the two hulls "boats" because they still couldn't visualize the two being joined together to form one vessel.

Terry ignored their comments as we worked nonstop to level up the support cradles on the asphalt parking lot. We had to align the hulls precisely parallel at the right distance apart so the crossbeams could fit in the chocks on the deck that held them in place. I know this sounds easy, but it wasn't. The final adjustment was done inch-by-inch, using car jacks and pieces of wood for blocks and skids. It took the rest of the afternoon to get them leveled and set up exactly the way Terry wanted them. If we moved the front end of one hull one way, the back end would get out of line all over again. We adjusted them at least a hundred times before they were right.

By the time we finished and started disassembling the lift frame for the last time, the onlookers had gotten bored and left and I was exhausted and couldn't wait to get back in the truck to go home. But as we left, I realized that Terry hadn't been kidding all this time, and now this boat was going to *be* home. The house we were going back to tonight would soon be a memory left behind, that thought made me more than a little nervous and sad. What was it really going to be like, living on a sailboat? I realized I was about to find out, for better or worse.

Our next trip to Bay Springs Lake was our last one. We didn't get going until early in the morning the day after coming back from unloading the two hulls, because it took most of the afternoon before to load the four crossbeams, two masts and other assorted boat parts onto Mr. Jenkins' trailer. Even though most of the stuff we were taking with us to live on the boat was already aboard in the two hulls, Mom and Janie still managed to pack her car so full that I once again had to ride in middle of the truck seat between Terry and Mr. Jenkins. The Camry wasn't really hers anymore anyway, but my cousins had agreed to rent it back to her for the day if she knocked off half the three hundred they owed for the house rent that month. They said she could just leave it with the key in it at the lake and they would come get it that coming weekend. Terry was furious with her for giving them a break on the rent, but we couldn't all fit in Mr. Jenkins' truck anyway, so he finally shut up about it.

We were back at the boat ramp parking by mid-morning and set to work immediately unloading the parts off the trailer so we could finish the final assembly. It wasn't long before a crowd gathered again, this time bigger than before, especially now that we had Mom and Janie with us, as well as a big assortment of strange looking parts painted the same color as the two "boats" everyone was talking about. Getting the heavy crossbeams from the trailer up to the decks would have been a difficult job, but one advantage of having all these gawkers was that Terry was able to recruit some of the men to give us a hand. With all that manpower, the beams and decks were quickly lifted into place and then Terry set to work lashing them firmly into position.

"You ain't gonna just tie it together, are you?" one of the fishermen asked. "That rope'll break soon as you get down to the Gulf and hit some weather."

"Not this stuff, no sir!" Terry answered. "This is low-stretch Dacron rigging line, with a breaking strength higher than an equal-sized steel cable. But even if it weren't, these lashings wouldn't fail due to quadruple redundancy! The Polynesians were colonizing the Pacific four thousand years ago on big double canoes lashed together with rope made of coconut fiber. A catamaran like this has to give to the sea, that's what a lot of today's designers don't understand. Bolt it together so it can't and the waves will work the connection points until you get stress cracks and broken hardware. The old way, as usual, is better and cheaper too!"

A couple of the other fishermen were standing at the stern of the starboard hull, snickering as they moved the big rudder back and forth, and mumbling something about how "they must not have been able to afford proper hardware."

Terry ignored them. He had already explained the rudder-lashing concept to me, Mom and Janie so many times I had it memorized word for word. Yes, the rudders will be lashed on. No, the lashings won't wear out for at least twenty years because there is no chafe and the rope will be painted over like everything else. No, stainless steel hinges wouldn't be better, because they would require screw holes drilled into the hull and every hole below the waterline is just another place to invite rot to get started. Those were the main points, but ultimately the reason that trumped everything else was that James Wharram designed it that way, and whatever James Wharram said, Terry believed. The only thing he believed in more was epoxy resin.

"I hope you don't think y'all can just sail that thing down

to the Gulf," another of the fishermen said, as he followed Terry around the hull, watching him tighten the lashings with additional wraps of smaller line called "frapping turns" to cinch them down. "It's more'n three hundred miles down the river. Then you got the locks to go through. And then there's all the bends and sandbars, not to mention barge traffic and bridges and power lines to go under. You just can't sail a boat down the Tenn-Tom. What you've got to have is a *motor*."

Terry rolled his eyes as he looked at the man and explained what he thought was obvious. "We never *planned* to sail down the river. That's why we do have motors; two outboards as a matter of fact!"

"I hope they're big ones. You're gonna need a lotta horsepower to push a boat this big."

"Once again, looks can be deceptive; it actually doesn't take much at all. Look at the lines of the hulls at the waterline. See how fine the entry is? They'll slice through the water like a knife and with little effort. Two fifteen-horsepower motors would be ideal, but I've got one nine-point-nine and one eight for now. All we need to do is push it at hull speed, and they'll do just fine for that."

"A nine-point-nine and a eight! Hell, I got a Mercury 150 on my seventeen-foot Nitro! And it still ain't fast enough! I can barely hit fifty with it wide open on flat water!"

Terry didn't answer, but just turned to me and Janie with a look of ill-concealed contempt for the fisherman written all over his face, winking as he whispered a reminder to us not to forget what he had said before about go-fast bass boats. I thought the old used motors he had bought looked awful small for such a big ship too, but I didn't dare say anything. Questioning Terry's judgment on anything to do with the boat was the same as flat out begging him to launch into one of his rants. I kept quiet and helped as much as I could in getting them out of the back of Mr. Jenkins' truck and lifting them up to the decks.

When they were up there, Terry installed them one at a time in the two motor well openings in the decks on either side of the steering wheel. Each motor well had a hinged wooden sled with a place to clamp the motor mount brackets to on the back of it. The sleds looked like miniature wooden boats themselves, and Terry said the reason we needed them was to have a way to lift the two motors clear of the waves when we were sailing. When they were lowered down, the bottoms of the sleds would rest on the water's surface and the propellers would stay submerged like they were supposed to. It seemed complicated to me, but Terry insisted the sleds were necessary. He said we didn't want any drag from the props slowing us down when we were sailing, and with this arrangement the motors would be stowed high and dry under the decks when we were crossing the ocean to the islands. I finally just had to believe him, because I still couldn't quite picture what sailing was going to be like anyway, having never been on a sailboat. Terry said it was like a religious experience, and that once I felt the boat come alive and harness the power of the wind I'd be hooked for life and never be able to get sailing out of my system. I wasn't sure about that, but I was looking forward to finding out if I'd really like it or not.

After we got the motors mounted securely on their brackets, there were still a bunch of big parts on the trailer that had to be lifted up to the decks and lashed in place. These included the long cockpit seats that had storage boxes underneath for all kinds of gear like extra anchors, fishing spears and life jackets. We also had all our bicycles and the extra jerry cans of gas to lash to the railings, and the blue tarps to set up as temporary awnings until we got the masts up and could rig them properly. Then there was all the steering mechanism that included the tillers that attached to each rudder head and a bunch of ropes and pulleys to control them from the big steering wheel in the center. I knew from hearing Terry correct me a thousand times that "ropes" on a boat were really "lines," and that 'pulleys' were called "blocks" and the steering wheel was the "helm." But I still didn't think of them that way when I saw them. I thought we were sailing away to get away from all the dumb rules on land, but Terry had so many rules on the boat I didn't know if it would be better or not. We had been building the boat for so long that I sometimes forgot that he was a teacher when we met him, and a teacher's job was to make people learn dumb stuff and follow dumb rules.

The last parts to go on board were the two masts, but we

weren't going to "step" them (Terry's nautical term for standing them up) here at Bay Springs Lake. He said that would have to wait until we reached Mobile Bay because there might be power lines and bridges to go under on the Tenn-Tom that were too low, and besides, the waterway was too restricted for much sailing anyway. He said the masts were going to be in the way until we got them stepped, but we would just have to work around them. He had built a couple of two-by-four cradles to support them in the horizontal position, and with the help of some of the men at the boat ramp, we got them up there and got them lashed down securely. Both of them were as long as the boat, so they didn't stick out at either end, but we had to duck under them to go across the bridgedeck from one cabin to the other.

Janie wasn't much help during the assembly process, especially later that afternoon when whatever school was nearby let out and two older boys showed up at the boat ramp with a ski boat. They zeroed in on her right off and, after gawking at our catamaran and asking a few stupid questions, asked her if she wanted to go fishing. I knew Janie hated fishing and wouldn't know what to do with a fish if she caught one, but I could tell by the way she was looking at him that she liked the oldest-looking of the two boys. He was the one driving the four-wheel-drive Silverado they had towed the boat with, and to me looked like he was at least eighteen and maybe twenty. If he was still in high school, I thought he must have flunked a year or two somewhere along the way.

I didn't really care what she did because when she was around, Janie was just in the way most of the time anyway. She would have her chores on board once we got to sailing though; Terry and Mom had already talked about that. Terry said there were no passengers on a sailing ship and that everyone had to do their equal share of the work, which he assured us there was a lot of. I didn't see how sailing could possibly be as much work as building the boat, but I knew I was about to find out one way or the other soon enough. I was just ready to get underway and see what it was all about. Some parts of the building had been fun, but I was tired of it and especially tired of sanding and painting. I still had dried paint under my fingernails and in my hair from the week before, and I was glad I wouldn't have to paint any more, at least for a while. But Terry said a boat was never finished, no matter if it was sailing or not. He said there were always improvements to be made and maintenance to keep it from falling apart.

"It's *entropy*, Robbie. Entropy never slows down and never sleeps. You can't beat it but if you stay on top of things you can keep it in check.

"What is it?" I had asked, never having heard that strange word in school or anywhere else.

"Disorder, Robbie. All things tend towards disorder, including us. The whole world is falling apart. That's why we've gotta keep moving. If you don't work fast enough building a boat, the damned thing will start rotting before you ever splash her. And once she's launched she's already in the process of decomposition. There are the U.V. rays from the sun, breaking down the paint and the epoxy, and even the sails and rigging lines. There are the cycles of hot and cold that cause the plywood to check and crack the fiberglass over it, letting in rainwater and dew. Then there are bacteria in the rainwater and later the mildew and fungus starts to grow in the wood. Then below the waterline there's the weed that starts growing on the hull first, and then the barnacles. Let it go and pretty soon it turns into a reef. Every bolt, screw, nail and fitting will rust, even the expensive stainless steel they put in the fancy yachts. Wiring in the interior corrodes from the inside out and pretty soon navigation lights and instruments won't work. The list goes on and on, Robbie. Everything on a boat from the bottom of the keel to the top of the masthead will self-destruct and in short order. It's the Law of Entropy."

"So what's the point of even building a boat then? All this hard work is for nothing if it's all gonna fall apart anyway."

"Not as long as we don't let it, it won't, Robbie. That's what I'm trying to tell you. You won't see a lazy crew on a voyaging ship, Robbie, especially not a wooden ship. No sir, back in the days of the *real* sailors all ships were made of wood and it took men of iron to sail them!"

"Then we can beat the *entropy*?"

"Absolutely! The only other choice is to die. All we have to do is keep moving and keep working. Anybody that isn't is dead already."

I kind of understood what Terry was saying. I felt like most of the people back in Calloway City where we'd been living acted like they were half-dead. They didn't go anywhere and they sure weren't building any ships like we built, or doing much of anything else. I thought we did a pretty good job even if our ship didn't look like the fancy yachts in Terry's books. I still didn't see how it was going to start falling apart anytime soon, but from the way it sounded Terry was going to make us work on it all the time anyway. I wondered if I was even going to have any fun when we finally got to the exciting places he promised us we were going. It didn't suck as bad as going to school, but it would still suck if we went to some island somewhere that had coral reefs and crystal clear water like I'd seen on Animal Planet and I still couldn't go swimming and snorkeling because I had to work on the boat.

Janie said we'd be the only ones down there in the islands on an ugly old homemade boat. She said she'd seen a movie back when we still had a TV about some people that cruised around on a big yacht. She said nobody used sails anymore and that real yachts were like small, private cruise ships and they had air conditioners and real showers in them and even washing machines and dryers.

"You know Terry said we're going to have to wash our clothes in a bucket! And that we're going to have to bath in seawater because we can't waste freshwater."

"He said seawater is clean," I countered. "Especially way out in the middle, away from land."

"Clean? How can it be clean if fish take a crap in it? It's nasty, Robbie! Hell, even *whales* crap in it! Can you imagine how big a whale turd must be?"

I didn't know for sure, but I figured it must be pretty big. Terry said where we were going we were certainly going to see whales. He said some of them would be longer than our boat too, and forty-six feet is pretty long. He also said we were going to see a lot of sharks, but that we wouldn't have to worry about them because they wouldn't mess with us if we didn't swim at night or stay in the water a long time with a bloody fish when we were spearfishing. I couldn't wait to go spearfishing, but I knew I was going to be scared of the sharks when I did.

I wasn't worried too much about what other people thought of our boat like Janie was though. I knew some people might think it was ugly, but I was proud of it because I helped build it. Maybe it was homemade and maybe it wasn't perfect, but I could see what Terry meant when he said she had "nice lines." He said James Wharram's catamarans were his interpretation of the originals that the Polynesians sailed thousands of years ago. He pointed out the upswept bows and the long overhangs on the bow and stern of each hull and talked about how they would lift to the seas and ride over them rather than plunge through them like a lot of modern catamarans. He called most of the modern catamarans "condomarans" anyway and said they weren't good for anything but tying up to the dock to have a place to

60

drink margaritas right next to the rest of the shore bastards.

When we finally had all the pieces and parts lashed down, our catamaran really did look like a ship sitting there near the edge of the lakeshore, her twin bows pointed towards the water like she was ready to go somewhere far away. There was still a lot to do to get organized and ready to splash her. Terry said we had to have a christening ceremony to give her a proper name and invoke the blessings of the various gods of the sea and wind. It was already too late in the day for that by the time we were finished though, so he said we would sleep aboard with the boat still "on the hard" and get up at first light for the christening and launch.

When they found out they weren't going to get to watch us try to get our huge catamaran in the water that afternoon, most of the fishermen and campers who had been hanging around wandered off or went home. Terry told them to come back in the morning if they wanted to be a part of it, and most of them said they would, but I didn't believe them and neither did Terry.

Janie finally showed back up just before dark when the two boys she'd taken the boat ride with came back to the ramp to haul their boat out on the trailer. I knew she'd been drinking beer with them because I could smell it on her breath just like I sometimes did when she came home from Friday night football games at school. I'm pretty sure Terry knew too, but he never said anything about it because he just figured it was easier to get along with Janie if he let her do whatever she wanted. Mom would have been mad, but she couldn't smell much of anything most of the time. She'd had a stopped-up and runny nose ever since we moved south to Mississippi and said it was allergies due to all the stuff blooming here year round. Terry told her that once we got out to sea the salt air would clear that right up.

"Salt is the cure for everything, and there's no purer place to get it than out on the open ocean, far from the pollution, filth, and stench of industrialized, commercialized and urbanized land! Where we're going, you'll breathe better than you ever have in your life, Linda, that's a promise!"

I didn't know if that was true or not, but when it got dark in the boat ramp parking lot where the boat was assembled, even the lake air felt different than the air back home in Calloway City. It was cooler and scented with pine from the surrounding forest. This was going to be our first night to sleep on the boat; even if it was high and dry "on the hard," as Terry said was the proper nautical term for a ship out of water. I was excited about it and nervous at the same time. My bunk was in the forward part of the starboard hull in my own tiny cabin, which was separated from Janie's cabin in the back of the same hull by a small central area where we had a built-in desk and bookshelves and where a wooden ladder went up to the hatch opening onto the decks. Although it sounds like a lot to say that I had my own cabin, the truth is the whole thing wasn't much bigger than the closet I had in my bedroom back home. A cabin in a boat is different than a room in a house though, and like Terry said, with the built-in bunk and every little space and nook and cranny utilized for storage, there was enough room. After we sat outside eating the sandwiches Mom had made at home before we left, I finally climbed down to my bunk when it was time to go to bed. For some reason I kept calling the old house in Calloway City, home. It was going to take a while to think of the boat as home in the same way a house was.

Four

I DIDN'T SLEEP MUCH that first night on the boat. My bunk wasn't as soft as my old bed at home, and wasn't as wide either. Janie was listening to her dumb music on her iPad with her stupid Bluetooth speakers instead of her ear buds, so that made it hard to sleep too because the sound carried right through the thin plywood bulkheads separating our cabins. Mom and Terry couldn't hear it because they were way over in the other hull, completely separate from ours. I knocked on the bulkhead to her cabin but she just yelled at me to leave her alone.

On top of all that, when she finally did turn it off way after midnight, there were all kinds of weird sounds coming from outside around the lake and the surrounding forest. I knew what most of them were: croaking frogs, singing cicadas and crickets and hooting owls, but once in a while there would be a big splash in the lake and I wondered if it was an alligator. Then I wondered if an alligator could climb up onto the boat if it wanted to, and it seemed to me like it probably could, especially once we got it in the water. Terry said we'd see lots of alligators on the Tenn-Tom Waterway, especially when we got down south near Mobile. I wanted to see them, but I sure didn't want them to get too close. What I really wanted to see though was a real live shark. Terry promised me there'd be plenty when we got to the Gulf, and even more in the tropical islands we'd eventually sail to. He said we'd see whales and giant manta rays and all kinds of cool stuff. He said he'd seen all that and more so many times he couldn't remember them all.

I must have fallen asleep despite all the noise because the next thing I remembered, I was seeing daylight streaming through the tinted lens of the hatch over my bunk and hearing Terry's voice somewhere up on deck. I stuck my head out and found him sitting in the cockpit drinking coffee with Mom.

"All hands on deck, Robbie! Tell your sister that means her too! We've got time for a quick breakfast and then it's time to do the ceremony and launch!"

Terry had told me several times before how important it was to do a proper christening ceremony when you launch a ship. He said most traditions and rituals like this were nonsense if they had to do with anything on land, but for sailors things were different. He said that seafarers couldn't be too careful, and anyway, whether it did any good or not, we weren't about to forsake the time-honored way to launch our own ship after all the hard work we put into building it.

Janie was in a bad mood about having to wake up before sunrise, especially since Terry had promised her that neither one of us would ever have to get up early and go to school again.

"I don't see what the big deal is," she said. "You could have let me sleep through the launch."

"No way, Miss Janie, you've got the most important role here. You're the virgin maiden who gets to do the honors!"

Janie didn't look impressed or honored, but I thought it was a good thing we got the boat built when we did. At the rate she was going, hanging out with older boys like those two from yesterday afternoon, she probably wouldn't be a virgin much longer, if she even was now. Terry had told me before that normally when you launch a ship, the young woman who was selected to do the christening had to break a bottle of champagne across the bow. He said we weren't going to use champagne though because it was too expensive and pretentious, and that the gods of the winds and seas probably preferred rum anyway. And since our ship was a catamaran, breaking a bottle across both bows at the same time wasn't feasible, so he thought that it would be all right to just open the bottle and let Janie pour some over each bow in turn.

By the time we were ready to do all this, two old gray-haired couples that were staying in their motorhomes in the campground, and had watched the assembly the day before, wandered back over with their coffee mugs in hand to see the show. Men driving pickup trucks with fishing boats on trailers behind them started showing up too, and I recognized at least two of them from the day before as well. Terry said they probably came to the lake every day and probably didn't care whether they caught any fish or not, they were just looking for something to do and a place to go to get away from their wives. Today the men just parked their trucks without launching their boats first, so pretty soon we had a small crowd gathered around to see what we were going to do next.

When all of us were ready and waiting in front of the boat where Terry said we needed to be for the ceremony, he reached up high to the front side of the starboard hull and pulled off the big piece of cardboard that he'd taped to the side with blue painter's tape. Then he walked to the port hull and pulled the cardboard off that one too, finally revealing the painted ship's name that had been hidden under them until now! When he did, you could hear whispers among the people watching:

"*Apocalypse!* Ain't that from the Book of Revelations?" one of the fishermen asked.

"Yes, that's what most people associate it with," Terry answered, to no one in particular. "The End of The World As We Know It and the promise of impending doom!"

"Now why would anyone want to go and name a boat a funny name like that?" someone else wondered aloud.

"Maybe he's a preacher," another fisherman said.

"Probably so, look at him now:"

Terry was standing in front of the boat, with Janie beside him. He had both arms upraised to the heavens, the bottle of rum held high in one hand:

"I name this ship, *Apocalypse*!" he declared as he lowered his gaze and stared long and hard at the creation resulting from all our hard work. "May she bring fair winds and good fortune to all who sail on her, and may Neptune, king of all that moves in or on the waves; and Aeolus, guardian of the winds and all that blows before them, look after her and her crew wherever she may sail!"

With that, Terry opened the bottle of rum and handed it to Janie. "Just about a third on each bow, Janie. Save a swig for each of the crew, it's part of the good luck!

"Reckon he ain't a preacher then," I heard one of the men say. But another said he probably was and that his preacher liked to take a drink of whiskey now and then too.

"If it was me, I'd be sayin' a prayer to *Jesus*! Especially if I was about to get on a homemade boat named the *Apocalypse* with my whole family and head to the Gulf!"

Janie reached up and poured a splash of the rum over the upswept stem of the starboard hull. When Terry said that was enough, she walked over to the port hull and did the same. Then, she raised the bottle to her lips and took a big drink, contorting her face and coughing a bit as she did, but swallowing it all. Terry told her to save some for the rest of us and she handed the bottle to him. He passed it to Mom, who said she didn't really want any rum this early in the morning, but Terry insisted that she should at least take a sip to make the ceremony complete. Then he offered it to me.

"Terry! He's just twelve!" Mom said.

"He's my navigator!" Terry snapped back. "In the days of wooden ships and iron men, boys not much older than Robbie were earning their own commands. Not to mention everybody on board, even the scrawniest cabin boys had their daily ration of rum. It's not going to kill him, Linda!"

I took the bottle from him with some trepidation. I'd never tasted rum before, but Janie had let me have a sip or two of beer she sneaked into her room one time. I tipped the bottle cautiously and let a bit of it flow between my lips. It burned like fire, but I couldn't look like a sissy in front of all those fishermen, especially if Janie could do it. I swallowed it and stood up straight and tall as I could as I swaggered back over to Terry with the bottle and offered it back to him like we did this all the time. Mom just shook her head, clearly disapproving, but I knew that from now on, Terry was the captain of this ship and he would probably get his way over most of her objections about most things. I figured that would be a good thing sometimes, and probably a real bad thing at other times.

With the christening done, Terry was anxious to get on with the launching. He'd counted on bystanders and fishermen being around to help, and so when he explained his plan to the group, one of the men, who said his name was Jimmy went and got in his truck and backed his bass boat down the launching ramp. Terry had asked him if he could take our main bow anchor out to deep water and drop it, and Jimmy had readily agreed. As Jimmy was getting his boat off the trailer and moving his truck back out of the way, Terry was already giving orders to the rest of us, including the other strangers who offered to help.

"When I get the port bow high enough, pull that cradle out from under it, Robbie," he said to me as he pumped the handle of the small hydraulic floor jack we'd used yesterday to level the hulls up for assembly. "We'll get both bows lowered on the rollers and then do the same for the sterns."

What he meant by rollers were the two dozen or so three-foot sections of round fence posts he'd cut to length in the backyard shortly after we'd finished construction. The support cradles didn't have wheels on them and Terry didn't want to put any on because he said we needed to keep the deep-V hulls as low to the ground as possible when launching so that they would float as soon as they had a couple of feet of water under them. "This is the way ships have been launched since before the Vikings, Robbie! Do you think they had trucks and trailers in those days? We'll set an anchor in deep water and then winch her right in. It won't take much persuasion; because once we get her started, gravity will do the work."

"TAKE IT OUT ANOTHER FIFTY FEET, JIMMY!"

71

SAILING THE APOCALYPSE

Terry yelled to the man in the boat.

When Jimmy was in a position Terry was happy with, he dropped the anchor with a big splash at Terry's signal. Terry clambered up on deck and began hauling in the slack in the heavy nylon anchor line. We couldn't call it an "anchor line" though because Terry said the correct term was "anchor rode." It was another one of those stupid nautical words I had to memorize, and I wondered if he made it up at first, but then I saw it written in one of his sailing books.

"Janie, I need you on deck to tail the winch as I crank it in. Robbie, you and your mom need to watch and keep moving those rollers from the stern to the bow as she starts going forward. But stay out of the way, because once she starts moving, nothing's going to stop her until she splashes!"

I got into position on the outside of the starboard hull and mom took the port side. Several of the bystanders wanted to help and Terry said that was okay, just as long as they stayed out of the way and didn't get run over when the *Apocalypse* started rolling.

At first, nothing much happened. You could hear Terry grinding on the big winch he'd installed to handle the anchor rode, and you could hear the rope creaking and stretching. I wondered if it was about to break as I saw it stretch tight, dripping with water where it made a taunt, quivering line from the big roller on the forward crossbeam to the sunken anchor two hundred feet out in the lake. It didn't break though, and suddenly the whole ship began to inch forward.

Terry kept cranking the winch and the round posts under the keels began to roll. The part of the parking lot where we'd assembled the catamaran was pretty flat, but in just a few more feet, it started sloping downhill the rest of the way to the boat ramp. That was the part Terry was talking about when he said once it got moving, there would be no stopping it. I just hoped it wouldn't go faster than Mom and the rest of my helpers could keep up with the rollers. If it did, it would slide on the concrete. We had built up the bottoms of the keels with extra fiberglass and layers of what Terry called sacrificial wood in case we hit a reef, but I still didn't want to take a chance of springing a leak. The last thing I wanted was to be way out on the ocean somewhere with all those sharks in a leaky boat. Terry said it wouldn't sink even if we hit something and knocked a hole in the bottom because of all the watertight bulkheads that segmented each hull into lots of separate sections. But I knew any ship could sink, just look at the *Titanic*. They said it was unsinkable too when they built it. We didn't even know if our boat was going to float to begin with. Thinking about that made me nervous too, and I heard some of the fishermen whispering about it. That's probably why most of them were here, just to see if it was going to sink or not when we put it in the water for the first time.

But Terry wasn't worried about that and he kept cranking away on the winch. The hulls rolled forward, and as they moved off the rearmost rollers, we hurried to shuffle those to the front so there would always be something for it to roll on.

SAILING THE APOCALYPSE

After a few times of doing this, the *Apocalypse* was moving downhill on her own.

"STAND BACK!" Terry shouted, and we all did. The big catamaran picked up speed and Terry couldn't turn the winch fast enough to keep the slack out of the line. When the bows slid into the water, the keels ran off the last of the rollers at about the same time. You could hear fiberglass and wood grinding on the concrete ramp, but the ship was still moving, and only a little slower than when she was rolling. Terry caught up with winching in the line and kept pulling the *Apocalypse* towards the anchor with the winch, dragging her down the ramp. I winced at the sounds of inevitable damage but Terry didn't seem to care. It was like that was why he'd added the sacrificial keel strips, just to grind them off during the launching.

Finally, both hulls were completely afloat and it looked to me like they were mostly level with each other. I saw Janie looking over one side at the water, and then back at all of us like she couldn't believe this thing we'd built was actually a boat. But it was, and boy was I was excited now! The *Apocalypse* didn't show any signs of sinking, and I was ready to get on board.

"Come on, Mom! It's time to go!"

"Now hold on a minute, Robbie. Terry and your sister have got to get that boat under control and back to the dock. Then we can get on board."

Watching them closely now, I could see that mom was

SCOTT B. WILLIAMS

right. Terry was now trying to lower the two outboard motor sleds into the water and Janie was just standing there like she didn't know what to do, which she didn't. The ship was drifting sideways now and the anchor rode was slack. When he finally got the motors down in the water, Terry climbed down on the starboard sled and started pulling the rope starter cord. He pulled and pulled and nothing happened. I heard him cuss and say something about crappy ethanol gas and then he pulled some more. The other people watching started talking about all the things that could be the problem: dirty spark plugs, clogged fuel filter, maybe he forgot to pull the choke, and this and that, on and on. As we watched, Terry gave up on the starboard motor and went over the one on the port side. He pulled that one a dozen times and nothing happened with it either. I heard him cuss some more. I remembered that he hadn't tested either one of the motors since he bought them several months ago, but each one was working when he did, because the sellers had demonstrated that they ran before he handed them the cash.

When it was clear that he wasn't going to be able to get either one of the motors started on his own, Jimmy, the man who'd taken the anchor out in his fishing boat said he would go out and help. I asked him to take me with him and he said okay. We got in his boat and he pulled it up alongside the *Apocalypse*, but not without banging his aluminum boat against our hull, scratching our new paint. Terry didn't say anything about that now though, he just handed me a line and told me to tie the fishing boat off alongside our ship and hold it steady while Jimmy climbed aboard. Later, when we were alone he said that Jimmy's carelessness and lack of boat-handing skill was typical of landlubbers and just proved you couldn't put a farmer on a boat.

When we were all in the cockpit, Jimmy asked Terry some questions about the motors and Janie just sat there looking bored like she always did. I watched as Jimmy climbed down and took the cover off the starboard motor. It was the bigger one, the ten-horsepower Evinrude. He asked Terry if he had any tools and pretty soon he had taken the spark plug out, cleaned it and put it back in.

"It oughta fire right up now," Jimmy said. "Give it a try."

Terry did and the motor sputtered and came to life, then smoothed out and ran normally when he adjusted the throttle. Jimmy had a big grin on his face and Terry thanked him for his trouble. I wanted to ask Terry what we would have done if somebody who knew what he was doing when it came to fixing motors weren't around, but I figured I'd better not. Jimmy checked the port side outboard as well and soon had it running too.

"Them motors are old, but they'll run a long time long as you don't get water in the gas and you run a clean filter to keep trash out. It don't do 'em no good to set up, so try to run 'em most every day if you can."

Terry said there was no doubt we would, at least for the next few days as we had hundreds of miles of motoring ahead of us to get down the Tenn-Tom Waterway. He said after that it didn't matter if the motors ran or not and that he might toss them overboard to get rid of the weight anyway once we got under sail out on the high seas.

"That'd be crazy right there," Jimmy said. "You can't count on the wind blowing all the time and you can't figure out which way it's gonna be coming from most of the time anyway."

"It's different out on the ocean," Terry said. "Without the effects of land, the wind at sea is predictable and quite reliable. How you do think they settled the New World back in the day? They didn't have motors then."

"They didn't have no choice like you do," Jimmy said. "It ain't like they threw 'em overboard. I reckon ole Christopher Columbus wouldn't a thrown an outboard like that over the side if he had it, even if it *was* a little wore-out ten-horse two-stroke!"

Terry just gave him a blank stare, but I knew from seeing that look time and time again that it was full of contempt. He thought he was smarter than everybody, especially somebody who talked like Jimmy. Maybe he was, but that didn't give him an excuse to look down on everybody. I wondered if he'd always been that way or if was because he was a teacher, or maybe because of all the places he'd said he'd been and things he'd said he'd done. Whatever it was, as long as I'd known him I had never seen him admit that somebody else might know something he didn't. Even now, after Jimmy fixed the motors, Terry didn't give him credit for it. He told me later he would have checked the spark plugs next but since Jimmy insisted on helping, he had let him. He said guys like that who spent all their time fishing and working on old motors and trucks liked to do it so much that letting Jimmy fix it was doing him a favor. He could now brag to his buddies about how easily he'd figured it out and the other onlookers who saw it would look up to him like he was some kind of genius.

Jimmy asked if we needed any help getting the anchor up and Terry said we didn't. He said we'd haul it in and then motor alongside the small wooden dock beside the boat ramp so Mom could get on board and he could check everything and make sure the ship was good to go before we set off to go south. Jimmy climbed back down into his boat and untied his lines from the *Apocalypse*, letting his boat drift nearby while he watched us make ready to go to the dock. My job was to keep the anchor rode straight by laying it down neatly in three or four-foot sections in the built in anchor rode storage box under the forward deck. Terry called this "flaking" the line and said it was critical to do it right so that if we had to anchor fast in an emergency the line would pay out without tangling up. I didn't have any problems until the last thirty feet or so came on deck. This part of the rode was a piece of heavy chain shacked between the anchor and end of the nylon rope part. Because it was heavy, Terry said it would stay down on the bottom and keep the pulling forces against the anchor at a low angle, which would make it hard

SCOTT B. WILLIAMS

for the anchor to pull out of the seabed when we needed it to hold in a storm. He said that chain was also necessary for that last part of the rode because any kind of rope would be sliced right through the first time we anchored over a coral bottom in the tropics.

The chain had stayed on the bottom all right; that was obvious because as he winched it on board, it was covered with black, stinking mud that got all over my hands. I didn't know what to do, so I wiped them on my trousers, and Terry yelled at me, saying that now I would get the mud all over the decks and in the cabin. Janie yelled too, telling me to stay away from her, but I raised my muddy hands up and lunged at her like some kind of swamp creature. She ran screaming down below and locked herself in her cabin.

"What you've got to do, Robbie," Terry said, "is have a bucket full of water and a scrub brush on deck so that when than chain comes aboard, you can wash the mud off." He dug around in the cockpit storage lockers until he finally found a bucket. The first thing he did was tie it to a small piece of line so he could dip it over the side to fill it, then he poured all the water on me, attempting to wash off the mud. The water smelled almost as bad as the mud, but I didn't care, I just wanted that thick, gooey muck off me. We finished cleaning off the chain and the decks and by this time the ship had drifted close to the bank to about a hundred feet from the dock. I heard something thump loudly against the hull closest to shore and ran to the side only to see that we'd banged into the protruding stump of a big dead tree. More paint was scraped off, worse than the place on the other hull where Jimmy had hit it with his boat.

Terry put the starboard engine in reverse and slowly backed away from the shore to deeper water. I figured he did it just in time or we would have been stuck in the mud near the bank. He shifted it to forward and adjusted his course and the *Apocalypse* slowly started moving towards the dock, where Mom was standing, watching our every move. As we got closer, I wondered aloud when he was going to start slowing down.

"Don't worry, Robbie. I'll back down in reverse at the last minute and she'll lie right alongside that dock just perfect."

I didn't say anything, but when he went to put the outboard in reverse, there was an awful racket as the whole motor kicked up out of the water, the prop still spinning and the boat drifting forward just as fast as ever. I saw him frantically trying to wrestle the motor back into the water but it was stuck on its bracket in the tilted-up position and he couldn't get it down again. I didn't know what I could do to help, and Terry was cussing so much he couldn't hear me ask him. I glanced back at Mom and saw that she was backing up fast to get out of the way just before our catamaran crashed into the dock. I heard the sound of wood splintering and cracking and I lost my balance and fell to the deck when the boat came to a sudden stop. By now Terry had the engine shut down and he was climbing up out of the motor sled to try and get to the dock and fend it off.

Janie screamed from down below because she didn't know what happened and was scared, and I heard yelling and laughing from some of the people watching from on shore. I got back on my feet and handed Terry the mooring line he asked for, as he stood on the dock hanging onto the side of the hull to keep it from drifting back into deep water. Mom came back out on the dock to help too, and when I looked down from the deck, I saw that our boat had broken the ends off of several of the dock planks and pushed one of the pilings over enough that it was leaning at an angle. When I stepped down there, I saw that our hull side had cracked too, and there was an ugly, ten-foot long scrape right down the side where the paint was missing. With this and all the other scrapes and bangs we'd gotten in the first half hour, I resigned myself to a life of hard work. Just keeping the damage fixed all the time was going to be bad enough, never mind the *entropy*.

Terry said it was no big deal and the crack was nothing epoxy resin couldn't fix one evening when we were at anchor on the way south. I asked about the damage to the dock and he said it was old and shoddily built or else it wouldn't have broken so easily.

"A dock is supposed to be able to stand up to a little impact, Robbie. What do you think happens when ships come alongside in bad weather? Whoever built this one clearly didn't understand proper construction techniques. We

81

were barely moving when we touched it."

"Maybe they didn't build it for ships as big as ours, though."

"Then that's their fault, Robbie. Like I told that ranger the other day, the only reason this lake exists is because it is part of the inland navigation route of the Tenn-Tom Waterway. They should have known bigger vessels than these bass boats would be using it."

"It looks like you've got a chance to tell him that again," I said, pointing in the direction of the parking lot, where the ranger had just parked his truck and was getting out to come and see what all the commotion was about. Terry pretended to ignore him and kept fussing with the dock lines and checking for more damage to our hull.

The ranger walked right through the small crowd directly to the dock, but I could hear some of the fishermen telling him what happened as he did. I figured we were in big trouble for messing up the dock, especially since this was the same ranger who didn't want to let us launch the *Apocalypse* in the lake to begin with. He looked at our ship like he was surprised it was actually floating, then walked out on the dock and saw all the damage we did.

"How did this happen?" he asked Terry.

"Failure of the locking pin on the motor-tilt bracket," Terry answered. "When I put it in reverse to back down, the motor kicked up out of the water and then hung up in the tilt position so that I couldn't get it back down in time to slow our drift."

"I told you that thing was too big for our launching ramp! Look what you did to my dock!"

"How is it *your* dock?" Terry countered. "Did you personally pay for it and install it yourself, or was it provided by the federal government for the users of this park with proceeds collected from taxpayers such as myself and all these other fine folks out here today?

"It's under my supervision. Who paid for it doesn't matter! What does matter is that you're going to have to pay to have it fixed, or at least your insurance company is."

"Insurance? Do you actually think I have insurance on a vessel like this? You ought to try and explain to an insurance company what wood and epoxy composite construction is. They don't have a clue. All they hear is the word "wood" and they say they don't insure "wooden" boats. Then they find out we built it ourselves and they say they don't insure "homemade" boats. So I had to say to hell with insurance! They won't sell it to us and we couldn't afford it if they would! We don't need it anyway because if we could build the boat in the first place, we can fix anything that happens to it."

"Well, I hope you can afford to fix what it broke out of pocket too. I'm going to have to fill out a report and issue you a citation, and that includes taking down your vessel registration information and mailing address. I'll get a contractor out here to give me an estimate and I'll send you the bill once the work is complete."

SAILING THE APOCALYPSE

"We don't have a mailing address because where we live is wherever this ship is, which won't be here. I'm not paying some crooked contractor who'll charge double what a simple job like this is worth. If you're going to get all bent out of shape about a few broken boards, I've got the tools and know-how to put them back myself, and it won't take long. Just let us get the boat secured and my stepson and I will get started on it right away."

"Fine, but I'm still filing a report. If you don't fix it, or you do a half-assed job of it, I'm not letting it slide, just so you understand! It doesn't matter if you have an address or not. Those numbers on the side of your hull are going to follow you wherever you go, so don't think you can just sail away and skip out on your responsibility for this! It wasn't broke before you got here with that raft, and it better not be broke when you leave!"

Five

WHEN THE RANGER AND most of the bystanders left, I didn't think Terry would ever stop ranting about that officer's threat and the stupidity and the injustice of a system that assigns numbers to everything, including our ship.

"You see what I told you about being nothing more than a number, Robbie? That's all the *Apocalypse* is to them, all I am, all you are; all any of us are! They make us buy the damned numbers for the hull and then use the same numbers to keep track of us wherever we go to extract even more money by threats of jail! But what he doesn't know is that this Mississippi state boater's registration number doesn't mean much where we're going, and they'll never find us once we get there. If it wasn't for those damned locks downstream, and all those river miles we've got to motor, I'd raise sail and disappear over the horizon right now! Why should I waste my time and money fixing something that was broken by accident?"

"Probably because you were the one who broke it," I said.

"It doesn't matter who did it! With as much tax money as they get for funding parks like this and paying morons like him to enforce their stupid rules, they should have plenty left over to allow for maintenance and minor repairs. I imagine some of these idiots in their fishing boats have hit a dock or two in their day too. And look what they spend just on all the signs they've put up all over this place telling you what you can and can't do! It's bureaucracy, Robbie. Mindless bureaucracy! The only purpose for its existence is to spend the taxpayers' money by making rules, and then spend even more money enforcing them. With all the tickets they write, not to mention extorting honest folks like us to do their repairs for them, they have even more money to buy their fancy trucks and patrol boats! I'm telling you, Robbie, the only answer is to get as far away from here as fast as we can before we go broke! But now we're going to lose a whole day going to get lumber and fooling around with saws and hammers to fix this pathetic excuse for a dock."

I thought we were lucky that Mom's car was still here, parked at the lake until my cousins could come and get it. Without the car, we wouldn't have had a way to go get the boards we needed for the dock repairs and may have had to pay one of the fishermen who had a truck to take us. The car wasn't ideal, but since we didn't need anything heavier than a few eight-foot two-by-sixes, Terry said we could tie them down to the roof of the car. He asked Jimmy where the nearest building supply store was and Jimmy said it was in Booneville, a little over twenty miles away. Terry cussed some more about how long it would take to go that far and back but asked Mom for the spare key she still had and told me to come with him. Mom and Janie would stay with the ship.

"I thought I'd seen the last of American roads when we launched our ship this morning, Robbie. But here we are again, once more behind the wheel of a car and at risk of instant death by blunt force trauma at every mile, all for a few boards! If we survive this last car trip, I'm ditching my driver's license for good."

"Don't you need it to drive the *Apocalypse*?" I asked. This was something we hadn't really discussed. I knew Terry was going to be the official captain, even though he said we'd all be taking turns steering. I figured he'd at least have to have a driver's license.

"No, Robbie. As long as we leave now before they make a new law, we don't need a captain's license to pilot our own ship, at least as long as we're not taking passengers for hire."

"But I figured whoever was in charge would at least have to have a driver's license to drive something that big. Just look what it did to that dock, and we were barely moving when it hit."

"That dock was half-rotten and should have been torn down. If it hadn't been there in the way, the bows of our catamaran would have just dug into the mud a bit at the lake's edge and she would have come to a stop without a scratch. Now you're going to have to repaint the topsides on both hulls."

"Great! I figured it was going to mean more work for me."

"Not work, just keeping entropy at bay, Robbie. Don't forget what I said. By keeping on top of maintenance you're making sure the ship beneath us won't let us down when she's put to the test by the sea. Thinking of it as work is the wrong attitude."

I knew we had to do it, but it was *still* work. Work was anything that wasn't fun, like riding my bicycle or swimming and diving when we got somewhere with the nice water that Terry had promised. I hated doing chores because they had to be done over and over again and they never got done for good. I could see now that painting the boat over and over and over was going to be almost as bad as having to mow the yard every week all summer long. In Mississippi, it was so hot and rained so much in the summer, by the time you got through mowing it once, the grass was already growing again in the first place you started.

We finally found the lumber store in Booneville, and Terry picked through the pressure-treated two-by-sixes until he found what he estimated he needed. Using some spare Dacron line he'd brought from the ship, he lashed the boards directly on the roof of the Camry by passing several turns through the open front and rear windows. I asked if the boards wouldn't scratch up the paint and Terry said it didn't matter since Mom had sold the car to my cousins for such a ridiculously low price.

"They shouldn't even get to keep the wheels for what they paid, not to mention they'll still have almost a half a tank of free gas in it when we get back to the lake. I should siphon it out and sell it to one of those fishermen to make up for some of the forty-five dollars we had to pay for lumber and nails for that stupid dock!"

On the way back, Terry launched back into a tirade about registration and licensing. He explained that he'd done his research on this and determined that despite what most other voyaging sailors did, he wasn't going to apply for federal documentation of the *Apocalypse* with the U.S. Coast Guard. He said state registration was simpler and faster, and that while it might raise some eyebrows with customs officials in some countries, where we were going he didn't plan to check in at any official ports of entry anyway.

"That's another beauty of a Wharram catamaran, Robbie. Even though it's a big liveaboard sailboat, it doesn't draw much more water than a skiff. All those deep-keeled conventional boats have to follow the established and predictable routes. In most places sailors go, the port cities and their greedy customs and immigrations officers are located right next to the only deep harbors and channels that funnel in marine traffic and the money that comes with it.

SAILING THE APOCALYPSE

Those yachties sail right in and pay whatever is asked without question, but not us, Robbie! We don't have to. We can slip through the back door and enter the most remote island groups by simply sailing over the shallow banks and coral reefs that keep everyone else out. We can find our own private anchorages in tropical lagoons practically no one else visits. We can stay as long as we want for free and leave without telling anyone. Once we reach the South Pacific we won't be going back to any place where registration, documentation or license numbers matter."

"How do you know it hasn't changed?" I asked. "Maybe now they have webcams at those places and they know when you get there."

"You still don't understand just how isolated some parts of the Pacific really are, Robbie. Some of those island groups are so remote that the nearest other rock is hundreds of miles away...a thousand or more in some cases. There are *no* people on those kinds of islands, Robbie; no one to put up a webcam and nowhere to plug it in anyway, even if there was a way to connect it to the Internet. You'll see. There *are* still places where everyone doesn't have an iPhone in their pocket! There wouldn't be much longer, if things keep going the way they are going, but there's no way they can, Robbie. All this technology is bound to self-destruct! Even here, the ones who are left alive will be back to calling their neighbors by beating on a drum, if they call them at all."

We made it back to Bay Springs Lake in the early

afternoon and Terry rushed to get out his tools and replace the damaged boards on the dock so we could leave. I helped him measure and cut the new ones and we pried off the broken ones and stacked them in a pile near the boat ramp. Mom was busy organizing all the things in the galley to starboard and the big cabin she and Terry shared in the port hull, and I figured Janie was in her bunk with her ear buds in, blasting music. We didn't need any help anyway, and after a couple of hours we were done. Terry told me to run up to the ranger's office and tell him he could come take a look at our repair. The last thing we wanted was to get stopped somewhere on the river by a water cop he called because he claimed we didn't fix it right. I couldn't find the ranger though and the office was closed. When I went back to the dock to tell Terry, he said it was probably because the ranger was off writing tickets and hassling someone else. He said we would go ahead and leave and that we didn't have time to sit around wasting all afternoon here when we had so many miles to go to get to the Gulf.

I was super excited that we were finally casting off. Terry made Janie come on deck to help, and when he finally got both outboards started again, he told us to stand by at the bow and stern where the lines were still looped around the dock pilings and to untie them when he said to. Leaving the dock was a little easier than pulling up to it, but Terry still managed to scrape the hull again. The new dock boards didn't break though; they just took more paint off our topsides in an ugly scratch I knew I would have to fix later.

When we were clear of the pilings and in deeper water, Terry couldn't make the catamaran go backwards in the direction he wanted it to. It would veer off to the side and then he would shift into forward to straighten it up and it would veer off the other way next time he put it in reverse. He said it was because sailboats were never designed to go backwards and that trying to back one up was stupid anyway.

"Once we're free of this inland waterway we won't ever need to back her up again, Robbie. Docks are for shore bastards who want to put on nautical airs to impress their friends. Real sailors drop the hook and anchor out; they never go into marinas and tie up in slips like a bunch of cars in a parking lot! It's idiotic to try and make a boat go in a direction she wasn't designed to go."

"So are we going to anchor out tonight?" I asked.

He said that of course we were, tonight and every other night and said there were several coves in the lakeshore between here and the big lock and dam at the end. He wanted to spend one night on the hook in the lake and then lock through going downstream early in the morning. Although Terry explained to me how the locks worked, I had never seen one in person much less been through one on a boat. He said the one at Bay Springs Lake was the highest one on the Tenn-Tom Waterway and that it would lower us eighty-four feet to the next level. Motoring across the lake surrounded by woods that you couldn't see through, it didn't seem like we were that high above anything to me, but he said there were several more smaller locks that we had to go through too in order get all the way down to sea level.

Terry was right about anchoring out being easier than docking; at least that first night. We turned off the main lake into an area of quiet water surrounded by tall pines and oak trees and he just put the motors in neutral and let us drift. When we eventually came to a stop, about a hundred feet from the wooded bank, he showed me how to slowly let out the anchor rode so the plow-shaped anchor would settle on the bottom and dig into the mud. The lake was calm, with barely a ripple, and the big, wide catamaran was so stable it was almost like still being on land or a small island. It didn't rock or move at all when you walked around on it, even out on the ends or near the edges. Terry said that was one of the advantages of sailing a catamaran, especially a Wharram.

"She won't roll and make you puke your guts out like those lead mine monohulls, Robbie. You'll understand the difference when we get to the Gulf and sail in a seaway. Catamarans have an easy motion for their size, and this Tiki 46 is big enough to handle any weather we're likely to see."

I didn't know about that, but I liked the calm water just fine. It was quiet and peaceful out there except for the occasional sound of a distant outboard from one of the fishing boats. Later that evening just as it was getting dark, we saw our first barge go by. It was huge and all lit up like a small town or something. Terry said for what the government spent building the locks and canals on this waterway, there should have been a dozen of them going by every hour. But we only saw that one, and then I heard one more go by sometime in the middle of the night. When I woke up the next morning the woods were noisy with the sounds of chattering squirrels and birds. I heard splashes from fish jumping too but nothing as big as that first night at the boat ramp when I was sure I heard an alligator.

Terry was going on and on telling Mom how great the *Apocalypse* really was now that we finally had her afloat. He was happier than I'd ever seen him since he first came into our lives, probably because he was finally doing what he'd been talking about the whole time. He had us all right where he wanted us too; a full crew to help him make his dream a reality and keep it moving. But even though he was grinning now, I knew it wouldn't be long before he was back to ranting, complaining or worrying about something.

All it took was the sound of a motor coming our way to completely change his mood. Somehow he just knew even before he looked through the big binoculars he kept by the helm, that the approaching boat was a law enforcement vessel. He was right, of course. As the dark green aluminum skiff drew near, I could see the blue light mounted on a short pole at the bow. It wasn't turned on, but the man steering was wearing a uniform and a hat, and he had a big pistol strapped on his belt.

"Good morning! How are you folks doing?" he asked as

he idled up close and tied alongside our starboard hull, probably scratching the paint even more I guessed since he didn't have any fenders on his metal boat and didn't wait for Terry to deploy ours. "Boy, this sure is some boat! It's what you call a catamaran, ain't it?"

"Sure is," Terry said. "It's a Wharram Tiki 46."

"Well, it's the biggest one I've ever seen. From distance, it looked like an over-grown Hobie Cat like the ones you see on the beach down in Pensacola. But the closer I got, boy-oh-boy! This thing's like a ship!"

"It *is* a ship," I said. "It's *our* ship and we built it ourselves to sail it to the other side of the world!"

"Is that right? Well, I reckon if you're sailing it'll take you about as long to get there as it did to build it. I hate to bother you folks so early in the morning, but I need to come aboard and check your registration and safety equipment," the officer said.

"We're completely legal," Terry said. "This vessel is fully compliant with the law and properly equipped to go to sea."

"Yes sir, I'm sure it is, but I have to take a look around. It won't take but a few minutes."

I could tell Terry was furious, though he was trying to hide it and act civil. The officer declined Mom's offer of a cup of coffee and instead asked to see our PFDs, emergency flares and fire extinguishers. He said that although we had the correct number of life jackets—one for every person on board—we were missing a Type IV "throwable" PFD and that he was going to have to write us citation for that. Then he checked Terry's boat registration card to verify that, and finally asked if any of us were planning on doing any hunting or fishing. Terry said we weren't but the officer, whose badge read "A. Riley, Mississippi Department of Wildlife, Fisheries and Parks," saw the fishing rods, landing nets and spearfishing equipment stashed in the cockpit lockers.

"All that stuff is for when we get to the Gulf and later to the islands," Terry explained. "We're not planning on doing any fishing in freshwater."

"The fact that you have it in your possession aboard a vessel in Mississippi waters is reason enough for me to write you a citation for fishing without a license. But since you're already getting one for a safety equipment violation, I'm going to give you a break this time on the fishing. It's a real pet peeve of mine when I see a fella like you out here with his family, not having everything you need to stay safe."

Terry said that considering the size of the *Apocalypse* and all the safety netting and guard rails around the decks, he didn't think it was likely anyone was going to go overboard, especially not here on the Tenn-Tom. He said he'd forgotten about the Type IV PFD and that he'd pick one up at the next place we stopped.

"You'd better, because you're going to be running across wildlife officers and marine police patrols wherever you go, Mr. Bailey. I'd advise you to keep this fishing gear put away and out of sight while you're in state waters too. Now, I've got to ask you one more question, have you got any firearms aboard?"

I knew the answer to that and so did Mom and Janie, but we all knew the drill too, because Terry had repeated it so many times that there was no way any of us could forget. Of course he had guns on board: a Colt .45 semi-automatic pistol, a bolt-action .22 hunting rifle with a scope and a Chinese SKS carbine that looked as old and beat-up as most of Terry's boatbuilding tools. He had all these on board, along with plenty of ammo for each one, but he had them well hidden in a secret storage compartment he designed and built into the boat during construction. He said that we might need them most anytime for defense against modern-day pirates. He said there were plenty of those in some parts of the world, like the Western Caribbean, through which we would have to pass on our way to the Panama Canal and the Pacific. But he said the main reason he had the guns is because we would certainly need them *after* the collapse, both to fend off attacks from the desperate shore bastards, and for hunting food, especially if it happened before we reached the atolls of the Pacific. He said it was vitally important that the weapons stayed hidden and that no customs or immigrations officials ever suspected we had them. He said most countries nowadays wouldn't allow them in, and if they did, they would take them and place them under lock and key until we cleared out, and what good would that do us if we needed them while we were still in those countries? Although the guns weren't illegal to have in Mississippi, I figured Terry was practicing his response to this question on Officer Riley. His face held no expression that betrayed his flat-out lie when he answered:

"No sir, absolutely not! Why would we need guns? I'm taking my family sailing on a trip of a lifetime. It's going to be an educational experience for the kids and I figure there's no place safer for us to be than out on the water, away from the drug-dealing, robbery, rape and murder of the mainland. Besides, I'm a teacher, not a policeman or soldier."

"If I was you, I would be packing something, Mr. Bailey. There are crazies out on the water just like everywhere else. But at least you won't look like some of these rich-assed Yankees we have coming through here on their way from the Great Lakes to Florida and the islands. You ought to see some of those yachts: Eighty, ninety-footers—some maybe a hundred—gotta be worth a few million, at least! They're just targets of opportunity once they get away from developed areas. And they're getting robbed and attacked more than you hear about in the news too, you can believe that."

"Well you won't see vessels like that where we're going. They don't have the fuel range to cross whole oceans the way we can with our sails. And after what's coming, those big yachts won't be anything but derelicts blocking the channels when they run their tanks dry. The oil will all be gone and that will be that."

"I don't see us running out of fuel anytime soon, Mr.

Bailey. We're doing more drilling in this country than we have in forty years. All that talk about the oil running out is just environmentalist nonsense. But I would still carry a means of protection on this boat if I were you, no matter where you're going. Now get that throwable PFD as soon as you can and think about your wife and kids before you do anything stupid. The Coast Guard recovers bodies every day lost off sailboats and powerboats, big and small; mainly the inexperienced, unprepared and overconfident who don't take the weather seriously. I've personally pulled a few floaters out of the drink right here on the Waterway. It happens a lot more often than you think!"

"Well we're not any of those things and we're not going to end up in the drink, either," Terry said. "Don't worry about us, we'll be fine. Now if there is nothing else you need to inspect, we'd like to finish our breakfast and get underway. We've got a long way to go today."

When he left, Terry cussed Officer Riley for writing the safety citation.

"At least he didn't write us one for fishing without a license," I said.

"That's just because it's so early in the morning and he's probably still in a good mood. If it was later in the day near the end of his shift and he hadn't written his quota, he would have given us one for sure. That's all they do; ride around in their boats looking for somebody to write up. They have to because the fines fund their salaries. But my money won't.

We'll be out of state waters soon and over the horizon like a mirage." With that, Terry tore the ticket in half and threw it overboard.

"He still seemed like a pretty nice guy," I said in Officer Riley's defense.

"What if he had found those guns?" Mom asked. "I still think it's a bad idea to have guns on board."

"They're perfectly legal, Linda, especially here, since I bought them legally as a resident of the state of Mississippi. He couldn't have said anything about them even if he had found them, and you heard what he said about thinking we *should* have at least one gun for self-defense. I started to tell him what we had, just so he wouldn't think I was too dumb to know I needed one, but decided against it because I figured it would be a good test of my hidden compartment if he searched the vessel."

"These redneck cops around here aren't looking for guns," Janie added. "All they want to do is bust somebody for having a joint, which is *exactly* what I wish I had right now!"

"Janie! Stop talking like that! You know you don't have any business even thinking about illegal drugs at your age," Mom said. Janie just rolled her eyes. Terry and I knew Mom was fooling herself. But Terry had had a long talk with Janie before we left about trying to sneak anything like that aboard our ship. He told her that most places where we might stop at first, like the Bahamas, had a zero tolerance policy against illegal drugs on vessels because of the drug smuggling crackdown that happened back when Reagan was president. He said they confiscated boats for having just one marijuana seed on board in some cases, and that we weren't taking any chances with losing the *Apocalypse* over some stupid joint after all the time and money we spent building her. He told Janie she could smoke all the pot she wanted while on shore and that it would be easy enough to find down there. But he also told her that if he found out she brought any of it back on board with her he would send her to Arkansas to some boarding school for girls he knew about. He said if that happened, she would wish she had listened to him when she found herself spending her days memorizing Bible verses and learning how to sew.

After we ate, and Terry finished his coffee, we started the two outboards again and pulled up the anchor. Once again, the chain was covered in black mud and I had to scrub it down as it came on deck. We headed south, straight in the direction of the huge lock and dam, which you could see in the distance from the marked channel in the middle of the lake. Terry called the lock master on the marine radio mounted near the helm, and a man replied, telling him there was no other traffic and the lock would be ready when we got there.

I still wasn't sure what to expect when we entered the lock, even though Terry had explained how it worked back when we first started talking about taking the Tenn-Tom Waterway route. Two huge gates like double barn doors closed behind us as we entered the box-like structure, with concrete walls on both sides and the same kind of double gates on the other end. A man working at the lock leaned over the railing above us and told Terry where to tie our lines. He said it was very important to tie them to the floating mooring bits that went down with the water, rather than the fixed walls of the lock, otherwise, the lines would either break when the water dropped or we'd be left hanging from the top. The man watching didn't leave until he was sure we'd done this correctly. Then a horn blew and the water around us started swirling and gurgling. I could feel the turbulence and the *Apocalyspe* moved back and forth against her lines as the water began to go down. It was kind of like we were being flushed in slow motion down a giant commode and I wondered what would happen if the gates broke or something. They didn't though; the walls around us just got higher and higher until it felt like we were way down in the bottom of a well. Finally, the water stopped dropping and calmed down, and then the horn blew again and the big gates on the downstream side started to slowly open. The man on the top of the wall who had been watching us waved as we untied our lines, and then Terry put the motors in gear and we headed out of the gate.

Everything looked different now that we were out of Bay Springs Lake. The Waterway looked more like a river now, except as we continued on, there were places where it widened out in a series of small lakes and then got narrow again. Most of the shoreline was nothing but woods, but in some places there was wide-open marsh with tall reeds and cattails. Just about every time we rounded a bend, water birds like ducks and herons would scatter and take flight at our approach. Most of them would land father downstream and then just do it all over again when we closed in on them the next time. They were too stupid to fly around us and go upstream where we wouldn't bother them, and I wondered if the same birds would keep flying ahead of us all the way to the Gulf.

We were in one of these narrow sections, when all of a sudden we came around a bend and there was a huge towboat pushing a long line of barges in front of it. The barges were tied up two wide and at least five long, with the towboat way in back. It was going a lot faster than we were and coming straight at us, and it didn't look to me like we had either the time or the room to get out of the way. Terry called the barge captain all kinds of nasty names, as if he could hear him that far away and over all the noise of his engines. He steered the *Apocalypse* hard to starboard to try and get out of the way and we hadn't gone thirty feet before the catamaran slammed to a stop, her bows plowing into the mud in an area of shallows.

The barge passed by just a few yards off our stern, but we couldn't see anybody inside the pilothouse through the dark tinted windows. Terry flipped them the bird anyway and was answered by a loud, prolonged blast of the towboat's horn. When the barge was gone, he tried putting both

103

outboards in reverse to back off the mud bottom, but even at full throttle they didn't have enough power to budge us. Terry cussed some more and said we'd either have to jump in at the bow and try and push it off, or waste an hour unpacking and inflating the rubber dinghy so we could set an anchor off the stern and try to winch ourselves off.

I was in favor of jumping in and pushing until I did. Since the *Apocalypse* only draws a little over two feet, Terry said we wouldn't even get wet much past our knees, but when I jumped in, I found out he was wrong. The problem was the bottom was nothing but yucky, soft mud. I could feel it when my feet hit it, but it didn't stop them from sinking at least another foot into it. I was in the water over my waist now and couldn't move my feet. When I pushed on the boat to try and free it from the mud, I just pushed my feet in even deeper. Terry was bogged down in it too, but he said the way you get out of mud like that was to stop fighting it because that just made you sink deeper. He said we weren't going to be able to budge the ship anyway, so we might as well focus on getting ourselves back on board. It didn't seem like it would work to me, but Terry said the trick is to just get down all the way into the water and try to swim. He said it would get the weight off your feet and help you break free of the mud. When I saw it work for him, I tried it too and I was finally able to pull my feet out. The only problem was that one of my shoes got left behind, buried in the muck. Terry didn't let us bring a lot of extra clothes and shoes with us, and these were my favorite sneakers, so I held my breath and dove under, feeling around blind until I had my missing shoe and pulled it loose. Terry said I shouldn't have jumped in wearing shoes in the first place, but I told him that in muddy water like that you never know what you might land on. I was glad to get back up on the boat anyway; thinking all our splashing around might have attracted some alligators. If there were any around, you sure couldn't see them in that kind of water until it was too late.

With the boat still stuck as firmly as ever, we had no choice now but to try and use the dinghy to set an anchor as far out from the stern as the rode would reach and try and winch it off. Terry said none of this would have happened if it wasn't for that towboat, but it looked to me like the captain didn't have much choice with all those barges he was pushing. He had to stay in the channel or run aground too, and it sure would have been a mess trying to get all those heavy steel barges out of that mud.

Terry wasn't joking when he said it would take at least an hour to get the dinghy ready and get an anchor set out. We had to unroll it on the foredeck of the catamaran, and then inflate all the separate air chambers with a foot pump. Then we had to take the smaller of the two outboards off its motor mount on the retractable sled, and carefully lower it into place on the transom of the inflatable without dropping it overboard. Then one of the spare anchor lines had to be unpacked and I had to carefully pay it out to keep it from getting tangled while Terry motored away with the anchor in the dinghy, pulling out the line behind him. It was a lot of trouble, and I wondered if it was even going to work.

But once the anchor was set and the line was wrapped around one of the big sheet winches in the cockpit, the *Apocalypse* had no choice but to back off the mud bar into deeper water. We had to be careful too not to let her drift back to either of the banks and get stuck again though. There were some tense moments while we retrieved all the anchor gear and remounted the outboard on its sled, but we did it. By the time all this was done, we heard the engines of another towboat coming around the bend, and as Terry cussed, I wondered if we were going to have to do it all over again.

Six

THE SECOND TOWBOAT WAS much smaller than the first and was only pushing a single barge that was carrying a big construction crane strapped down on its flat platform. I could tell Terry was relieved not to have a repeat of the last incident and he even gave the captain of this boat a friendly wave instead of flipping him off. He said it was ridiculous how many barges that other boat was pushing and that there ought to be regulations against it. He said they'd rather fine people on small craft like ours for something stupid like not having a throwable PFD on board than to bother the commercial vessels. He said it was the same as on the highways, with all the overloaded eighteen-wheelers blatantly breaking every kind of regulation and getting away with it most of the time.

"It's all about the money, Robbie. The corporations that

own the shipping and trucking industries pay off the right people and they can get away with murder. The police on the roads and on the water are all the same; it's easier for them to go after the low hanging fruit. They pick on private citizens like us because they know we can't afford to fight them in court. It's the same old story of corruption, Robbie. You can't get away from it anywhere there's organized society and that's why we're going where there isn't!"

The towboat and its barge with the crane disappeared around a bend upstream and then there was nothing to be seen but woods all around the waterway on both sides. Terry talked about how remote the islands where we were going were, but it seemed to me that we were already in the middle of nowhere. We didn't see another barge all day, and only passed one other person, a man fishing out of a small aluminum Johnboat. Terry said the isolation out here was just an illusion, because you couldn't go far in any direction without coming to a road, a house or some other manmade structure. He said there were no good places left in America where you could survive very long after the breakdown that was coming.

"Some people think they can bug out to the deep woods, or head for the hills, but they're mistaken, Robbie. There are simply too many people in the United States and too many of them are armed to the teeth. The ones that survive the initial crisis will be hunting each other down; first to steal food and supplies and when that's all gone, to eat whoever they can catch. Sure, there are a few big wilderness areas up north and out in the Rockies where a few tougher holdouts could make it for a while, but certainly not long-term. Times are going to be too hard in the high country for most people these days. Most of them are too soft to live like that anymore, especially in the winter. The only hope is to get as far away from all of it as possible. Halfway around the world is a good start! Having a ship that can take us there on our own and provide a platform for fishing and foraging is what gives us the edge. We won't need anything the mainland has to offer ever again!"

I still didn't understand how Terry was so sure everything here in America was going to collapse. I had flipped through some of his books on the subject and seen all the other ones he pointed out in the bookstore. But if those books were true, it seemed strange to me that most of the people I saw every day weren't worried about something like that happening. If things were really that bad, and life as we knew it was about to end, then why were so many people out camping and fishing at the lake like they didn't have a care in the world? Why was everybody else still going to school and work like normal? I didn't know a single other kid whose family had taken them out of school like Janie and me. I sure didn't know anybody else who had built a big catamaran sailing ship to leave the country on. But Terry was confident he was right and everybody else was just living with their heads buried in the sand, as he put it. He said they didn't want to think about things like that because then they would have to start doing something about it, and he said none of them wanted to do that. He said what they wanted to do was keep spending their paychecks and talking on their smart phones and burning up gas driving around in their big pickup trucks. He said all that, but I kind of envied all those other people who weren't so worried about running away. I hoped we weren't just leaving for no reason and I wondered how we would ever find out what happened back here if anything ever really did. If it was really like Terry said and there was no Internet or TV or phone service out there among those atolls, I figured we probably wouldn't.

But on the other hand, I was still excited about the adventures that we were going to have. I figured we were already having one now compared to most people. Every time we went around a bend on our way down the Tenn-Tom, I never knew what I was going to see next. It was like being an explorer, and I was glad I wasn't stuck sitting in some stupid classroom, at a desk, studying about old-time explorers in a boring history book. I was living the real thing, and I knew most of those kids back in Calloway City would never get to do this. Most of them had never even heard of the Tenn-Tom Waterway, much less all the islands Terry said we were going to see.

Terry said most of the locks and dams on the Waterway were in the upper section, and it didn't seem like we'd gone far at all since we ran aground before we came to the next one. This one was at the small town of Fulton, but you couldn't see much of anything from the water because of the levees on both sides. The man on the radio who answered Terry's request to let us through said we would have to wait because a northbound barge was coming through first. This agitated Terry because all we could really do was drift and motor around in big circles while we waited. After our experience with the dock at the launching ramp, he didn't want to go anywhere near the pilings that were available for waiting vessels to tie off, but it made him furious that we were wasting gas. It was an hour later before we were finally able to enter the lock. We knew what we were doing this time, so it wasn't as scary, and besides, this lock only dropped us twenty-five feet; a lot less than the big one coming out of Bay Springs Lake.

Once we got past Fulton and crossed under a tall highway bridge, we were back in one of the narrow areas but it didn't last long until we were in another series of lakes with more locks ahead. I couldn't believe how many locks there were. We spent the rest of the day until almost dark going from one to another, until we were south of a pretty big town called Columbus, and finally back in the woods again. Terry said that the rest of the way down to the Gulf the Waterway would be a river, with only a couple more locks and dams. He said we would anchor at the first good place we came to and tomorrow the route would cross the state line into Alabama.

All along the way we occasionally passed barges tied up to

the banks. Sometimes their cables were connected to pilings and other times to unseen anchors or trees on the bank. Terry said we'd do the same just as soon as we found a good place, and we finally did just before it got too dark to see. He steered the *Apocalypse* around in a big circle and pointed the bows back upstream, the way we had just come from, as he eased over close to a clay bank with big trees growing on top of it. He said the chart showed deep water right to the edge here and he intended to get close enough for me to jump over to the bank with one of the mooring lines and tie us off.

I was just about to make the jump when I saw a big snake wrapped around a stump on the bank. Terry didn't see it and was yelling at me to hurry up before the current swept us backwards, but there was no way I was jumping ashore anywhere near a snake like that. Terry yelled some more but by then we were already going backwards and I felt the stern of the hull closest to the bank hit something under the water and cause us to spin around. Terry was really cussing by this time and I climbed back into the cockpit to tell him why I didn't jump.

"A sailor puts his ship first, Robbie! That snake was probably just a harmless water snake."

"No, I'm pretty sure it was a moccasin, and if there was one there's probably more!"

The *Apocalypse* had bounced off whatever we'd hit with the stern and was now drifting sideways down the river. Terry was going back and forth between the motor wells and the helm as he fought to get the ship back in control.

"We might as well just anchor," he said, still clearly mad at me for failing to do what he said was a simple task. "It's too dark now to see what we're doing well enough to tie up to the bank, so we'll have to take our chances on the hook."

By this time he had us pointed downstream and he said we'd look for the first wide spot in the river to drop the anchor that was outside of the barge channel. When we found a place I had the job of going forward to release the anchor so it would drop to the river bottom in the right spot, while Terry tried to hold our position in the current. It was really dark out here now that the twilight had faded away and it was hard to tell whether we were too close to either the bank or the channel. But there wasn't a whole lot we could do about it anyway by now, because pulling it up again and moving in the dark would be a major operation. We just sat there in the quiet after Terry turned the engines off and waited to see if the anchor was going to hold or not, and to determine which way the current was going to push us. I went below and switched on the masthead anchor light because I was still scared a barge might hit us. Terry said that even if we were out of the way, you just never know if some captain driving one might be sleepy or even drunk, like some people on the road at night in cars.

But I was mainly scared because of a story that Terry had told us all one night over dinner back when we were still building the boat. He had been talking about the advantages of shallow draft vessels such as our catamaran and had used the story to illustrate how we'd be much safer than most people traveling on sailboats. He had been talking about this mainly to reassure Mom, who was worried that almost anything could happen to us out there. The story didn't do much to reassure her though and it sure wasn't something I would forget about anytime soon. What happened was that right down at the end of this river, at a place called Mobile Bay, which we were going to have to sail across, a family had anchored their sailing yacht out in the middle when it got dark. Terry said that unlike most places on the coast, you could do that there because the water in that bay was shallow enough to anchor almost anywhere. Since they were well away from any marked navigation channels, they thought they were safe from getting hit by big boats and ships, wrongly assuming all of them would stay in the channels. What they didn't know was that in that big bay, the barges and all kinds of other big commercial boats sometimes took shortcuts that were outside of the channel. After all, the water depth was about the same everywhere, and there was nothing out there for them to hit—except an anchored sailboat some towboat captain was never expecting to be there. It turned out that the whole family was drowned right there when their boat sank after being run over in the middle of the night. Terry said that even if they had their anchor light on, the towboat captain probably wouldn't have noticed it against the background of confusing lights both ashore and on oil platforms, as well as other boats.

It was scary to contemplate something like that; one minute you're sound asleep in your bunk and the next thing you know, you're swimming underwater in the dark. I hoped Terry was right thinking that we could avoid that danger by anchoring the catamaran closer to shore. But here we were already, our first night on the river, anchored out in deep water where some barge straying out of the channel could do us in. And if that happened, it would partly be my fault for being too scared of a snake to jump ashore with the mooring line.

Needless to say I didn't sleep too well that night. At first, I didn't hear any barges, but every time I heard motors in the distance from cars or trucks or any kind of machine, I couldn't help but stay awake listening, just to make sure the sounds weren't coming closer. Then, sometime after midnight, there *was* a barge coming. The sound of its big engines was unmistakable, but even louder in the dark than the ones we'd passed the day before. I yelled for Janie and Mom and Terry to get up because I didn't want us to all die like that family in Mobile Bay. If nothing else, we could all jump overboard and swim for it, but I planned on saving our ship if at all possible. I got Terry's big twelve-volt spotlight he kept near the helm and plugged it into one of the cigarette lighter outlets he'd installed in the cockpit. I turned it on to make sure it worked and then turned it off again while I waited for the barge. There was no sign of Janie, but Mom and Terry came up on deck, asking what was the matter. Terry said there was no need for alarm and that the anchor was still holding and we were well outside of the channel. But I wasn't taking any chances. When the towboat and its stack of barges finally came into view, it was huge. It was one of those pushing too many barges for this narrow river, just like that first one that forced us to run aground.

I aimed the spotlight right at it and a few seconds later I knew the captain had seen us because he swept his blinding searchlight right back at us, lighting up our decks almost like it was daylight. Terry yelled at me for shining the light in the captain's eyes, but compared to that searchlight our little spotlight was like a penlight. I didn't care if that captain was mad or not, or Terry either, for that matter. What was important was that I made sure he saw us before he ran us down. I heard him revving up his engines as he made a hard turn to miss us, and I was sure that if I had not warned him with that light, he would have probably made a wider arc outside the channel just because it was easier.

"See how close that was? That's why I shined him," I told Terry as the massive wall of black steel barges slid by us in the dark, far ahead of the towboat itself. I could tell Mom was shaken up. She had been upset by the story of the sailboat in Mobile Bay too. Terry just grumbled about how nobody would have to worry about things like that if the commercial boat captains would just stay in the channels like he said they were supposed to. I could tell he didn't want to admit that where he decided to anchor wasn't a good choice. He knew it when he did it the night before, but he was just ready to stop. And after I messed up our attempt at tying up to the bank because of the snake, he didn't want to try that again.

Now we were all wide-awake, even Janie, who finally stuck her head out of the hatch to see what was happening. Terry said there was no use just sitting there waiting for the next barge to come along and hit us, so we might as well get the anchor up and keep moving downriver. He said we'd have a better chance of staying out of the way if we weren't on the hook and that the sooner we got to the Gulf and off this waterway the better off we'd be anyway. I wasn't sure about that, but I did know I wouldn't be able to go back to sleep after that close call, so it was just as well with me if we got going. Besides, the idea of motoring down the river at night was kind of exciting. I figured that I might finally get to see an alligator or something if I shined the spotlight along the banks.

I didn't see any alligators that night, but I did see a couple of raccoons at the water's edge and one deer that stood there watching us go by. It turned out we didn't pass any more barges until daylight, so we could have just stayed where we were, but I was glad we didn't. It was kind of mysterious going down the waterway at night, never knowing what might be around the next bend. Closer to daylight, there was a low fog hanging over the water too. Going through that was really neat because you couldn't even see the water. It was like we were floating on a blanket of smoke about three feet thick that our bows sliced right through. Terry didn't like it because he said there could be logs or something out there we might hit, maybe even a fisherman, invisible in some low-sided little Johnboat. He slowed the outboards down to just a little over idle, and we were moving about as slow as the boat could go without just drifting. Terry said it was about two or three knots.

Like everything else on the boat, he wouldn't let us use measurements from land that we all understood. He said speed on a boat, whether we were talking about boat speed or the strength of the wind was always measured in knots rather than miles per hour. Janie thought it was stupid and Mom didn't seem too interested one way or the other, but after Terry explained it to me, I could see that it kind of made sense. He said that navigating by nautical miles rather than the statute miles the shore bastards used was what made us sailors, and that all sailors, and airplane pilots too, used this method. A nautical mile was longer than a regular old statute mile on land though, so if we were going five knots, which was five nautical miles per hour, it was really like going almost six miles per hour in a car or on a bike. Janie said it was pointless to even bother keeping track since a dumb sailboat went so slow she could almost walk as fast anyway, but Terry said she would understand when we got out to sea and he showed her how keeping track of speed was vital to navigation. Even though we had a GPS to show us where we were, he said we'd still use dead reckoning as a backup. That was another term that was as mysterious to me as all the rest, but I figured I would learn what it meant too when we finally got out on the ocean.

Terry also said we hadn't seen anything yet with regard to what the *Apocalypse* could really do. He said that under sail out on open water, she would really come alive and that depending on the wind speed, we would be going two or three times faster than those old outboards could push us. He said that sailing was nothing like motoring.

"A proper sailing ship comes to life in the wind, Robbie. She's like a living creature, splendidly evolved to harness the breeze and ride the waves, taking her crew wherever they care to go. No engine-powered boat or ship can compare. A sailor plays the forces of the wind with fine-tuned skills instead of trying to fight it with brute strength. Motors were invented because most people are too impatient to develop the skills it takes to sail. The wind will take you anywhere you want to go, but you've got to understand the patterns, the currents, the storm systems and the seasons. It's not for the lazy or the ignorant. But people who go to sea in the future are going to have to go back to sail whether they like it or not. Those of us already doing it will be ahead of the curve."

Terry was always talking about how the world was going to run out of oil, and that all the technology built around the internal combustion engine was doomed to obsolescence

119

when it did. He said the oil running out was as big a reason as any of the others that most of modern civilization was going to collapse. He said people didn't want to give up being dependent on it to try to develop alternatives, and that they would be killing each other over it until the last drop was extracted. But running out of oil was just one of the many problems facing civilization that would doom it, according to Terry. Even if there was enough oil, he said things couldn't keep going on like they were. He said there were simply too many people in the world, competing for far too few resources, and that we had done so much damage to the environment that it couldn't be undone now. One of the biggest results of this damage was creating the global warming trend that was now unstoppable. Because of that, he said sea levels were going to rise everywhere and a lot of people were going to have to move away from coastlines, unless they lived on a boat like us.

Terry had gotten in a lot of arguments with some of the other teachers and parents in Calloway City when he talked about this kind of stuff in the classroom. People around there didn't believe in global warming and they didn't want him trying to teach it in school. He said he would have quit his job there anyway because of that even if he hadn't married Mom and started building the *Apocalypse*. It still seemed odd to me that he was ever teaching there in the first place after traveling all over the world like he said he'd done. I knew he said he came to Mississippi to teach at Ole Miss, but he never really told us why he left there. I wondered if maybe he got fired or something, and I figured that must be it. Why else would he move somewhere to teach at a university and then leave that job to teach at some little small town junior high?

Mom didn't seem to care one way or the other what brought him there, she was just infatuated with him and swept up in his big dreams and ideas. Mom seemed to get that way every time she met someone new, like our old stepdad, Wayne Delaney, the last one before Terry. I hadn't ever realized she wasn't like most moms because she had always been this way as long as I could remember. I wouldn't have known what it was like to have a mom who didn't get divorced and married again pretty often, and I sure didn't know what it was like to have a mom married to my real dad like most kids I knew. Mom just had a restless side to her, and she loved adventure and excitement. Terry was more adventurous than anyone she'd ever met so he was just what she was looking for when he came along. Mom seemed to believe everything he told her, at least enough to decide to help him build the ship and sail it away. She believed him when he said the country was going to fall apart, and she believed him when he said he knew the best places to go before it did and the best way to get there. I couldn't have changed her mind about it, even if I'd tried, which I didn't, and Janie couldn't either. Unlike me, Janie did try; real hard at first, pitching fits and threatening to run away, but she finally gave in to the inevitable and reluctantly started helping us.

We still had a ways to go before we could see firsthand what Terry was talking about when he said the *Apocalypse* was going to come alive under sail. The river just went on and on, with one bend after another unwinding in front of us. There was mostly nothing but the same kinds of trees on the banks on both sides with little to break the monotony as the outboards droned along at the same slow speed. I studied the river charts and flipped through Terry's boater's guide to the Tenn-Tom, trying to visualize just where we were in relation to where we'd started and where we had to go to get to the end of it. But it wasn't as easy to tell out here on the river as it was on the road in a car. We had been in Alabama for a while now, but we didn't pass any sign on the riverbank saying so, like those big signs you see on the highway when you cross from one state to the next.

It seemed to me like there was even more woods here than there was in Mississippi. There was just mile after mile of nothing but trees and I imagined this must be what it was like everywhere in America back when the Indians were still wild and nobody else lived here. I was beginning to imagine that the eerie fog we had passed through was some kind of portal back in time when we finally came to a huge power line stretched far above the river on tall metal towers that glinted in the light of the morning sun. Later on we passed under a bridge that was almost as tall, and throughout the day a passing barge or some other reminder that we were still in the right century would appear. But even if we were in the right time and there weren't any wild Indians along the bank, there *were* alligators. I started seeing so many that after a while they got boring to look at because all they did was sleep in the mud all day. I never did see one swim or even move, but I knew if there were that many on the bank, there must be even more in the water.

Terry figured it would take us three or four days to get the rest of the way down the Tenn-Tom to Mobile Bay, but that was if the old worn-out outboard engines continued to work like they were supposed to. They didn't, of course. First it was the ten-horse Evinrude to starboard; then the eight-horse Mercury on the port side. The symptoms were always the same: they would run rough and sputter, then finally go dead altogether. Terry was getting good at getting them going again by the third day, mostly copying what he'd seen Jimmy do the day we launched. He would take the covers off, remove and clean the spark plugs, change the fuel filters in the lines between the gas tanks and the motors and then we'd be off again until it happened the next time. The worst time was when it happened just as we were in the middle of the river, drifting helpless in the current while a barge was headed straight for us from upstream. Terry cussed the motors, the barge captain and the river current as he worked frantically to get the starboard motor to running just in time to get us out of the way.

"Maybe we should've hired Mr. Jenkins to haul the boat

all the way to Mobile," I said.

"And paid him what, an extra three thousand dollars? Look what he charged us just to go a little over a hundred miles! Besides, it would have been too risky, Robbie. All it would take is one idiot pulling out in front of Jenkins' truck at the last minute and we could have lost our ship. No sir, not on your life could we take that chance. I'd rather go down the river even it takes us a month!"

It seemed to me that we were just about as likely to get our ship run over by a barge, as to be in a wreck on the highway with Mr. Jenkins. But I didn't argue with Terry; there was no use. He was always right about everything, according to him, and I guess he really was right about this too, because finally, six days after we launched the *Apocalypse* at Bay Springs Lake, we reached the end of the Tenn-Tom Waterway.

The first sign we were near the Gulf was the change in the way the air smelled. Since I'd never been to the ocean before, it was new to me, and Terry said it was the salt. He took deep breaths in and out as he stood at the helm grinning, steering us through the last stretches of river where the woods gave way to a wide expanse of grassy marsh on either side of the channel. Soon we were passing the tall buildings and dirty commercial docks along the waterfront of Mobile, and I stared in awe at the big ocean-going freighters tied up there. They were the first real ships I'd ever seen, and they made our catamaran look small, kind of the same way the *Apocalypse* had made those fishing boats at Bay Springs

Lake look tiny.

Terry wasn't impressed, no matter how much Janie and Mom and I stared at all the new sights we passed going by the city. He said cities held nothing of interest to him and that he'd be glad when he'd seen his last. What really got him excited was when we finally reached open water just past the Mobile waterfront and the bay stretched out in a wide expanse before us. It looked huge to me after being on the river for so many days. The land on both sides was far away and blue looking in the distance; ahead of us, there was nothing on the horizon but a long line of channel markers that seemed to stretch to infinity. Here and there, scattered on the far horizon, I could see what looked like some kind of towers. Terry said they were oil-drilling platforms.

"They'll keep drilling until they tap the last drop," he said. "Then those rigs will rust away like every other machine made possible by fossil fuels. But we're about to be done with internal combustion engines, Robbie. After a quick stop at the boatyard to step these masts, the *Apocalypse* will become the sailing ship she was built to be!"

Seven

TO GET TO THE place where we had to stop to have the two masts raised, we had to turn off of the main channel leading out of Mobile Bay and go up a side creek called Dog River. Compared to the river we'd just come down, Dog River wasn't much of a river, but there were lots of boats there. I couldn't believe all the sailboats I saw tied up in the marinas ahead of us. It looked like a whole forest of masts, and besides all those boats in the water, even more were hauled up on the land at the boatyard where we were headed. Some of the boats were huge compared to ours, but only one other one that I could see was a catamaran. Most of them had a single hull that was much wider and deeper than either one of our two. I knew they were monohulls because Terry had lectured us for hours about the differences between monohulls (he called them lead mines) and multihulls (like

127

our catamaran and the three-hulled boats called trimarans).
He had talked about it constantly while we were building the
Apocalypse and often when we were eating dinner, or driving
somewhere to get supplies.

"Keel boats like that will sink like a stone if you hole the
hull, Robbie. They can't sail to windward without all that
ballast of lead or iron that weighs half as much as the boat
itself. Going to sea in a boat like that is just a drowning
waiting to happen. All it takes is hitting some kind of debris
out there in the water and down they go. There's no practical
way to build one with enough positive buoyancy to float if
the hull is ever holed and takes on enough water."

Terry had ranted on and on about this, also explaining
that monohulls and multihulls were two entirely different
philosophies of how to design a boat in which to go to sea.
He said that monohulls were a product of European and
Mediterranean seafaring cultures and that the thinking behind
them was to build a heavy ship that could plow its way
through the waves the way armies from those places plowed
across the new lands they discovered. Multihulls, on the other
hand, were more delicate and graceful, a product of tribal
islanders who lived in harmony with nature and built double
canoes and outriggers to float lightly, skimming over the
surface of the sea with little effort. I read all the same things
Terry told us about them in his copy of *The Wharram Design
Book* he kept on his desk. Everything he said was right there
in the book, so I don't know if he got all his information just

from reading what James Wharram said or if he actually had some experience with all the different kinds of boats he talked about.

The one thing negative he'd said about big catamarans was that most marinas and boatyards didn't like them. From what I could see as we motored up the Dog River, that seemed to be true. He said they could make more money off of monohulls because they could fit more of them into a given space along a dock by making the slips just wide enough to accommodate them. With our catamaran being twenty-four feet wide, we would take up as much space as two regular sailboats the same length.

"Like everything else the shore bastards do, Robbie, it's all about money. They can make double the money off all these idiots who follow the herd and buy the same old white-plastic Clorox-bottle boats. Show up with a real ship and they don't know what to do. But all we need is a few minutes of the yard crane's time. It'll cost us dearly, but with all the stupid laws and regulations in this country, we have no other choice."

Terry had complained bitterly about this when we first finished the masts. Even though they were hollow, built up by laminating long boards together in a box section, then cutting them down to round with Terry's planer and sanders, they were still really heavy, weighing hundreds of pounds apiece. Each one was forty-six feet long, just like the two hulls of the *Apocalypse*. Getting them to stand in the upright position on the finished boat seemed impossible to me, but Terry said it would have been easy thirty or forty years ago before everything that made sense was either outlawed or forbidden.

"They're so worried about somebody getting hurt and filing a lawsuit they just made everything they could think of illegal. Back when I started sailing, if you wanted to step or lower a mast, you just pulled your boat up to bridge overpass and tossed a line to your buddy on top. Then you'd rig a simple block and tackle system and any mast could be up or down in a jiffy. Now if they catch you doing something like that the fine would cost even more than these boatyard pirates will take us for. We'll have to pay their ridiculous price this one time, but once we get away from the land of litigation and legislation, we can maintain our ship the way the natives do everywhere."

During the planning stages of the trip, Terry learned that most people taking sailboats down the Tenn-Tom stopped at Dog River to have their masts stepped before sailing into the Gulf. One of the bigger yards there had the facilities to do it and the cost was supposedly less than it would be anywhere farther south, especially in Florida.

I could tell Terry was nervous as he steered the *Apocalypse* into the restricted channel of Dog River, passing close to those huge, gleaming motor yachts and the concrete docks and pilings they were tied up to. He tried to hide it, but I'm sure he was thinking about how badly he messed up trying to land at that dock at Bay Springs Lake that first day. I stood there waiting for him to tell me what to do as he steered into an even narrower channel at the entrance to the boatyard. Finally, he told me to take the helm and hold it straight while he cut both engines to idle and put them out of gear. His plan was to drift the rest of the way into the big slipway where there was this huge machine called a travel lift with gigantic wheels that rolled on two parallel docks on either side. Terry said the travel lift was used to haul boats out of the water, but when he'd called the boatyard before we left, they told him they had a crane mechanism built onto their lift that could also step or lower a mast. All we had to do was get into position under it and tie the boat off securely so it wouldn't move.

A man working in the yard saw us coming and walked out onto one of the docks to take our lines and help us tie off. He yelled at Terry that we were coming in too fast, but it was too late to do any good. The *Apocalypse* kept drifting even with the engines in neutral and didn't stop until our starboard bow slammed into the concrete wall at the end of the slipway. The impact nearly caused me to lose my balance, but I didn't fall this time. Terry just cussed and blamed an invisible current he said had swept us forward. Whatever the reason, I knew that fixing whatever damage had been done to our bow was going to be another job for me to have to do when we got somewhere and stayed long enough to work on it.

Once we were tied up, Terry and I followed the boatyard worker to the office to find out what it was going to cost to raise the masts. They quoted us a price of five dollars a foot, which came to four hundred and sixty dollars plus tax for both of the masts. Then there was a labor fee for rigging on top of that: a minimum of one hour at boatyard rates of eighty-five dollars an hour. Terry just about flipped out when he heard this. He said we didn't need a rigger and that we'd built the boat ourselves and we knew how to rig it ourselves. All we needed from the yard was the use of their lift to hoist the masts up into the vertical position. The manager said it was fine if we did the rigging, but we still had to pay one hour for the labor, because a skilled worker had to be there with us to operate the lift. He said he was being generous because with us doing the rigging ourselves, it would probably take a lot longer than it would if their rigger did it.

Terry also argued that stepping two masts on the same boat shouldn't be as expensive as stepping two masts on two different boats and that he ought to cut us some slack on the stepping fees. He said since we were already tied up under the lift that it wouldn't take hardly any more effort to raise the second one while we were there. He said that the second one ought to be free and when that didn't work, he suggested half off. The boatyard manager wouldn't budge though, other than to say he would let us slide on the sales tax. He said sailboats such as ketches and schooners with two masts came down the river all the time, and if he started discounting the second mast for one boat, word would get around and he would have to do it for all of them. Terry muttered something under his breath and counted out the cash.

"Over half a grand just to stand up a couple of wooden poles!" he said as we walked back to the boat "We probably should have taken our chances and done it at some bridge. The fine would probably be less than what these bastards are taking us for!"

I was beginning to see that having a ship was expensive. Even though we built it ourselves, we still had to pay for all kinds of stuff like this. I looked at the gleaming fiberglass yachts all around the boatyard and figured that the owners of boats like that had to be really rich. But whatever we had to pay for or buy for the *Apocalypse*, Terry always seemed to have enough money, even though he complained. He always paid in cash too, and I wondered how much of it he had stashed away somewhere on board for our travels.

Getting the two masts up took a lot longer than Terry expected, not because of the boatyard, but because of all the complicated adjustments he had to make to the rigging wires that held it up. While the man operating the lift waited, Terry sorted through the tangle of wires and lashings, and tensioned and re-tensioned them as he worked to get the masts standing straight up and in line with each other. These wire cables that held the masts up had special names too, of course, like "forestay" and "port shrouds" and "starboard shrouds." I would be expected to learn all the names, just like everything else on board.

The men at the boatyard said they'd never seen a sailboat rigged the way Terry rigged ours. They said we should have bought something called "turnbuckles" to tighten the rigging wires, but Terry said that was ridiculous and that the way we were doing it was simpler, less likely to break and cheaper besides. I didn't know the difference about that either, but I knew Terry got it from James Wharram's plans and he wasn't going to change his mind. At the bottom of each wire cable, there was a loop, and we had to pass several turns of the super strong Dacron lashing line through these and around the big wooden lashing plates we'd bolted and glued onto the hullsides. They had to all be tightened more or less evenly on both sides of the ship, so the two masts wouldn't lean one way or the other. It looked like it was working to me, and when we finally left, the two huge masts towered above the decks, completely transforming the look and feel of the *Apocalypse*. Despite his earlier complaints about how much money the yard charged, Terry was grinning from ear to ear as we motored away out of the Dog River channel and headed back to Mobile Bay.

"Now we have our freedom!" he proclaimed. "The *Apocalypse* is complete and we have the means to ride the wind wherever we want to go. We've finally broken away, Robbie! Once we raise sail on that bay we can leave these shore bastards behind for good!"

Raising the sails for the first time was a lot easier said than done, though. The first thing we had to do once we got out into the open water of the bay again was to find a place to anchor out of the channel and out of the way of boat traffic so we could sort them all out. I didn't like the idea of anchoring out in Mobile Bay at all considering what happened to that one family, but Terry said we'd be fine because it was daylight. The sails were all down below, folded and stowed in bulky nylon bags that we had to drag on deck. Even though they were just made of cloth, they were so big they weighed a ton. Getting them unfolded and ready to attach to the rigging wasn't easy either, but Terry said it was a lot easier on a catamaran with all that deck space than it would have been on a monohull, rolling in the waves. None of us but him had ever been on any kind of sailboat though, so we didn't know the difference. To me it was still hard work, even if it was easier.

The wind was blowing and the sails were flapping around and making a lot of noise even before we raised them. We had to hold them down to keep them from blowing overboard while Terry sorted out the lines called "halyards" that he said were used to pull them up the masts and the other lines called "sheets" that he said we would control them with. There were huge piles of rope everywhere on deck, but I couldn't call it that because Terry said "ropes" were for shore bastards and "lines" were what sailors used on a ship. I didn't see why it mattered but I sure didn't want to get Terry going again. I also didn't see how we were ever going to keep all these sheets and halyards straightened out and untangled. It looked to me like sailing the *Apocalypse* was going to be a lot harder than just motoring down the river. But the smell of the ocean on the breeze was exciting, and all around us there were big seagulls and pelicans, and sometimes, even fish jumping out of the water. And this was just the bay. It was exciting to think about going even farther out, where we would see no telling what out in the Gulf.

From where we were anchored, we could see other sailboats sailing around out in the bay. Some of them were little boats that were going back and forth close to land, and others were bigger, but so far out there all you could see were little white triangles of sails moving across the horizon. Mom said they looked peaceful and that she was looking forward to being out there too. But we soon found out that the peaceful appearance of sailing was an illusion. When Terry finally finished sorting out all the sails, we hauled in the anchor and started hoisting them up. That's when all hell broke loose.

The first one we tried to put up was the mainsail; the one on the aftmost mast that stood closest to the helm. Both the mainsail and the foresail on the other mast had short poles at the top of them that were called "gaffs." As soon as we had the main just a few feet off the deck, the wind caught it and the gaff started swinging back and forth like a runaway baseball bat or something. Terry yelled at us to watch out or it would kill somebody. When it was high enough above the deck to no longer be a threat, the heavy Dacron sail started flogging in the wind and when it popped, it made a sound almost as loud as a gunshot. It took me and Terry and Janie hauling on the halyard line to get the mainsail all the way up, while Mom did her best to steer us into the wind like Terry told her to. We were still running one of the motors; otherwise it would have been impossible for her, because the wind in the sail kept trying to push the boat away from the direction it was blowing.

With the mainsail up but the sheets still loose and flogging, Janie and I had to hurry forward all the way up to the slatted deck in front of the foremast and untie the jib sail where Terry had it strapped down, so he could hoist it next. When he did, it flogged around even worse and one of the sheet lines whipping in the wind hit me so hard in the arm that it raised a big red welt and stung like fire. Terry yelled for us to get out of the way and yelled at Mom to steer us off to starboard enough to fill the two sails. When she did, there was a loud "bang" as the jib sheet on one side snapped taut and the sail suddenly went from a baggy piece of cloth to something solid, like a wing. The same thing happened with the mainsail when Terry hauled in on its sheet. I felt the ship surge forward much faster than she had ever moved before, and then Terry shut off the engine. It was weird how we kept going just as fast and all you could hear was the sound of water surging past the hulls.

"Feel that? That's the power of the wind and we've got it in control, baby!" Terry exclaimed, grinning bigger than ever. He said we didn't even need to set the foresail in this much breeze because we were going plenty fast enough under just main and jib. He said all we had to do now was steer and enjoy the ride. We were heading straight out towards the open Gulf at the end of Mobile Bay, and our boat speed was nearly twelve knots. As we sailed south, I looked back at the skyline of Mobile several times, seeing it get hazy in the distance, along with the land we'd left behind at Dog River. This catamaran we'd built in Grandpa's old barn really *was* a ship, and she was taking us out to sea! My arm was still stinging from the slap of that jib sheet, but I didn't care about that. I just wanted to see what it was like out in the Gulf where we were headed.

The wind was blowing out of the west, and we were going pretty much straight south. Terry said we were sailing on a beam reach, which he said was the best angle to the wind to sail fast. It did feel fast, especially since both of the motors were off. Even Janie seemed impressed. Compared to land speed we were still doing less than fifteen miles an hour most of the time, but the water rushing by and the wind in your face made it feel faster. That and you could tell we were getting somewhere, because of the way the land behind us got hazy and new oil rigs and channel markers kept appearing on the horizon ahead of us. It didn't seem long at all until we were near the pass to exit Mobile Bay, and you could see the open Gulf of Mexico dead ahead.

The opening to get out there wasn't nearly as wide as the main part of the bay. There was an island on the west side called Dauphin Island, and the land on the east side stuck way out on a point towards Dauphin Island, leaving a gap just about two miles wide between them. It was through this gap that the Mobile ship channel went, and the way we would have to go too. By now though, the wind was blowing a lot harder, and we were going even faster. The wind pushing on the sails caused all kinds of noises all over the ship. There were creaks and groans and rattles and pops, a lot of them coming from where the beams were lashed to the hulls and where the bottoms of the two masts sat on the beams in the big wooden hinges Terry called "tabernacles." I didn't like all that noise and neither did Mom and Janie. It sounded like something was going to break any minute, but Terry said the sounds were normal and that we'd get used to hearing them. I asked him what would happen if the rigging broke and one or both of the masts fell down, but he said it wouldn't. He said James Wharram knew what he was doing when he designed it and that he had followed the plans. I didn't doubt that Mr. Wharram designed it right, but seeing how Terry cut corners to save money on everything else, I doubted he bought the best rigging wire and rope and wondered if it was even the correct size or strength. Even though he didn't answer my question, I was sure that if either one of those heavy wooden masts fell, it would kill anyone it hit just like a falling tree. I sure hoped it didn't happen, but with the wind howling the way it was, I figured it was bound to if it kept up.

On top of worrying about the masts falling down, I was also nervous about the three huge ships we could see dead ahead of us, all of them lined up one after another to come into the bay following the same channel we were sailing out of. Terry said we ought to put a reef in the mainsail, to slow down and get more control for when we passed them. Reefing was the sailor's word for making the sail smaller, so it would catch less wind, but doing it wasn't nearly as easy as it sounded. The first thing we had to do was turn so the bows were pointed upwind, just like when we raised the sails. But doing that caused the jib to flog like crazy again and after the way that sheet slapped my arm the last time, I wasn't about to go up there and try and tie it down to the deck. Terry yelled at me to, but with this much wind, the flogging was worse than before and I was too scared to do it. By this time the mainsail was slamming back and forth too and the ship was turning all the way around and tying to go the opposite way from where we'd come. The jib filled up with a huge pop as it strained against the sheet tying it down from the wrong side, then I heard an awful ripping sound as it tore along a seam all the way from top to bottom.

"Now look what happened!" Terry screamed, but I didn't care. I didn't think it was my fault anyway because as hard as the wind was blowing I couldn't do anything about it. Besides, I knew he recut the sails from old used sails he ordered from somewhere online for cheap, so they were bound to tear up anyway, the way I saw it. What was worse than Terry's cussing and yelling about it though was that we were being blown out of control, and straight into the middle of the ship channel where the first of those freighters was bearing down fast.

Mom yelled at him to do something before we got run over and he yelled at me to start the engines while he struggled to get the main down.

I could have started them no problem if the sleds they were mounted to were already in the water, but they weren't. Terry had pulled them up and lashed them in place under the deck when we started sailing, saying we wouldn't need the motors again for no telling how long. Besides that, all this wind had made the waves really big. I'd never seen waves anywhere near that big and the *Apocalypse* was really moving up and down in them. The wave tops slammed into the bottom of the decks between the hulls and soaked me with salty water when I tried to untie the lashing line holding up the starboard sled. When I did finally get it loose, the whole ship came down hard off a big wave and the sled fell into the downward position so fast that when it hit the water, the ten-horsepower Evinrude bounced right off its mount. It happened so fast that I barely caught a glimpse of the top of it before it sank out of sight in the dark brown water of the bay. Terry was still so busy fighting the mainsail down that he didn't even know what happened, and I was scared to death to tell him. I crawled across the deck to the port motor well and hollered at Janie to help me. She'd seen the other motor fall and the look on her face told me that she was even more scared than I was. If we didn't get this motor down and get it running in time, that big ship was going to run over us for sure!

SAILING THE APOCALYPSE

Before I lowered that port side sled, I grabbed the screw clamps on the motor mount and turned them as hard as I could to make sure they were tight. I sure didn't want to lose this motor the same dumb way. I got Janie to undo the lowering line from its cleat and help me hold it so we could both let the motor down slowly. One thing that helped was that the eight-horsepower Mercury was a little lighter than that bigger Evinrude. We managed to get it in the water without dropping it, and I climbed down to where I could get in a good position to pull the starter rope. Just doing that was harder than I could have ever imagined. With the waves washing over me and the whole ship pitching up and down, it was hard enough just to hang on, but I finally got myself in a position to pull the rope. Nothing happened the first three times I yanked on it as hard and fast as I could, but the forth time the motor cranked right up.

"Hurry Robbie! That ship is almost here!" Janie yelled.

I heard my mom screaming: "Oh my God! Do something, Terry!"

"Grab the helm!" I yelled at both Janie and Mom. "Steer us out of the way!" But as soon as I said it, I was out of the motor well and on the deck to take the helm myself. Terry was just now emerging from the pile of tangled halyards and wadded-up Dacron mainsail that he had finally wrestled to the deck and managed to lash to the aft crossbeam to keep it from blowing away. He just now realized how close the big ship was and screamed at me to open both motors up to full

142

throttle. Even as he yelled it, and was about to jump down to the starboard well, he saw that the Evinrude motor was gone. The look on his face was one I knew I would never forget, but I was a lot more scared of that ship than I was of Terry. By now, it was so close that all you could see was the oncoming gray "V" of solid metal that was the ship's massive bow. It towered over us like a giant building and way up at the top I could see a railing around the deck where the crew could look over, but nobody was up there looking down at us. They didn't even know we were there, and that was more frightening than anything. It was weird too how you couldn't even hear the motors that were pushing the ship. It was coming at us really fast but making no noise except for a rushing sound of water parting at the bow. Terry said later that the reason we couldn't hear the engines from where we were was because they were so deep in the hulls and so far back from the bow. The ship was at least three hundred feet long.

All we had to save us from certain death was the little eight-horsepower Mercury, and I prayed that it wouldn't quit until it got us out of the way, and it didn't. Before I knew it, the view of the ship changed from a giant knife-like bow splitting the water in front of it to a cliff-like wall sliding just behind us in our wake. I could feel a push from the big wave the bow made as it went by, and then all of a sudden the wind stopped blowing completely. I realized a few minutes later it was because the ship was blocking it, because when it went on by, the wind came right back, howling as strong as ever. Looking up at the stern of the ship now, I could see three men way up there on one of the upper decks, staring down at us. They didn't wave and we didn't either. I know they didn't see us until after they went by and somebody on board just happened to look down and see they nearly ran over a sailboat. Terry said later that if they had hit the *Apocalypse* they probably wouldn't have even felt the bump in such a big ship and would have never known they'd cut us in half and sent us straight to Davy Jones's Locker.

Eight

WE WERE ALL JUST sitting there kind of stunned as we watched the ship continue on to the north and the port of Mobile. Terry steered us on a course straight away from the ship channel at right angle, so now we were going east instead of south. By the time the second and third ship in the line passed us, we were a good half mile from the channel and he finally backed the throttle off to idle and let us drift for a bit until he could decide what to do next. I'd expected him to be mad enough to just about throw me overboard for losing that starboard motor, but he didn't do it and he didn't scream at me either. Instead, he just gave me a look that made me feel about two feet tall; a look that told me he thought I was an idiot and that I'd let him down when he needed me most. It wasn't quite as bad as getting thrown overboard and keelhauled, but it was worse than getting yelled at.

SAILING THE APOCALYPSE

I felt bad about losing that motor, but I didn't think it was completely my fault, especially in those big waves. Even if Terry was trying to put all the blame on me, he had to know it was as much his fault too because he failed to secure the motor properly. One day back when we were still on the river he'd mentioned that it would be a good idea to rig a safety line on each of the outboards in case they came loose. He just never got around to doing it.

But even though he didn't direct it specifically at me, he made a comment we could all hear about how close we'd come to losing our ship and probably our lives too because we only had one outboard now, and the smaller one at that. He said next time we might not be so lucky and that as soon as we could find a good deal on a used one, he was going to have to buy a replacement for that Evinrude. He seemed even more upset about the torn jib and the difficulty he'd had getting the mainsail down in a blow than he was about the lost motor though. Later on I figured out that was because he had thought he knew everything there was to know about sailing and that he had built and rigged the *Apocalypse* to handle anything. Having so many problems on her maiden voyage under sail felt like an utter failure, and he was disappointed, to say the least. Not only that, but Mom and Janie were now scared of sailing and both of them said something about wanting to go back home. Terry dismissed that as nonsense and reminded them we *were* home.

But home or not, one thing was for certain. After what

happened, we would not be continuing on into the open waters of the Gulf that day. Terry said the jib had to be repaired before we could sail anywhere, and he had to get the mainsail rigging sorted out so that the sail could be dropped instantly when necessary. He said we could do all this at anchor somewhere nearby, and that we might as well keep going until we found a good spot to hole up. We couldn't stay where we were; out in the open expanse of Mobile Bay, so he said we would motor on to the east with the one outboard we had left. We would use the Intracoastal Waterway to take us in the direction of Florida, which is the way he had planned to go once out in the Gulf anyway.

We finally got across to the east side of the bay and then we were once again motoring through a narrow channel kind of like on the Tenn-Tom Waterway. But the Intracoastal Waterway wasn't a river. Terry said it was a mix of manmade canals, bayous, sounds and bays that were connected together to form an inside route along the coast safe from the storms and big waves of the Gulf. Like the Tenn-Tom, towboats and barges used the ICW, but at least there were no huge ships like the one that almost ran us down. For the first time on the trip, we also passed other sailboats underway, most of them motoring like us but a lot faster, their sails down and neatly furled and stowed away under colorful canvas covers. All of the ones we saw that first day were monohulls, and most of them were shiny and expensive-looking, like the yachts back at the marina on Dog River.

147

SAILING THE APOCALYPSE

"They're making fun of us," Janie said.

I had no doubt she was right as I looked at the staring crew of a gleaming white sailboat that overtook us, easily cruising twice as fast under power as we were.

"We're the ones who should be laughing," Terry said, adding a derogatory comment about the company that built the particular yacht these snobby people were aboard. "They're all about building what looks impressive at the dock. All that piece of crap is good for is piddling around in protected waters like this. One trip out to bluewater in some weather, and a plastic pool toy like that would be crushed like an egg and swallowed whole by the waves."

Looking at the yacht, I couldn't see why Terry thought it wasn't well built. It had a massive looking aluminum mast that was a lot taller than either of ours, and the metal railings at the bow and stern looked like polished stainless steel, as did the winches and other deck hardware. Everything on board was neat and organized, and there were no bicycles lashed to the decks, or faded blue plastic tarps stretched out in the rigging for shade like ours. Instead, the crew of two middle-aged men and two women who were probably their wives were all seated in a comfortable-looking cockpit behind a big shiny steering wheel, with a sharp-looking Navy blue awning overhead to keep the sun off. Compared to their boat, the *Apocalypse* looked like it was built from mismatched marine salvage parts and miscellaneous bits and pieces of junk, which was about the way it was. From the way the people aboard that boat looked at us, I could tell they had never seen a ship like ours before. Janie said she didn't care if Terry thought their yacht was a bad sea boat. She said she would trade places with them any day.

"I'll bet they've got a big screen T.V. in every stateroom," I said, doing my best to fuel her envy. "And they probably have satellite Internet and cell phone service no matter where they go."

"What they have is an affront to Mother Ocean!" Terry countered. "See that ridiculous walk-through transom and the total lack of overhangs at the bow and stern? Combine that with way too much beam for her length and you've got a tub that would be happier on the bottom than trying to stand up to her rig in a seaway! It's all completely wrong; everything about it!"

Janie finally shut up about it when the yacht was so far ahead of us it was out of sight. We kept going until the middle of the afternoon, passing through some areas that were nothing but woods like along the Tenn-Tom and other places where fancy waterfront homes with private docks lined the channel on both sides. There were places to stop and eat and places to buy fuel, as well as more marinas like the ones on Dog River where lots of boats were tied up. When we finally came to a place called Ingram Bayou, we turned off the ICW channel heading north into a small bay, and at the end of it entered a winding channel into more woods. Terry said the bayou was a designated anchorage, and that its location would provide good protection from the wind while we made our repairs.

When we first got there, we had the anchorage all to ourselves and it looked perfect. Terry steered us around several bends until we were completely surrounded by the woods, then he told me to go forward and drop the hook while he held the ship in position from the helm. The water was really shallow here and it didn't take much rode to set the anchor securely. Mom was especially relieved that we were off the bay and out of the wind, and she said she wished we could just sail in places like this all the time and not have to go out in the ocean at all. Terry said that if all he wanted to see were places like this he would have built a houseboat instead of a proper ship. Then he told her that once she saw the islands she would never want to look at muddy brown water like this again.

We cleaned up the decks that afternoon by washing them with buckets of water dipped up from over the side, and the next morning we started working on repairing the jib, spreading it out on the decks and hand-sewing the ripped seam back together. We were no longer alone as we did this, because that second day was a Saturday and the wind had calmed and the weather turned out really nice. All kinds of boats started coming and going in the bayou, some of them fishing boats and others houseboats or pontoon boats like some we had seen on the Tenn-Tom. Twice during the afternoon a big pontoon tour boat full of people with cameras visited the bayou, the man driving it pointing out the sights on a loudspeaker to his passengers who were all snapping pictures and taking videos, including plenty of us.

Everybody that came by in a boat stared at the *Apocalypse* like they'd never seen a catamaran before, and I knew it was because they probably *hadn't* seen one like ours. Some of them stopped to talk and ask where we were going, but most of them just looked at us like they felt sorry for us or something. Janie said they probably thought we were poor and homeless because we were living on a homemade wooden catamaran with lots of old parts, torn sails and one little worn-out outboard.

Terry was getting more and more agitated as the day wore on and the bayou became more crowded. He especially hated it when the jet-skiers started showing up that afternoon. They were speeding by in all directions, yelling and revving their motors and throwing spray everywhere, some even getting close enough to get us and the sail we were working on soaking wet. Terry cussed and shook his fist and flipped them the bird, but this just made them laugh and do it again and again. Most of the riders were boys about Janie's age or even younger. When they saw her, they did even more showing out which just made Terry madder. Janie waved at them and said it looked like fun to her and that she wished she could ride one. I wanted to ride one too but I knew better than to ask Terry if we could. If I didn't pretend like I hated them as much as he did, he would probably never speak to me again.

SAILING THE APOCALYPSE

The jet-skiers finally scattered and left us alone when a big gray powerboat with a row of blue lights mounted on top of the pilothouse came cruising into the bayou. We knew the men on the boat were policemen of some sort, and sure enough, they were coming straight in our direction. Two of them were standing by the gunwales with lines already in their hands, waiting to tie off to our rail, while a third man steered, the boat now barely idling. By then I could read the lettering on the side of their hull, which said: "Alabama Marine Police."

"Water cops!" Terry whispered loudly, but not so loud the men on the boat could hear him. That was probably a good thing, as he couldn't hide the disgust in his voice.

The man at the wheel maneuvered his boat alongside our starboard hull and one of the others standing ready said that they needed to come aboard for an inspection. It wasn't a request—even I could tell that—and I knew far less about things like water cops than Terry did. Like when the game warden came aboard on Bay Springs Lake, there was nothing Terry could do but stand aside and let them. But these guys looked more serious and a lot less friendly than that game warden. All of them were wearing big black pistols on their belts, and they had short crew cuts and clean-shaven faces like they were in the military. They didn't seem to be in the mood for friendly conversation like the game warden in Bay Springs Lake either. It was clear that they were sure when they came aboard that we were breaking some law and they were determined to find out what it was and fine us for it. I already knew one thing we were missing, and that was the Type IV throwable PFD that Officer Riley had already written us a ticket for. Terry had told him he would stop and buy one at the next marina or marine supply we came to, but he didn't because he either forgot or just never got around to it. Now, I figured he was going to regret it, and I was right.

The two policemen standing at the forward end of their boat stepped up to the decks of the *Apocalypse* without waiting for an invitation. The other man at the wheel remained where he was, keeping a close watch on his partners and us at the same time.

"We have all the required safety gear on board," Terry lied. "And our boat registration is up to date, as you probably saw from the stickers on the hull."

"We'll check that for ourselves," the first officer to come aboard said. "I need you to show me your head and holding tank facilities first of all."

Terry had told me back when we were building the boat that water cops everywhere in the U.S., and especially in Florida, made a big deal out of boat toilets. He said they had a bunch of stupid rules and regulations to keep people from peeing and pooping in the ocean, even though the ocean was so huge he said it couldn't possibly hurt anything.

"They make it illegal for one human on a boat to flush his crap overboard, while entire cities along the coast run their sewer lines straight into the bays and sounds. But get caught

153

flushing a turd out of a boat and they fine you hundreds, if
not thousands of dollars! All for doing what billions of fish,
dolphins, whales and other sea creatures do every day in every
square mile of the ocean! I'm telling you, Robbie, marine
waste regulations are among the stupidest laws ever devised
by man, and are nothing but a source of revenue for the local
bureaucrats!"

Terry had gone on to explain the various complexities of
a legal marine head system, and ranted about the expensive
and dangerous arrangements found on almost every "proper
yacht." He said such installations required drilling holes in the
bottom of the boat, below the waterline; holes for water to
come in and holes for water and crap to be flushed out. But
flushing it outside into the water was only allowed out on the
high seas anyway, beyond a certain distance from shore.
Along the coasts, all the pee and poop had to be flushed into
what was called a "holding tank."

"Holding tanks take up huge amounts of valuable room
on board and they stink and they leak. And pumping a toilet
overboard, even offshore is insane, considering you have to
drill holes right through the bottom of the boat and then
install a bunch of pumps and hoses and valves and vents to
route all the crap in the right direction when you flush. At
best, you get a stinky, crappy boat if one of those hoses or
fittings inside the hull bursts. At worst, you sink if one
leading to the outside fails. More boats end up on the bottom
because of faulty toilet installations or plumbing failures than

sink in storms, and all because people want to have a flush toilet like they're used to ashore. All you need on a boat, Robbie, is a bucket. Put a toilet seat on the rim and you're good to go. When you finish your business, dump it over the side and feed the fish!

"Buckets are cheap, foolproof, and they don't stink and they don't leak. But the government hates them for all those reasons. Anything that's simple and works as it should is an abomination that must be banned and outlawed! But we're going to use a bucket anyway; we just have to keep an eye out for the water cops when we do, at least until we get out of U.S. waters and get somewhere people still use common sense."

Ever since we had launched at Bay Springs Lake, we had been using a big plastic bucket with removable toilet seat; at least all of us except for Janie. She had refused, saying it was disgusting, and had been constantly using the Porta Pottie toilet that Terry had bought as a compromise specifically to comply with the law while we were still in the U.S. He didn't want us using the Porta Pottie because he said it was a pain in the butt to empty and clean. He said all it really was anyway was a glorified bucket that just had a lot of parts to make it look like a shore bastard's commode and to hide the sight of one's own crap until it was emptied. Keeping it from stinking required the addition of expensive chemicals, and when it was full the whole mess was supposed to be flushed down a toilet somewhere on land. Terry didn't like it, but he had given in and let Janie use it, at least for now. But he said it was going over the side as soon as we were away from U.S. waters for good.

I didn't mind using the bucket myself, but I only used it to poop. It was much easier to pee right over the rail, and that's what Terry and I did whenever Mom and Janie weren't looking. Terry said that's what all men did on boats whether it was legal or not, but the silly toilets had to be aboard just to satisfy the law. The Porta Pottie, at about eighty dollars, was the cheapest legal option, and that's why Terry bought it. He said he wasn't about to drill a hole in the bottom of the *Apocalypse* for a marine head, and that we sure didn't have room aboard for a real holding tank.

But the Alabama Marine Police officers seemed really surprised that we didn't have one of those marine toilet installations that Terry hated so much. They said that a Porta Pottie like ours was just for weekend sailors and wasn't big enough for a family of four living aboard a boat full time. They questioned the fact that the small built-in tank underneath it was completely empty and wanted to know how that was possible. I knew Terry had dumped it over the side and washed it out right after we had anchored at Ingram Bayou, and that Janie hadn't used it since, but I kept my mouth shut. Terry lied and said we had gone ashore at a marina we passed a few miles back and that he had emptied it ashore in the toilet there.

The questioning officer was skeptical of this and asked to

see Terry's logbook to see if he was telling the truth. When Terry said he didn't keep a logbook, the officer lectured him on the importance of maintaining a captain's log for safety and navigation purposes. Then he wanted to know where we got the *Apocalypse*, where we came from, and where we were going. He also wanted to know why Janie and I were not in school even though it was right in the middle of the fall semester and not a holiday or break time. Terry told them that he was a certified schoolteacher and that he was home schooling us on the boat.

"We moved aboard so they could get a *real* education," he said. "Do you think they could learn anything in a small town public school in Mississippi besides how to do drugs? The public school system is so hopeless I gave up trying to teach other kids. I decided to focus my energy on my immediate family and get them the hell out of that zoo before it's too late!"

The officer who was asking most of the questions looked skeptical of Terry's explanation. "I'm not sure how you figure they're going to get a well-rounded education living on a homemade raft! And I don't know where you think you're going, but if you're headed to Florida you're going to find out that you can't just anchor out somewhere and live for free. Not anymore! People are tired of looking at anchorages full of derelict liveaboards who don't pay taxes or contribute to the local economy. You'll have a hard time finding a marina slip that allows full-time liveaboards too. And even if you do,

157

it'll cost a lot more than living in a nice apartment ashore to tie up something this long and beamy."

I could tell Terry was seething from the comment about our ship being a "raft." He didn't try to convince the officer otherwise though, because he probably figured there was no use. He said we weren't headed to Florida anyway and if we stopped there at all it wouldn't be for long. He said we were on a world cruise and that the education Janie and I would get would be better than any school on the planet could offer. He said that besides that, there wouldn't be any functioning schools to go to in the United States much longer anyway.

"Why do you think I named this vessel the *Apocalypse*? Do you officers of the law not keep up with what's going on? Do you think everything can keep rocking along like it always has and not come to a screeching halt? I'm not waiting around to see how long it takes! I can't take a chance that it might happen before we can get out, so we're staying ahead of the curve, leaving now to find a place where we can ride it out in safety."

Both of the policemen just kind of laughed at this like they thought Terry was joking. You could tell that like most everybody else who heard our reasoning for leaving, they didn't believe anything like that was going to happen. It seemed nobody did, except for Terry and the people who wrote all those books he read.

Just like I figured they would, those Alabama water cops wrote Terry another ticket for that missing PFD, saying we'd better get one on board as soon as possible. And before they left, the one who had been doing most of the talking had another stern warning for Terry:

"I don't have any proof you've been dumping that Porta Pottie overboard, Captain, but I can tell you that we will be back soon for another inspection. You won't know when we're coming either. It could be this time tomorrow or it could be at oh-four-hundred in the morning. If you're still here when we get back and that little five-gallon tank is still empty, you *will* be fined for illegal overboard discharge, and you're not going to like what it costs! If I were you, I'd stop at the next boatyard and have a real marine head installed in this vessel if you insist on continuing to live aboard. But the best thing you can do is get these kids back in school and quit filling their heads with all these ridiculous ideas about the world coming to an end. People have been saying that stuff since the beginning of time and it hasn't ended yet, so I doubt we have to worry about it happening in our lifetimes, either. You're a lot more likely to get your family drowned out there trying to run away from it all than you are to have problems just living a normal life on land. Especially on an ill-equipped homemade raft!"

"*Normal life on land?*" Terry muttered as the officers motored away in their patrol boat. "What the hell does he call *normal?* Slaving away at some underpaid job to make some faceless corporation rich? Selling more than forty hours a week of your precious time on earth for money to buy all the crap those same corporations want you to believe you can't live without? Those cops are just part of the machine that keeps people from knowing what real freedom is. They spend their days keeping the herd in line, worrying about enforcing the most ridiculous rules ever devised. They should change the name of their agency from "marine police" to "pottie patrol!" Can you believe they get paid for riding around all day in that boat, burning up fossil fuels to make sure everybody else on every other boat is crapping in a plastic tank? A plastic tank that gets pumped out at a marina so it can then be pumped into a sewer line that takes it to the sea? And they think this is *not* going to collapse? Insanity!"

After this visit from the Alabama Marine Police, Terry said it wasn't worth it for us to hang around here any longer than necessary and that it wasn't worth stopping in Florida, since we could avoid it.

"What we need to do is get out of this country ASAP and go somewhere people are still living in reality. We need to finish getting our sails and rigging in order and then leave on the first weather window to sail across the Gulf. We can lay a course for Key West and then sail around the bottom end of Florida without touching land. From there the door is wide open: Cuba and the Bahamas, through the Windward Passage past Jamaica and on to the Panama Canal and the blue Pacific that awaits!"

"But I *wanted* to go to Florida!" Janie protested. "I've always wanted to go to Florida. You promised us we would!"

160

"Florida's nothing but sand and condos," Terry said. "You won't see anything there you haven't already seen here in south Alabama. Florida is just an over-hyped old-folk's state for people who want to get away from winter. There are so many snowbirds living there now they've driven the price of everything through the roof and made more rules and regulations than any state in an already rule-happy nation! We haven't lost a thing in Florida, and you'll see better beaches than any to be found in that overcrowded tourist trap as soon as we make our first island landfall. Giving Florida a miss is the best idea I've had all week, and thanks to those water cops, I've made up my mind. As captain of this ship, I can't subject my crew or my vessel to the hazards that sailing to Florida would entail!"

At this, Janie sulked off to her cabin, saying that was nothing but a bunch of bullshit, but I knew that when Terry made up his mind about something, there was no changing it. Mom didn't argue with him. As usual, she believed whatever he said even if it contradicted something he'd told us all before. That left me, and I wasn't about to protest because I knew all it would get me was another long rant, probably lasting for hours, about the evils of Florida. It kind of made me sad that we couldn't go, but I knew Terry wouldn't let us see anything fun there like Disney World anyway, so what was the point? For better or worse, I was stuck on the *Apocalypse* sailing wherever Terry wanted to sail unless I ran away to live like an orphan on the street somewhere, and that didn't sound any better. At least we were going back out into the Gulf once we got the boat ready again and I would get to see what it was like out on the ocean. Mom was worried about that, and I have to admit, it made me nervous too after what happened the first time we sailed. But Terry said it if we didn't go on across the Gulf, we'd probably end up in jail if we stayed near the coast. He said nobody here wanted to see us because seeing our ship reminded them of all the things they wished they could do but were afraid to. He said a ship like ours represented freedom, and that most people were afraid of the idea because they wouldn't know what to do if they didn't have somebody to tell them, especially the cops. He said they would think up so many things we were in violation of that we couldn't possibly pay all the fines. In the end, I was okay with the idea of sailing on across the whole Gulf to get to some island somewhere, but I sure hoped the wind wasn't blowing as hard as it was that day on Mobile Bay when we did it.

Nine

WE STAYED AT INGRAM Bayou while working on the sails and sorting out the problems with the rigging. Terry had to climb both of the masts to change out some blocks at the top that the halyard lines ran through. He said they were getting in a bind when the sails were full of wind and that was part of the reason he'd had such a hard time getting the mainsail down when it was blowing so hard on Mobile Bay. We had to all help him when he climbed up there, because there were no steps or anything else to make it easy. The two masts were just round wooden poles cut down from the huge chunks of square timbers we had glued together from the old wood salvaged out of Mr. L.C. Pickens' barn. When we were making them, Terry said James Wharram's sail design was different than those used on most ships because the leading edges of the sails went around the masts like sleeves. It was an innovation designed to clean up the airflow and make the boat go faster. Terry said they were called Wharram wingsails and that they acted just like airplane wings. Janie said that was stupid and that a dumb, slow sailboat didn't have a damned thing in common with an airplane.

"That's where you're completely wrong," Terry had countered. "A sailboat is actually very much like an airplane and operates on the same principle. But instead of using the lift to get off the ground like an airplane wing, a well-trimmed sail uses it to go to windward. Figuring out how to harness the wind to sail to windward is one of mankind's greatest achievements. Sailing ships that could go to windward changed history in every way you can think of!"

Terry admitted that while the Wharram wingsail design was efficient, the wrapping of the sail around the mast had some drawbacks. It meant that the masts had to be smooth and unobstructed, and certainly could not have the ladder-like steps to the top that many sailing vessels were equipped with. It also meant that there was sometimes a lot of friction with all that fabric in contact with the mast, and getting the sails to slide up and down properly was not easy. This was especially true in strong winds, when the pressure was increased. Terry was confident this wouldn't be a problem once we were out to sea in the steady trade winds of the Pacific, because he said we wouldn't have to be raising and lowering sails all the time. But regardless of the reason, climbing the rig to work on things aloft would never be easy.

To get up there, he had to sit on a flat board called a bosun's chair with straps hooked to one of the halyards. We had to hoist him up using the big winch in the cockpit. This was slow, hard work, even with me and Janie and Mom taking turns. And because our boat was a schooner, he had two masts to climb, which meant double the work for us. Terry said that going aloft was going to be my job most of the time because I was way lighter than him and most jobs up there were simple, like replacing the bulb on the anchor light. But all this rigging work was something he had to do himself and it took just about a whole day to do it.

While we were at Ingram Bayou doing all this work, Terry made us all go to the bathroom in that stupid Porta Pottie so we could show those marine police when they came back that it was full of crap. And they did come back the very next day after that first visit, just like they said they would. And we did show them the crappy toilet, which seemed to surprise them because they were no doubt expecting that they would find us in violation of the no-discharge law. The one who wrote Terry the ticket for not having a throwable PFD had brought one to give us this time. He said it was an old one he'd found floating in one of the bays and that we still needed to buy a better one, but this one would be good to have until we did, in case someone fell overboard.

"Does that mean I don't have to pay the ticket, then?" Terry asked.

"No sir. I can't let you slide on that because that ticket is supposed to serve as a reminder for you, as captain of your vessel, to put the safety of your crew first. But having this one on board will save you from another citation the next time you get stopped."

Mom thanked the officer and I thought it was pretty nice of him too, but Terry was still furious about the ticket and didn't say another word to him. The next time they came back, the day after that, the Porta Pottie was nearly full to the lid and the entire head compartment was starting to smell like it too. The other officer that had questioned Terry so much that first time wanted to know where we planned to empty it, since it was now too full to use. He warned that with four people on board, we'd better start thinking about that and probably should be moving on right away. It was clear from his tone that he didn't like our ship, didn't like our lifestyle and didn't want us anchoring in his district. Terry told him we were almost ready to leave and that we would be gone by sunrise and he would never see us again. He told him that we wouldn't need to use the head again until we were at sea, where it was perfectly legal to empty it.

Before dark that day, Terry announced that he was satisfied that the main and foresails would go up and down the masts easily in any kind of blow, and that with the jib repaired, we were ready to go.

"I'm not sure I am," Mom said. "I don't really like the idea of going way out there out of sight of land in the middle of the Gulf, especially after what happened right there in the bay. What if a storm comes? What if there's a hurricane?"

"There's not *going* to be a hurricane, don't be ridiculous! I already told you it was too late in the season. Statistically, the odds are very low of another tropical storm forming before the cyclone season is over. Just look around you! The wind is ten knots out of the southeast. What could be better? That's perfectly normal on the Gulf this time of year."

He said he had already checked the VHF radio reports for any warnings or other changes and there was nothing in the immediate future.

"The forecast is as good as it could get. What we should all do now is get a good night's sleep, because this will be the last night we're at anchor for several days or maybe even a week."

I tried to sleep, but I couldn't for the longest time. I just spent most of the night lying there listening to the night sounds from the woods surrounding the bayou, wondering if I would ever hear them again. Terry said that next time we made landfall, wherever that might be, it would be in the tropics or at least the subtropics and that everything would be different. He said it was going to be better in every way, and that we wouldn't have to deal with idiots like those Alabama Marine Police officers, but I was still nervous. What if the wind out there on the Gulf blew like it did that day on Mobile Bay? What if we were three hundred miles from land when it happened and the sails got tore up again, or we lost the other engine? There was plenty to worry about, but I was still excited about sailing the *Apocalypse* across the Gulf. I hoped we would see a whale or something cool like that. Terry said we probably would, but even if we didn't, he promised we'd see stars out there at night like we'd never seen them before on land. He said that being on a sailboat gliding across the sea at night made you feel like you were in outer space in a spaceship, surrounded by all those stars stretching from horizon to horizon with no land or anything else in sight.

Just when I finally fell asleep it was already time to get up. It was still dark outside, but Terry was banging things around on deck, checking that all our stuff was secure and making sure the bicycles and other junk couldn't fall overboard. He pulled on the outboard starter rope at least a dozen times, and I heard him cussing under his breath as it sputtered and refused to start. I climbed out of my bunk and went up there to help him. Mom was already up and making coffee in the galley, but there was no sign of Janie and I knew she would probably sleep until noon if Terry let her.

Once we got out there though, I knew he wasn't going to. No one on board was going to be able to get out of watch duty. Janie could care less, but Terry made it sound exciting— to me anyway—like we were on a spaceship mission or a Special Forces operation or something cool like that. The way it worked is that we would all be assigned to rotating three-hour watches. That meant that whoever was on duty had all the responsibility for the ship: making sure the sails were trimmed correctly, that we were staying on course, and most importantly, keeping a sharp lookout for other ships and dangers. Someone had to be on duty around the clock, because Terry said that a ship at sea never sleeps and we would be running twenty-four hours, day after day until we made landfall.

To make it simpler to keep track of time, we would be operating on twenty-four-hour military time. He wrote down the schedule for the first day: depart Ingram Bayou at oh-six-hundred, (6 a.m.) under his watch. At oh-nine-hundred (9 a.m.), Mom would take over the watch. At twelve hundred hours (12 p.m.), it would be my turn, and then Janie would come on duty at fifteen hundred hours (3 p.m.). This would mean that I would be back on duty for my next watch at twenty-four-hundred hours, or midnight, and Janie would come back on at 3 a.m. in the morning: oh-three-hundred. This was the only arrangement that Janie was satisfied with, because she definitely was not a morning person and being able to sleep until almost three in the afternoon suited her fine. She stayed up all night anyway; listening to her music on her iPad, so coming on duty again at three in the morning was easy too. That way, she would be done by the time it was getting daylight and could be back in bed before the sun came up.

Terry said we would all settle into the routine once we were at sea for a day or two. He said it was normal that everybody would want to be awake when we first departed, and we all were, except for Janie. I wanted to get one good last look at land because I wasn't sure I'd ever see it again, but I also wanted to see everything along the way as we made our way out of the bayou to the nearest inlet that would take us to the open Gulf.

That inlet was Perdido Pass, and to get there we had to go way east and then wind our way back southwest around a big peninsula built up with marinas, condos and seafood restaurants. Since it was so early in the morning, not many people ashore saw us go by, but the few joggers and fishermen and others who did all turned to stare at our ship as we passed. I saw a big McDonald's sign on the main road and wished we could stop so I could get something like an Egg McMuffin and a McFlurry before we left America for good, but I knew better than even mention that to Terry. There was no way he was going to stop for anything now, and all I could do was just stare at those Golden Arches and dream. It was better when it was finally out of sight around the bend, and I could see a much bigger arch—a tall, concrete bridge dead ahead, spanning the fairly narrow inlet that led to the open sea. It was as if it were a gateway to another world, beneath which we would pass, and beyond it, nothing would ever be the same again.

The single motor was running rough and pushing us really slow, but Terry said if it would just hold up until we got through the pass, it wouldn't matter after that. There was hardly any breeze and no way we could sail through this early

170

in the morning but he didn't want to wait for it to start blowing again because if we did, those cops would certainly bother us again. Terry said that once we got clear of land, we'd pick up steadier winds anyway and getting where we wanted to go would be no problem at all. What he didn't take into account though, is that the tide was still coming in when we left that morning. It had hardly been noticeable when we were just cruising through the Intracoastal Waterway, but once we made it to the inlet, it was like going upstream in a river. Terry had the throttle pegged wide open, and we were barely making headway against the rush of incoming water. Some old men standing on the rock jetties with fishing poles in their hands were watching closely to see if we would make it, one of them yelling that we needed to get a bigger motor or wait for slack tide.

All this tidal stuff was new to me, of course, since this trip was my first time to experience the ocean. Terry said that the tides were much stronger in other parts of the world and that the current here was nothing. He said the only reason we were having trouble is because that old Mercury outboard was a piece of junk and I'd let the better Evinrude go to the bottom. He said I'd better be glad we still had at least one or my job would be a lot harder. He said that in the old days before motors were invented, it was up to the crew to tow the ship through inlets like this by rowing the ship's boat. Since our ship's boat was that awkward inflatable dinghy that was so hard to manage, I knew that towing the *Apocalypse* against the

171

current with it using just the oars would be impossible. The crappy little motor was our only hope and I felt bad that I had not been more careful with the better one.

Even with the motor, it took us more than a half hour to get through the inlet and break free of the current into open water. At one point, I was sure we were not going to make it because it felt like we weren't making any progress at all and the big, sharp-edged rocks of the jetties threatened to tear our ship to pieces if the motor failed. But once we were in the clear, and free of the incoming tide, we picked up a couple more knots of speed. Terry pointed the bow straight south and told me to hold the helm steady. Then he opened the cockpit locker where our PFDs were and took out the throwable PFD the policeman had given us. Without a word, he flung it as far overboard to starboard as he possibly could.

"TERRY! What on Earth did you do that for?" Mom screamed.

"He said it was a *throwable* PFD! I was just testing it out, and yes! It is!"

"He gave us that because he was worried about us not having the required safety equipment. We might need it, Terry!"

"Don't be ridiculous! How could anybody fall off a ship as wide and stable as a Tiki 46? And with all those safety nets and rails besides? They can have their stupid PFD back!"

"And now we'll just get another ticket for not having it." Mom said.

"I told you already, Linda; they don't have laws about stuff like that where we're going. And we're not paying those tickets anyway!"

Mom finally dropped it and Terry took the helm back, steering us as directly away from land as he could. Looking back at the coast, you could see tiny cars moving both ways on the beach road, their glass and paint glinting in the sun, but they were so far away you couldn't hear any sounds they made.

The water out there looked a lot different than any I had ever seen before. Instead of being brown and impossible to see into for more than a foot or two, it was a pale green color that was so clear you could see the sand on the bottom even though it looked like it was ten feet deep. I was amazed at this, but Terry said the water here was nothing compared to what we'd see in the islands. He said where we were going that we'd be able to see the bottom a hundred feet down. He said that if you were swimming in it, you could see everything around you just like on those shows on TV where SCUBA divers are swimming around with thousands of fish and other undersea creatures. According to him, the coral reefs we were going to visit in the South Pacific were so remote most of them had never even been explored. He said they would have even more marine life than those on the nature shows because they were too far away from anything for fishermen to get there. But it was all those fish and crabs and lobsters that he was counting on to keep us fed and that was the reason he said we wouldn't need much if any money after we arrived.

I didn't care if he did think there was something wrong with the water here in the Gulf of Mexico. To me it was amazing and all I wanted to do was stare down into it. I went forward to the slatted wooden deck between the bows so I could lie down on my stomach and look over the edge as we sliced through it. I almost jumped straight up in surprise when something huge came up out of the water just a few feet in front of the starboard bow, but even though I'd never seen one in real life before, I knew it was a dolphin. Pretty soon there were five of them, and they seemed to want to play with the *Apocalypse* for a few minutes. They took turns jumping out of the water and swimming in front of our two bows like they were leading the way until they decided we were going way too slow with that one old motor. They were gone by the time Janie finally came up on deck, and even though we all told her we saw them, she didn't believe it. She just thought we were making it up just to get her interested in something besides sleeping and listening to music.

Once we were far enough out that we wouldn't likely drift back ashore before we could sail away, Terry shut down the engine because he said he was tired of hearing it. We just kind of drifted for about a half hour, but then with the sun well up and it getting close to oh-nine-hundred, a bit of a southeast breeze was stirring and you could see tiny ripples of waves forming on the surface of the water. Terry said it was time to set sail, and so we did, first hoisting up the mainsail on the mainmast and then the jib up forward, just as we'd done that first day we had tried to sail.

It was a lot different this time though, and with such a light wind everything went smoothly and stayed in control. Once we'd tightened up and trimmed the main and jib, Terry was ready to hoist the foresail for the first time. It was nearly identical to the main, and was set on the foremast that was in the middle part of the boat. Terry said that we needed all the sail area we could put up in this light wind. Once they were all set and trimmed and working properly, the *Apocalypse* slowly began gathering speed until we were moving at least twice as fast as we could with that outboard. It was a lot nicer sailing in wind like this than it had been that day on Mobile Bay, and once again I felt pride that I'd helped build a sailing ship that really worked.

I kept looking ahead for more dolphins but from time to time I would glance back at the land we were leaving behind too. I was surprised that it already looked so far away. After sailing for about an hour, most of what you could see from where we were was just a hazy blue outline of the trees and tall buildings on the beach. Terry said that soon we'd be completely out of sight of land and we wouldn't see anything else but water in any direction for days and days. He said we'd better get a good last look at the mainland if we wanted to now, because there was no way in hell he was going to be sailing back to America in this lifetime. Janie and Mom didn't seem happy about that because I don't think they ever believed this was going to be anything but a really long vacation until now. I knew that in the back of her mind, Mom still thought we were going to all be living in my grandmother's old house again someday, which is why she wouldn't sell it even when Terry tried to make her.

It hadn't really occurred to me that I might *never* see America again once we left, and hearing Terry say that made me a little sad. I thought we'd come back sometime, but the way he said it, I could tell he wasn't joking. I realized right then that I might have to grow up and get old enough to come back on my own if I ever decided I wanted to see it again. But even though I was sad about that, I was also anxious to get wherever we were going. Terry's excitement about finally being underway at sea was contagious, and now that we were heading straight out to cross the Gulf, I wanted to see what was on the other side.

It was a weird feeling when the land behind us finally disappeared completely from sight. I turned all the way around in a slow circle on the forward deck, looking for anything on the horizon and saw only a few oil rigs and distant boats and ships. Terry said we'd have to go at least a hundred miles out to get away from the oil fields and marine traffic, but that after that the horizon would be truly empty. Mom said that thinking about that made her nervous and she wondered what we would do if we had a problem with the boat and needed help. Terry said that wasn't going to happen and that compared to the Pacific, crossing the Gulf was just a practice run and that after we'd been out there a few days, we would all get used to the feeling of being alone.

The farther we got from land, the darker in color the water was, and before long it was such a deep, inky blue that it almost looked black. I kept looking for dolphins, sharks and whales but didn't see anything but a few seagulls and pelicans that came by to see if we were fishing and had anything for them to eat. By late that afternoon, we'd gotten so far from land that most of the birds were gone, and there were fewer boats and ships in sight. The wind stayed about the same all day, blowing just the right speed to keep us moving but not hard enough to cause problems with the sails. Terry said it was perfect, and that if this kept up we'd be across the Gulf in three or four days. We were steering a course to the south-southwest, because with the wind coming out of the southeast, that was as close to due south as we could go. Terry said that was fine, because on that course we might make our first landfall in Mexico, on the Yucatan Peninsula, which was just as good a route as any.

"The land of the ancient Maya! I was there in 1983 when I was in graduate Anthropology, excavating a just-discovered city in the jungle. It's a whole different world there, Robbie! Jungles…jaguars…monkeys… And snakes so deadly that if they bite you you'll die before you take three steps!"

"Are we going to get to go to the jungle?" I asked, wide-eyed at the thought.

177

SAILING THE APOCALYPSE

"You're going to see jungles aplenty, Robbie, but probably not in Mexico. Everything has changed there now. They bus tourists in to the ruins from the high-rise resorts in Cancun, and everywhere you go, everybody's got their hand out for gringo dollars. Get off the beaten track where the real people live, and you run the risk of getting caught in the crossfire of a drug war. We'll likely give Mexico a skip, but we'll be sailing close enough to get a glimpse. Then it's on to Belize where we'll make our first island landfall among the cays of the second largest barrier reef in the world."

Jungles! Jaguars! Drug wars, ancient ruins and barrier reefs! It was hard for all that to sink in and to imagine that such a different world was just a few days away and this ship that was gliding quietly over the water would take us there. It was a lot to think about, but even now we were in a different world. As the sun started to drop in the southwest, almost straight ahead in the direction we were going, I couldn't believe all the colors that appeared in the sky. Terry said sunsets were more spectacular at sea than they ever were on land, and after seeing my first one, I believed him. Even Janie was spellbound as she watched the changing colors and rays of light. When it finally reached the horizon, the sun looked like a fireball melting into the water. A few minutes later, it was gone and the bright reds and oranges turned to pale pinks and purples. In another half hour, the horizon grew much smaller as our ship was swallowed up in darkness all around, but overhead, a universe of stars opened up like I had never seen before.

All of us had been awake all day, despite the rotating watch schedule, and with so much to look at up in the sky, none of us wanted to go to bed now. We took turns with Terry's binoculars, lying on the deck looking straight up into millions of stars that were so thick they looked like clouds of light in some places. I never knew there were so many and Terry said that was because all the manmade lights of civilization on land made it impossible to see them. He said just seeing the world as it really is for the first time was reason enough to build a boat and go to sea, even if the country we left behind wasn't on the verge of collapse.

"Those shore bastards don't know what they're missing and never will! They've created an artificial reality that insulates them from nature. They live in climate-controlled boxes lit by fluorescent lighting and see only glimpses of reality through the windows or on a screen. They buy meat and produce from the grocery store but have no idea where food comes from or how to get it any other way. They take vacations on jets across the ocean and have no idea what they're missing down below. Getting somewhere in a few hours without navigating or seeing what's along the way is about as far from real travel as you can get, Robbie. Down here on the surface at the mercy of the wind, we're earning our passage mile by mile. When we make a landfall we'll have the right to be there because we found it ourselves and used the forces of nature to get there. Nothing is more real than

SAILING THE APOCALYPSE

sailing your own ship on a long ocean passage!"

As it turned out, Terry was right about us being at the mercy of the wind. Although the *Apocalypse* had maintained a steady speed throughout the afternoon and the first hours of night, by the time it was my watch at midnight, the breeze had completely died. With no wind to fill them, the sails hung slack, moving only slightly with the back and forth motion caused by the waves under our hulls. We were making zero progress, and Terry was up the rest of the night despite that it wasn't his watch. He adjusted sheets and tightened halyards, hoping to get something out of the sails, but there was simply not enough wind to fill them. Terry said that short calms were normal and that the wind would pick back up soon.

But daybreak came, and then sunrise, with colors almost as spectacular as the sunset the day before, and still there was no breeze. The surface of the sea was as smooth as the lakes along the Tenn-Tom Waterway, and we were just floating on it like a piece of driftwood, going nowhere. Terry tried to get a weather report on the VHF radio, but we were too far from the mainland to pick up a signal with that. He had another radio that he said would work anywhere in the world—a single-sideband receiver that could be used to listen to broadcasts, but not to talk—and he spent almost two hours that morning fiddling with it, trying to tune it in to a station that might give us an idea of the forecast. Watching him, I figured out pretty quickly that he had no idea how to use the radio and I wondered why not if he had done as much sailing as he claimed. He finally managed to pick up a station broadcasting weather info, but as we listened, it became apparent that the forecast was for an area of the Atlantic off the U.S. East Coast, not the Gulf of Mexico.

"What if this is a calm before a storm?" Mom asked. "I've heard there's always a calm before a storm, especially a big storm."

"That's an old wives' tale," Terry answered. "This is not a calm before a storm. There were no storms anywhere in the Gulf or the Caribbean when we left yesterday. You heard the weather report yourself."

Mom still wasn't convinced. She was certain the weather could change for the worse at any minute. She was clearly not comfortable being out here this far from land. It was a new experience for all of us, except for Terry, and I was a little nervous too at this talk of storms. It was after all, hurricane season, although Terry played that down when we left. He said that because it was already the first week in October when we launched the boat, the worst part of the season was already over. There had been no hurricanes in the Gulf of Mexico that year and Terry said that if one didn't hit between July and early September, then we wouldn't have to worry about it. He said the best part about leaving in the fall is that we would get to skip the winter in Mississippi, which meant that we wouldn't be needing our jackets, long pants and socks, or even shoes. He said that where we were going we would never see winter again and that the weather would always be warm enough to go swimming anytime we wanted.

A storm didn't come, but when the wind finally picked up again it was coming out of the south-southwest, in exactly the direction we were trying to go. It was blowing just enough to sail, but Terry said no boat could sail straight into the direction of the wind, so we would have to turn away at an angle of at least forty-five degrees to it to make headway. This meant either going nearly due west or east-southeast. West was not good, because Terry said that would take us to the huge offshore oil fields south of Louisiana and Texas, and put us too far away from the Yucatan anyway. He said it was better to go the other way, in the direction of Florida, at least until the wind turned again and allowed us to go more to the south.

Janie was happy to hear that we were sailing towards Florida even if Terry didn't want to. He said we weren't about to go there, no matter what, but as it turned out, Terry was wrong about that too.

Ten

I FOUND OUT ON our attempted crossing of the Gulf that sailboats don't always go exactly where you want them to go. It wasn't like driving somewhere in a car, where you just steer it the way you want to go and keep making the turns you need to make until you get there. On a sailboat, the wind dictates everything, and even though the boat can sail in every direction except straight into the wind, sudden changes in direction and intensity can make getting anywhere frustrating. No matter how much Terry adjusted the sails and tried to make progress to the south, the wind wanted us to go more to the southeast. We were getting farther and farther away from the land we left behind on the northern Gulf coast, but we just couldn't seem to get closer to Mexico or even to the big gap at the bottom of the Gulf between Mexico and Florida. Terry said that in addition to the wind, there were probably currents in the water pushing us the wrong way, even though you couldn't see them.

Although Terry had said we should be able to sail as close as a forty-five degree angle to the wind, it turned out that the *Apocalypse*, with her old, recut sails, just couldn't do that well. The best we could manage, according to the angle Terry estimated by looking at our compass course in relation to the direction the waves were coming from, was about seventy-five or eighty degrees. This meant that unless the wind really changed direction again, we were not going to be able to sail south straight out of the Gulf to the Yucatan or anywhere else. By the second night, we had been pushed so far to the east by these unfavorable winds that we were only a little more than a hundred miles off of the west coast of Florida.

Terry was furious at the thought of being so close to Florida and possibly having to stop there, but Mom and Janie both hoped we would. After the first night at sea, Janie said it was boring as hell out there because all you could see was water. Mom was nervous because we were alone out there and she kept wondering how we would get help if something happened to the ship or somebody got sick. I figured if anybody did get sick, it would be Terry because he would have a heart attack from staying so upset all the time. When the wind wasn't blowing enough to sail, he paced around the deck adjusting lines and looking up to the tops of the two masts or out at the horizon as if he might see a breeze coming. When the wind was blowing the wrong way, like it was now, he kept trying to make the boat point higher into it, either by trimming the sheets until we stalled or tacking to the other side to see if we could make progress that way. As he plotted our progress on a big paper chart using the numbers he got from the GPS, he got madder and madder that we were not where he'd hoped to be by now. Even though I had never been there, I could see on the chart that Florida was a long peninsula that we were headed straight for, and we were even with about the middle of it, in the area of Tampa Bay. Terry said the closer we got to the shore the harder it would be to sail around that long peninsula, and if the wind would just change a few degrees, we could go straight south and get out of the Gulf a lot faster.

The wind didn't change, though. It stayed steady out of the south-southwest and increased from a light breeze to about fifteen knots. We were moving pretty fast, running at around ten knots, and that would have made Terry happy if we could do it in any other direction. But the best we could do was aim for Florida at a point about halfway between Tampa and the bottom end of the state, meaning there was no way we could avoid nearing the coast soon, unless we wanted to keep tacking back and forth to stay offshore, going nowhere. Mom was dead set against that and so was Janie. Mom said that we should just stop in Florida and anchor for one night so everybody could get some rest, and maybe the wind would change so we could sail on south the next day.

"Maybe it will, and maybe it won't," Terry muttered.

SAILING THE APOCALYPSE

"That's the trouble when you get near any coast. The landmass affects the breezes and changes everything! The whole west coast of Florida this far south is mostly mangrove swamps and shoal water; with sandbars everywhere decently remote and all the harbors deep enough to anchor in surrounded by condos and marinas. Then there's Everglades National Park and all the government regulations that go with it. It's the same in most of the Keys. Don't ask me how I know because I've sailed there before."

Seeing the Everglades sounded exciting to me. I'd never even been to a national park before and I didn't see why visiting one wouldn't be a good thing. Terry said most of the park was just water anyway, so it seemed to me like it would be perfect for us, since we were on a ship. We had to go right by it anyway, and it wasn't like trying to get to somewhere in the middle of the state like Disney World, where you had to have a car. Janie didn't want to go to the Everglades at all because she said there was nothing to see there but snakes and alligators. She said she'd rather go to Miami Beach if we were going to Florida and she didn't see why we couldn't since we could get there by water too. Terry said Miami was out of the question and besides, if the wind *did* force us to make landfall in Florida, we weren't staying long enough to act like a bunch of "tourons" going around everywhere taking pictures. His fervent hopes that the wind would change did him no good, however. By the afternoon of the forth day after we'd left Orange Beach, Alabama, we caught our first glimpse of land dead ahead in the distance.

Terry's chart showed that it was Sanibel Island, and just to the south of it and behind it, you could see tall buildings that were the condos and hotels of Ft. Myers Beach. On the chart it looked like there was an area of protected water behind Sanibel Island, and it looked like there might be a good place to anchor just south of the short bridge connecting the island to the mainland. As we got closer to land the details of Sanibel Island came into focus. The first thing I noticed were the groves of tall, dark green trees that all looked alike but weren't like any trees I'd ever seen before. Terry said they were Australian pines and that Florida was full of them. He didn't seem to think they were neat at all, but he did get excited when we got close enough to see a few tall palm trees mixed in with the strange pines.

"Coconut palms!" he announced. "The icon of the tropics and a good sign that even if we *are* still in America, we're headed in the right direction!"

I didn't know much about palm trees of any kind because I'd never seen one before last week, except in pictures and on TV. There were several different kinds along the shore in Alabama, but they were nothing like these. The coconut palms were a lot bigger and more majestic looking. They had long, feathery fronds that waved in the wind from way up top of their tall trunks, some of them curved and leaning out right over the water. I knew why Terry was so excited about them, because he had been telling us the whole time we were building our ship that the coconut palm was one of the most important plants in the Pacific Islands, where we were going. He said not only was the coconut meat inside the nuts a source of food and oil, but the water inside the green ones was the purest and best-tasting water on the planet. He said the fiber from the husks was used for making rope and in some places people even still used the fronds for making the thatched roofs of their houses. But Sanibel Island sure wasn't one of those places.

I didn't know a lot about rich people because I didn't know any back in Calloway City or where we'd lived in Indiana before that. But even I could look at the houses on Sanibel Island and see that it didn't look like anybody who wasn't rich was living there. As we passed by the south end of the island to reach the protected cove behind it, I studied the houses through Terry's binoculars, marveling at how big they were and how perfectly landscaped everyone's yard was. There were all kinds of interesting plants and trees I'd never seen before, most of them palms and jungle plants of some kind, but a lot of them looked like cactus and other desert plants too. Most of the houses had big glass windows so the people that lived in them could get a good view of the Gulf, and there were big screened in porches attached to all of them. Terry said they had to have them to live here because Florida was a mosquito-ridden hellhole that would be uninhabitable without screens and air conditioners. He said that before those inventions, half of the state was a wilderness that still had wild Indians, and land was so cheap it was almost free. Now it costs a fortune for even the tiniest parcel of flood-prone dirt with a view of the water. He said most of the people that owned houses like the ones on Sanibel Island were so rich that these were just winter getaways and they really lived in places like New York or Boston most of the year.

When we got to the place behind the island, there were no boats anchored there and Terry thought that was strange. Looking at the chart in advance and now seeing it with his own eyes, he said it was a good, safe place to drop the hook in all but the worst weather, and he couldn't understand why it wasn't full of cruising sailboats like most good anchorages in Florida. As we motored farther north towards the bridge, keeping the island about a quarter mile off of our port side, we came to an opening in the land that turned out to be a channel leading into a small marina.

"That's why they're not anchored out," Terry said. "Money's not an object here, so they just take a slip in the marina when they come through."

"Look! There's a sign that says 'Free Overnight Docking!'" I said, excited about the possibility of staying there and getting to explore the island on foot before it got dark.

Terry saw the sign too when I pointed it out, but not believing it, he grabbed his binoculars to read the smaller print at the bottom: "With the purchase of five hundred gallons of fuel!" he spat with disgust. "*Five hundred gallons*! That's over two thousand dollars! How generous of them to offer to let you tie up for the night if you spend two thousand dollars on fuel!"

"What would anybody do with five hundred gallons of fuel?" Janie asked.

"Burn it up in a couple of days, if they're on one of those motor yachts with the on-board washer and dryer that you're so keen on! They'll go through five hundred gallons just to get as far as we've come since leaving Mobile."

"What do you think they'd charge us to dock there if we didn't buy all that fuel?" I asked, still hoping.

"We'll never know, because I'm not asking. But you can bet we can't afford it! And why would we want to, when we can drop the hook out here for free and have the whole anchorage to ourselves with a better view? Get ready to lower away, Robbie! I'm coming about!"

There were a few people in sight, most of them walking on the beach as we set our anchor and got settled in, and some stopped long enough to watch us for a few minutes but they didn't wave. Terry said we could still check out the island, all we had to do was blow up the dinghy and put the outboard on it. Mom was happy about that because she wanted to get back on dry land after being out of sight of it all those days, and she also wanted a meal she didn't have to cook. I just wanted to get a closer look at all those weird plants and trees, and Janie wanted to look at boys (and probably try to find one that had a joint he would share).

Since there weren't any other sailboats anchored there and we didn't know where to go to land the dinghy, Terry just headed for a narrow sandy beach where people were jogging and walking their dogs. It looked like a park of some kind and had a lot of shade from a dense stand of those dark Australian pines. We were just pulling the dinghy up on the sand when a man who looked like he probably lived in one of the expensive houses came over and said we couldn't land there. He said boats weren't allowed on the beach and that if we wanted to come ashore, we'd have to go to the marina. When Terry told him our catamaran was too wide for most marinas and that the docking fee was too expensive besides, the man said anchoring where we were near the island was prohibited.

"The Sanibel city council has just recently passed a 'no anchoring' ordinance. The only exceptions are for vessels needing emergency repairs or those seeking shelter from threatening weather. Overnight anchoring is not allowed."

"That's bullshit!" Terry told him. "Whatever city council you have here has no right to control the water. I don't care how much your shoreside real estate is worth. These are navigable waters and as captain of my ship I can come and go upon them as I please!"

"You'll get a chance to tell that to the marine police, then. All I'm doing is informing you of the law. And if you go ashore and leave this dinghy here, you're just going to make matters worse."

"Fine then! I was planning to take my family out to dinner in one of your overpriced restaurants, but if my money's not wanted here, I'll keep it! But we just sailed in from a four-hundred-mile passage across the Gulf. I'm not weighing anchor until my crew is rested and the wind is fair for the passage south!"

"Let's just go somewhere else, Terry," Mom said, as we headed back to the *Apocalypse* in the dinghy. "It's not worth another hassle with the police and the expense of more tickets. Can't we find someplace better to anchor? Someplace legal?"

"The hell with legal! We're doing nothing wrong anchoring here. Florida's definitions of what's legal and navigational reality are two different things. They've been trying to pull this kind of crap for decades. All those rich bastards from up north come down here and buy up all the waterfront property so they can see the ocean, then they get pissed off because somebody in a sailboat anchors in their view. They pay so much in taxes for their over-priced real estate that it burns them up to see people like us enjoying the same water without paying a dime. They bitch and complain to their city councils and local law enforcement agencies, and the elected officials give them what they want for fear of losing the salaries those ridiculous taxes enable. All you have to do is follow the money to understand it."

"What if they put us in jail?" I asked. "You said we'd

probably get put in jail if we went to Florida."

"Not for dropping the anchor! They won't and they can't! All these anchoring bans are good for is intimidation. It works on most boaters so they keep doing it. They might tow away some old derelict with a drunken bum living aboard in a canal, but they can't stop cruising sailors like us from taking a break!"

We found out Terry was only partly right when we got a visit just before sunset from a county sheriff's department patrol boat. The two deputies tied up alongside the *Apocalypse* and came aboard to do the usual search. When Terry asked them what the problem was, they informed him of the local anchoring ordinance and said that they weren't going to make us leave immediately without sleep, but that we could stay there no longer than twenty-four hours because we were in a restricted zone.

"Restricted for what?" Terry demanded. "We're well outside of any navigational channels and not in anyone's way."

"It's a Homeland Security restricted zone," the tallest of the officers replied. "It's our job to patrol these waters looking for suspicious vessels and this happens to be a buffer zone between the open Gulf and the ICW and Caloosahatchee River. We have to keep it clear and because of that, transient vessels are discouraged from anchoring here. But since you're already here, we're going to have to inspect your safety equipment and take a look around down below."

Naturally, the safety equipment list came up short—because we didn't have a Type IV throwable PFD on board! When one of the officer's pointed this out and pulled out his citation book to write the ticket, Mom gave Terry a look like she wanted to slap him for throwing that free one over the side. These deputies didn't like our Porta Potti any more than the Alabama marine policemen did either. They couldn't fine us just because it was empty though, because Terry showed them our GPS tracks which proved we'd just sailed in from the open Gulf. The deputy that did all the talking told us that we'd better install a real head if we were going to be staying in Florida waters, and he also informed us that we would need to purchase an out-state cruising permit or pay for Florida registration. Terry said we weren't staying here but one night and that when we hauled in our anchor tomorrow, we were leaving U.S. waters for good. The deputies weren't interested in where we were going or why, but before they left they said they would be back at the same time tomorrow and that we'd better be gone.

After they left, Mom wasn't happy about having to cook the same old rice and canned food we'd been eating while we were sailing. Janie and I weren't excited about it either after thinking we were going to get to eat in a restaurant, but food was the least of Terry's concerns. He was happier being on the boat than anywhere ashore anyway, but he was really fuming about the way people here were treating us.

"Second-class citizens in their eyes, that's all we are! Just because we don't fit into the mold and look, think and act like everyone else."

"I thought Florida was supposed to be a paradise for boaters," Mom said. "I'm shocked that they make it so hard on us."

"It was, back in the day, but all that's changed now. Like everywhere else in this country, it's completely screwed. I hope I don't have to keep telling you why it's imperative that we leave ASAP!"

I hoped he didn't either, because I got tired of hearing about it all the time, especially the part about everything collapsing. I did wish people would be nicer to us than they were, but I didn't think it was as bad as Terry said it was.

While we waited on dinner, Terry spread out his charts to plot our escape from Sanibel Island, the state of Florida and the United States, saying we were leaving at first light if the wind was even the least bit cooperative. He pointed to an inland route that he said the ICW took here at the Sanibel Island/Ft. Myers area, sneering at the thought of using it because it was the route all the powerboaters and sailors who'd rather motor than sail took.

"It's a shortcut to the East Coast, but it goes through canals and crosses Lake Okeechobee right though the middle of the state."

"If it's a shortcut, why don't we take it?" I asked.

"Because we can't sail it, that's why. It's an inland route

195

that's effectively a trap. With locks and drawbridges to go through, we'd be at the mercy of others just to transit. Imagine what would happen if we were there during the collapse and the poop really hit the fan. We'd be sitting ducks and never get out! No sir, Robbie, there's no way in hell we're taking that chance. It's back offshore from here for us. We'll just have to hope the wind is fair so we can sail south to the Keys and finally break out into the Atlantic where we'll be free of U.S. waters at last."

The Atlantic! It was hard to believe that we were about to be on the real ocean, maybe in another day or two, Terry said, if the wind was good enough. Things already looked so different here, I couldn't imagine what they would look like in the real islands. Terry said Sanibel Island wasn't a real island because it had a bridge connecting it to the mainland. He said half the so-called "islands" in Florida were like that, but where we were going, not only did the islands not have bridges to anywhere else; a lot of them didn't even have roads on them at all. He said there were people living in some of those places that had never even seen a car, much less ridden in one.

The next day when we woke up, the wind was still blowing out of the south-southwest, right in the direction we wanted to go. Terry had hoped it would change by now so we could bypass heading for the Keys and go straight to Mexico liked he'd talked about before, but that didn't happen. We left the anchorage and Sanibel Island at a pitiful two knots, the

SCOTT B. WILLIAMS

little eight-horse Mercury struggling to drive the *Apocalypse* along against a ten to twelve knot wind. Terry said if it got any stronger, we wouldn't be able to make progress at all. Once we got a half-mile or so from the coast, we raised the main and jib and tried to sail south along Fort Myers Beach. With the wind at the angle it was, we kept getting closer and closer to the beach and then we would have to turn and try and tack back out to get some room. With the way the *Apocalypse* didn't like to sail into the wind, every time we turned on this other tack, we were going north of due west just to make headway. It was frustrating because that was almost the way we'd come from. If it was going to be like this, it was going to take forever to get all the way south of Florida to the Keys and into the Atlantic.

The coastline here was mostly straight, running in a north and south direction. There were areas of tall condos and other buildings and other areas where there was nothing but woods. Terry said the thick, emerald green trees that grew right out into the water in these places were mangroves, and that we'd be seeing them from now on because we weren't going anyplace that wasn't tropical. He said there were a lot more of them in the Everglades, and that's where he'd now decided to try to get to that first day, because we couldn't make enough headway to the southwest to get around the end of the Keys. He said we could anchor somewhere along the Everglades coast, because there was nothing there but wilderness and the only cops we'd have to worry about would be the park rangers.

To get there we had to first go past a place called Marco Island. Terry said Marco Island was about the last place on the west coast of Florida that was a town or anything—everything south of that was just mangroves until you got to the Keys. Mom and Janie wanted to stop there, because they sure didn't want to go to the Everglades because they said they were scared of all the snakes and alligators there. Terry said that was nonsense and that Marco Island was even worse than Sanibel when it came to anchoring prohibitions. He had read in some of his sailing magazines before we left Mississippi that there was an ongoing legal battle over anchoring there and that the water cops in that area were the worst in Florida. He said he'd rather put up with snakes and alligators any day over more of that kind of crap.

But like it or not, we ended up stopping in Marco Island anyway. In fact, we ended up right on the beach. It happened when the steady southwest wind pushed us too close to shore like it had been trying to do all day. Terry tried to bring the ship about on the other tack so we could make some distance away from the land to deeper water. When he steered the bows through the wind so it could catch the sails on the other side, he did it too slow one time and we kind of stalled out, ending up in a situation that Terry said sailors call "in irons." We could have gotten it straightened out, no problem, but the trouble was, we were way too close to a long underwater sandbar that jutted out from the beach when it happened.

Even though the *Apocalypse* only draws a little over two feet, this sandbar area was so shallow that we got stuck when the wind and waves drove us backwards onto it.

Terry screamed and cussed like I'd never heard him do before. He was even madder than he was when that barge forced us to run aground on the Tenn-Tom. This *was* a lot worse, because the water wasn't calm like it had been up there, and the waves were causing us to bounce up and down on the bottom, jarring the whole ship every time it hit and making it hard to stand without losing your balance and falling. We weren't far from the beach at all and a bunch of people who looked like they were on vacation were staring and pointing at us like they'd never seen a ship like ours before, which they probably hadn't. Terry said to quit looking at them and help him get us off the sandbar. He said we had to do something fast, because the longer the ship was pounded there by those waves the harder aground she would get and we'd never get her off. I jumped in after him and he yelled at Mom and Janie to do the same. Unlike on the Tenn-Tom, the bottom here was sand, and we didn't sink into it much, but even with all four of us pushing, we still couldn't budge the massive *Apocalypse*.

One man from the beach who looked like he was about twenty-five waded out there to help us. He was one of those muscle guys you always see on movies and TV shows that hang around the beach in places like California. He wasn't wearing anything but a tiny little swimsuit that barely hid his private parts. I figured somebody with muscles like that could just about push our ship off without any help, but we still couldn't make any progress. As long as he was out there, Janie sure wasn't helping because all she was doing was staring at his body. One time I even noticed Mom looking too, but she turned her eyes away real quick when she knew I saw her.

It was clear that just pushing wasn't going to get us back to deep water, so Terry said we'd better get the dinghy inflated and try to set an anchor. The muscle guy, who said his name was Mark, offered to stay and help us, and Terry said that would be good, because it was probably going to take a lot of cranking on the winch to pull us off once we got an anchor set. The wind didn't show any sign of letting up either, and Terry said the biggest worry he had was that the tide was going to be turning and would start going out soon. When it did, there wouldn't be enough water to float the *Apocalypse* off that sandbar, and we would be stuck there for the night.

Just about the time we got the dinghy pumped up and had mounted the outboard to it, a big orange inflatable boat that looked like a cross between a giant dinghy and a big patrol boat showed up, slowing down in the deeper water about a hundred feet farther out from where we were stuck. When the boat turned sideways to us as it drifted, I could see big white letters painted on its side that said "Marine Towing." I was excited now, thinking we wouldn't have to do all that hard work with the dinghy and winch after all. I hollered at Terry that somebody was here to help us and when he looked up and saw the boat, he just started cussing again.

"No, he's not here to help, he's here to help himself to our cruising kitty! Outfits like that are nothing but modern day wreckers, the scourge of the coast, looking to take advantage of someone else's misfortune! He can go back where he came from, as far as I'm concerned!"

"Your insurance will cover the tow," the guy named Mark said.

Just as he said that, the VHF radio came to life with a call for the captain of the *Apocalypse* from *Marine Towing of Marco Island*. Terry was going to ignore it, but Mom pleaded with him to at least talk to the man.

"You never know," she said. "Maybe he won't charge us much. Maybe when he sees we're a stranded family, he'll pull us off for nothing."

"Keep dreaming!" Terry said. "Don't forget where we are. This is *Florida*, dear!"

He picked up the radio mic and answered the waiting towboat captain. The first thing the other man said was that he just needed to see our insurance policy and he'd pull us right off. Terry looked at the rest of us with an "I told you so" smirk and then spoke back into the microphone. "We don't have any insurance, and we can get ourselves off this sandbar, no problem."

"Roger, Captain. I understand. But I can accept cash or a

credit card as well. I can have you back afloat in deep water for five hundred dollars."

"Five hundred dollars!" Terry practically screamed into the mic. "We'll sit here all week before I pay you five hundred dollars for a five minute job!"

"Roger, Captain. Understood, but you are aware there's strong front coming through, aren't you? That southwest wind is going to clock around to the west and then northwest by midnight, and when the next high tide comes in before daylight, it'll put you right on the beach."

We didn't know about the change in the weather because Terry had been so focused on getting away from Sanibel Island and trying to sail south that he hadn't bothered to check the forecast again. The sun had been shining all day and the wind was the same as it had been for the past two days and nights, so he hadn't seen any reason to. He replied that with Mark's help and our winches and anchors, we could get our ship back off the sandbar ourselves.

"Roger, Captain. Understood. I'll stand by just in case you have problems and change your mind."

"See what I mean?" Terry said to the rest of us. "Just like a circling vulture waiting for its prey to die! He's going to sit there watching, just hoping we can't get it off ourselves so he can collect that five hundred dollars when we fail. Well, it'll be a cold day in hell when that happens!"

Two hours later, as the sun was nearing the horizon and the tide was running out, making our situation even worse, it was quite clear that we *had* failed in our attempts to free the *Apocalypse*. Even with an anchor set in deeper water out in front, and even with Mark's bulging muscles cranking on the winch handle, we were getting nowhere. And Mark said he had to go because he had a class to teach at the gym. Mom and Janie were begging Terry to let the *Marco Island Marine Towing* boat pull us off, and finally, just as the sun was setting, Terry reluctantly waved him over.

Eleven

ONCE TERRY HANDED OVER the five one hundred dollar bills, it was a simple matter for the marine towboat with its four huge outboard engines to drag us back to deep water. The *Apocalypse* had not been damaged in the grounding, thanks to the extra sacrificial layers of wood and fiberglass we'd built up on the keels during construction. The towing service captain said we were lucky, and that it could have been disastrous if the shore here was rock or coral like a lot of it was farther south in the Keys. He tried to give Terry a long sales spiel about his parent company's insurance policies that paid for statewide towing. He said everyone who boated in Florida ran aground frequently because of the shallow waters here. But Terry wasn't buying it. He said we couldn't afford towing insurance and the towboat guy kept saying we couldn't afford not to have it. Finally, the man pulled away in his boat, shaking his head, saying we'd probably be aground again in the Keys in a day or two.

Terry cussed and stomped around on deck as the towboat sped away, saying that five hundred dollars for something that took twenty minutes to do amounted to fifteen hundred dollars an hour.

"That's another reason this whole country is doomed," he said. "They pay teachers a poverty wage like they were paying me at Calloway Junior High, and any fool with enough money to buy a boat with four big outboards can earn what I made a year in a matter of days!"

"Well, it's not like anybody else was going to pull us off the beach," Janie said. "Isn't that how it works with something like that? The law of supply and demand or something? He can charge what he wants because he's the only one here to do the job. And if we didn't pay, we could have lost our ship in that bad weather that's coming."

Terry launched into her with all the reasons why it was still way too much money, saying the towboat guy could make honest wages charging a third of what he did. It seemed to me that whatever we had to pay, the most important thing was that we weren't stuck any more. Besides, no matter how much Terry cussed about it, he always seemed to be able to find however much money he needed just by going below in cabin where he and Mom slept and getting it out. He always paid in cash too. I wondered just how much more he had down there, but I didn't dare ask him.

With it dark out now and that frontal system approaching, the first thing we had to do was try to get somewhere that we could anchor for the night that would be protected from the wind. There wasn't a decent option close by, especially with the situation in Marco Island, so Terry said we ought to just keep heading south to the Everglades and stay far enough off the coast so we wouldn't have to worry about sandbars. We were all tired after the long day of tacking back and forth against the wind and then trying to get the ship ungrounded. I knew it was going to be a long night and I dreaded it, but there really wasn't much choice except to keep on going.

Terry said we couldn't sail near the coast in the Everglades area, because it was worse than Marco Island, as far as shoals go. He said there were lots of places where the water was just a foot or two deep and that on most of this coast there was little dry land, just mangroves growing out into the water far from the muddy shores that were there. At night, you couldn't see a thing on the coast, not even enough to tell there was land there, because nobody lived there and there were no lights of any kind except for an occasional small powerboat going by.

To make things a lot worse, it started raining at about twenty-one hundred hours and then you could hardly see a thing past the edges of the boat. It was so dark that it was hard to tell where the water ended and the sky began, and with all that rain coming down it didn't matter much anyway.

207

SAILING THE APOCALYPSE

It wasn't my watch and I didn't have to be up on deck, but I knew I wouldn't be able to sleep down below anyway, because I'd be too scared we were going to hit something or be run over in the dark by a ship like that one on Mobile Bay. I stayed out there in the rain with Terry, both of us wearing the plastic rain suits with hoods he'd bought for us at Walmart. Terry said there wasn't any use in worrying about ships because he said they would either pick us up on their radar or not, and there wasn't a damned thing we could do about it anyway.

The Walmart rain suits sucked because they were made of heavy plastic that didn't leak, but when they were buttoned up enough to keep you dry, it was so hot inside them you couldn't breath. It wasn't quite as bad at night as it was in the daytime, but it had been pretty hot ever since we got to Sanibel Island and Terry said it was just about always that way in south Florida. He said even though this change in the weather was caused by a cold front moving across the continent farther north, about the only difference it would make down here was that the wind would change directions and blow out of the north for a few days. He said the cold air wouldn't get this far south but that sometimes the fronts were strong enough to whip up dangerous seas.

It was a good thing that the wind was going to change direction and we'd finally be able to sail the way we wanted to go, but first we had to get through a stormy night. The rain was bad enough, but the change in wind direction also brought a change in wind strength. By midnight, it was blowing so hard we only had our smallest jib up on the forestay and the main was reduced to the second reef. That was about as little sail as we could have up and still be able keep the boat moving. Terry had planned on sewing storm sails too, but he just hadn't gotten around to it yet with all the other boat projects he had to do. The seas were getting really big all of a sudden and I was starting to get scared. They weren't big enough to flip over a catamaran the size of ours, Terry said, but they lifted the whole ship up and dropped it when they passed, making me think it might break apart or something. The ship's motion in the waves was an abrupt fore and aft pitching caused by the narrow ends of the hulls at the bow and stern. Terry said it was a lot better than the horrible rolling of a monohull that would make you puke your guts out, but Mom and Janie were feeling pretty sick anyway.

Terry told them they'd be better off up on deck, where they could get some fresh air, but they didn't want to come out there in the rain, and before long, they were both seasick. Janie was the first one to come up puking, and before she could make it to the aft end of the deck, she was spewing vomit everywhere in the cockpit and even got some on my feet. I screamed at her to use the toilet bucket, but it was already too late. Mom did use the bucket when she threw up, but I didn't get sick and neither did Terry, and he said it was because we were out there topside in the fresh air the whole time. They didn't go back below after that, and for the rest of the night the four of us sat out there in the rain, riding out the storm in those cheap plastic rain suits and hoping the waves weren't going to break the boat apart.

They never did, but a really big one swept across the deck and tore a bunch of stuff loose that Terry had tied down, including some of the extra gas cans for the outboard and Janie's bicycle. Terry and I hung on for all we were worth as we crawled out there and put more lashing lines on the rest of the bicycles. Janie was so seasick the bicycle was the last thing in the world she cared about. She said all she wanted was to get on dry land and if she ever did, she said she'd never set foot on a boat again.

We got through the rest of the night without losing or breaking anything else or getting hit by a ship, and when daybreak finally came, it felt like a miracle that we had survived. The wind was out of the northwest at a steady fifteen knots, and while there were still whitecaps and waves, they weren't as big as they had been during the night. Even though we'd been tacking back and forth to stay away from the shore, when Terry checked the GPS, it showed that we had been blown a considerable distance to the south along the coast. We were just off of a place called Shark River, one of the few good anchorages shown on the charts in the Everglades. Since we were all exhausted from staying up all night, Terry said we should go in there and drop the hook to get some rest. He said the wind ought to clock on around to the north by later in the day and probably to the northeast or east by the next day, making it easy for us to sail on south and get out of the Gulf for good. A stopover here wouldn't hurt anything and we could fix some of the things on the boat that needed fixing in a place where it was unlikely anyone would be around to bother us. It all sounded good to me, especially because we were anchoring in the Everglades and in a place named Shark River at that. I just knew I was finally going to see some full-sized alligators and maybe some sharks too! As we approached the coast under just our small jib, still making a good five knots, there was nothing in sight but dark green mangroves as far as you could see to the north and south. The green seemed to almost glow against the morning light with all that moisture from the rain still hanging in the air, and the whole place had a mysterious feel like nowhere I'd ever been before.

We entered the mouth of the Shark River following a channel marked with signposts and floating buoys. This was the first time I'd gotten a close look at all those mangroves we'd seen in the distance, and for the first time I realized how weird those trees really were. They looked almost like spiders or even something alien, with their long skinny roots branching out in all directions holding the rest of the tree up out of the water. And the way they were all tangled together reminded me of spider webs too. It was like an impenetrable wall of green, and I could not imagine trying to walk through it. Terry said you couldn't and that the best way to get through a mangrove forest if you had to was to climb from tree to tree like a monkey. He said you didn't have to be a monkey or Tarzan to do it either, because the branches and roots were so close together.

The seabirds seemed to love all that vegetation growing right out into the water, especially the herons that stood there in the shallows, hunting fish swimming among the roots. There were all kinds of other birds I'd never seen before too, some that Terry said never went north of this part of Florida. We saw lots of raccoons too, but even though I looked I still didn't see an alligator. Janie said she'd seen pictures on Facebook of giant pythons in the Everglades swallowing alligators, and that maybe there weren't any more left. Terry said that was nonsense, but it was true that pythons lived here now. He said it was just another stupid thing people did, introducing species like that where they don't belong.

"Even though it's supposed to be protected as a national park, and supposed to be a pristine example of a unique ecosystem, like everywhere else it's been screwed up by greed and idiotic thinking. It won't matter in fifty years though, because this entire part of Florida will be below sea level anyway."

"I don't see any land now," Janie said, looking at the flooded roots of the mangroves that surrounded us on both sides as we motored farther up the river.

"It's here, just farther inland. The mangroves form new land all the time, trapping sediment with the roots and making new islands, but they won't be able to keep up with global warming. Just a few feet of sea level rise will do them in, and it's going be a lot more than that eventually. That's why we've got to go to the Pacific, where the islands are really the tops of undersea volcanoes. Those islands with mountains and plenty of elevation near the coast will be the only safe place to be."

Terry said the Shark River was just one of hundreds of channels that flowed across the inland part of the Everglades to empty into the Gulf. It wasn't like a regular river, like the Tombigbee or the Mobile that we'd come down. He said farther inland, the water spread out wide and thin, running through a "sea of grass," and then narrowed back into separate channels that filtered through the mangroves at the coast, mixing with the seawater on the incoming tide. Because of that, there was just about every kind of freshwater and saltwater creature that lived in the region right there in those waters and I finally got to see my first shark. It wasn't a big one, maybe about six feet long, but it was fast! I could see it take off in the clear water when we surprised it, and Terry said that it probably thought our big twin hulls were two bigger sharks and needed to run for its life. He said that even though a six-foot shark wasn't all that big, it was plenty big enough to bite a chunk out of somebody or take off a hand or foot. It wouldn't be a good idea to fall in the water here because there were probably sharks a lot bigger than that one cruising around. He said they probably didn't just make up the name "Shark River" for no reason. I had been hoping I could go swimming ever since we got to Florida, but we never seemed to be in a good place for it. One thing I knew for sure though, was that I was not going swimming in a place named Shark River!

There weren't any other boats or people around when we found a good place to anchor on a side channel that went off through the mangroves. The water was calm in there because the trees protected it from most of the wind that was still blowing pretty good, and the opening was just wide enough for our catamaran to fit into. Terry cut the outboard to idle and let us drift in there, after first dropping our smaller anchor off the stern and letting the rode pay out as we went. He said that way when we got ready to leave, it would be a simple matter to pull ourselves back out the main river. That was much easier than trying to back up with the motor, because we'd already found on that first day at Bay Springs Lake that the *Apocalypse* did not like to go backwards.

Once we were in the side channel, the mangroves were so close that Terry was able to use our long boat hook to pass a couple of mooring lines around nearby branches on either side. One branch was rubbing against the starboard topsides, so Terry got out his machete and whacked it off. It was snug and secure feeling in there, and Mom and Janie especially liked it after being out in the Gulf at night puking their guts out in rough seas. It was kind of like being in the jungle, except that there was only one kind of tree—the mangroves —and nothing else to look at except the dark, but clear water below us and the sky overhead. Fish were jumping and splashing everywhere and Terry said we ought to try and catch our dinner. Mom warned him that we'd better not, since we didn't have a Florida fishing license and besides, this was a national park and we didn't know what the rules were. Terry said he wasn't worried about that because the Everglades was more than a million acres of mangroves and swamp and since we hadn't seen a ranger or even another boat since we got here, what were the chances of one finding us now? He said what we needed to do was inflate the dinghy and go farther up this little side channel, where we'd be completely out of sight, and then we could get all the fish we wanted among the mangrove roots where they swim in big schools.

Mom and Janie didn't want to go, but fishing sounded like an adventure to me, especially since Terry said we were going to do it with the spearguns he'd brought for underwater fishing in the islands when we got there. He said they would work fine from the surface in the shallow water among the mangroves, because the water was clear enough to see the fish we were shooting and all we had to do was tie up the dinghy and sit very still and wait. He said it was the same thing the herons did and it worked for them. We found a good spot after going around two bends in the channel up from the boat, and as soon as we tied up the dinghy, I started seeing fish. I couldn't believe how many there were. It was like the water was alive with them. It was only about three feet deep where we were, and it looked like it was going to be easy to get all the fish we could eat. It looked to me like all you had to do was shoot a spear down there at random and you were bound to stab one, there were so many.

It wasn't as easy as it looked though, once I tried. The spear guns used a long, metal spear that was propelled forward when you released the trigger by big tubular rubber bands like they use on slingshots. After each shot that missed, like all of mine did, you had to pull the spear out of the mud and load it back again, cocking the rubber bands. It was slow to reload and after every miss, the fish scattered and we had to wait for them to come back. I never hit one, but finally, Terry did.

"Yes!" he whispered as his spear connected. "I hope your mom's got the skillet ready! Fresh snapper for dinner tonight!"

I was expecting something bigger when he pulled his spear out of the water from the front of the dinghy and showed me his fish. It was about the size of my hand, and didn't look like it would be enough dinner even for Janie, and she was a picky eater who didn't eat much anyway. Terry said it was perfect though, and that there were a lot more where that one came from. He said it was a yellowtail snapper, and that it would be delicious. I told him we would need about ten more if they were all that size and he said we would get them because he was just out of practice when we started.

We were soon quiet and still again, watching and waiting for the fish to come back while the one Terry shot flopped its

216

tail as it lay dying on the floor of the dinghy between us. But before we got a chance to shoot at some more, the silence was interrupted by the sound of an outboard motor. It got louder and you could tell it was coming closer, but Terry said it probably was just some other fisherman going by on the Shark River and that they would never come up in this little channel. But he was wrong about that like he was about so many other things.

It turned out that the channel we were on looped around and connected back into Shark River on the other end. It had to, because before we knew what was happening, the boat we'd been listening to suddenly appeared around the bend farther up from where we were tied up in the dinghy, opposite the direction in which the *Apocalypse* was moored. And it wasn't just another fisherman like Terry thought. It was an Everglades National Park ranger in a patrol boat, and he caught us red-handed sitting there in that dinghy with our spearguns pointed into the water and the punctured Yellowtail snapper on the floor between us.

There wasn't any way to explain our way out of that one or pretend we weren't fishing. All Terry could do was claim ignorance and say that he didn't know it was against the law. The ranger said he didn't care whether we knew what the law was or not. He said it was our responsibility to find out if we were going to visit the park. It turned out that fishing with the proper equipment or licenses wasn't illegal, but doing it with a speargun sure was. It was illegal to even have spearguns in the park, much less to use them to spear game fish that we didn't even have a Florida saltwater license to catch. The ranger immediately confiscated the two spearguns, putting them in his boat, along with Terry's fish; then he told us he was going to have to search our main vessel as well. When Terry said that we didn't have anything else illegal, the ranger told him to shut up or he would take us both back to the ranger station and lock us up while they sent someone else out to have a look.

I was glad Terry kept quiet after that, because I sure didn't want to go to jail. I figured this whole mess was going to cost Terry some money, and I was right. The ranger followed us back to the *Apocalypse* and went through it from stem to stern, searching every locker in the cockpit, and every bin, cubbyhole and drawer in both cabins down below. He didn't find anything else illegal though, except for a big fishing net Terry had stashed that he said we couldn't have in the park, and he confiscated that too. The main thing I was relieved about was that he didn't find Terry's hidden gun compartment. I figured that if he made such a big deal out of a couple of spearguns powered by rubber bands, he would freak out over Terry's rifles and the pistol and probably have us all sent to prison. While he was at it, he checked our safety equipment and noted the absence of the Type IV PFD that we'd already gotten so many tickets for not having. Then he saw the mangrove branch Terry had cut with his machete.

"Cutting any vegetation in a national park is illegal," he

said, glaring at Terry. "Are you not aware too that cutting mangroves anywhere in the state of Florida is illegal? Just tying your boat to them is illegal, but you had to go and cut one too! This is going to cost you more than the fines for fishing without a license and using illegal hunting weapons in a national park!"

Terry mumbled something about how it didn't look to him like the mangroves were endangered, because they were the only trees you could see for a hundred miles up and down the coast. The ranger gave Terry and me a stern lecture about why national parks were established and how violators like us were no better than poachers out to destroy the whole ecosystem. He made me feel terrible just because I had *tried* to spear a fish, even though I never actually hit one. Then he started writing the tickets, although since I was underage, he said Terry was responsible for contributing to my delinquency and he would be fined double. Terry argued that we would have bought fishing licenses but we hadn't been ashore since we'd made it to Florida because we couldn't find any legal places to anchor or dockage that we could afford. He said fines and tickets for petty violations were breaking us and that the main reason we'd been fishing with the spears is because he didn't see how he was going to afford to feed his family much longer at this rate.

"I'd suggest getting a job!" the ranger said. "There's nowhere left in the world where you can live off the land or sea for free, I don't care where you go. You sailboat dreamers are all alike and I've seen plenty over the years. Everybody that lives in Florida has, because the warm winters draw bums like flies. You need to go to work and make sure these kids get a decent education. Teaching your son to break the law isn't the way to start him out in life and living on a boat is a dead end that's just one step up from homeless in the gutter."

Terry took the tickets and stuck them in his logbook with all the rest he'd been collecting, telling the ranger he'd be the judge of how best to raise his kids. He never mentioned that he was just a stepdad to me and Janie and went on like he'd raised us both from diapers and knew exactly what he was doing when it came to being a parent.

"When the economy in the country collapses, your wildlife and park rules aren't going to mean a thing to the hungry hordes that are going to be starving for anything they can catch. Where do you think the millions that live in Miami are going to head when the grocery shelves are empty? Right here to your sacred Everglades, that's where! They'll fish these waters bare and eat everything that swims, flies or crawls, including you if you're in their way! I'm just trying to protect my family from what's coming by getting them the hell out of the country before it's too late. We didn't come here to be Florida boat bums, I can assure you of that. Tomorrow at first light we'll be dropping this state astern and not stopping 'til we get to Belize."

The ranger left, but not before radioing back to his base about the incident and warning us that we were going to be under close surveillance until we were out of park waters. When he was gone Terry pitched a fit about how he'd stolen our spearfishing equipment and the big seine net he'd planned to use in the islands to fish the lagoons.

"Not only do they take our money with those ridiculous fines, now they're taking away the tools we need to make our living. It's only going to get worse, and if we don't get out of this country soon, they're going to end up taking our whole ship!"

I knew Terry had no intention of paying any of the fines from the tickets and citations he'd gotten since we launched. He'd already said that since the *Apocalypse* was not a federally documented vessel registered with the Coast Guard, they wouldn't be able to easily track us down to put a maritime lien on her for unpaid fines. With just a Mississippi registration number, he said they wouldn't know where to look for us once we got out of the U.S. and other "civilized" countries. Janie said that was crazy because she said that with the Internet and computers, they could easily find us and that no one could just "disappear" like that anymore. Terry told her she didn't know what she was talking about because her whole perception of the world up until now came from Facebook and other crap on the Internet, and she had no idea how big the *real* world was. He said that government agencies like the IRS wanted people to believe they had the power to know everything about everybody, but the reality was far different. He said that even with computers to help them, they didn't have the manpower to track every single person all the time, and that if you knew a few simple tricks for keeping a low profile, you could stay off their radar even living in the States. Besides, he said, even if they *did* know where we were, we'd be so far away by then it would be too difficult and expensive for them to collect those fines anyway, so they wouldn't bother.

I thought it would be better if Terry just paid them before we left, then we wouldn't have to worry about it. After all, he seemed to have enough money for everything that came up, even though he said he didn't. I didn't mention this though, because I knew what his answer would be. We would have to listen to another long rant about how it was the principle of it more than the money, and how he wasn't going to contribute to a corrupt system that already stole more money from honest citizens than it knew what to do with. I didn't want him to get into all that again because I was tired, and all I really wanted to do now that we already had enough adventure fishing, was go to sleep. We all needed sleep after being out there on the Gulf all night, but it was not to be.

Just about the time the sun started going down, the wind quit blowing too. That frontal system that had caused the change in direction from southwest to north had blown itself out, according to Terry. You would think this would be a good thing, at least at night when we weren't sailing and all we needed was a peaceful anchorage so we could all get a good night's sleep. But this anchorage was on the Shark River, right in the heart of the Everglades' mangrove coast. And what that meant was that with no wind to keep them away, we were in for mosquito and no-see-um hell.

It wasn't like we hadn't encountered any mosquitoes on this trip already. We had, especially on the lower Mobile River and around Ingram Bayou in Alabama where the woods were thick and swampy. But those mosquitoes had been few in number. Maybe a dozen or so buzzing around and a few bites on our arms or necks before we swiped them away or smacked them dead. Terry had some mosquito repellent that worked well on those too. It stank of chemicals, but it was better than getting bitten, at least all of us thought so except for Janie. She bitched and moaned about the mosquitoes and refused to use the repellent, instead retreating to her cabin where she shut all the port lights and was able to get away from them. But here in the Everglades, up in that river channel without the wind blowing, it was way too hot to go down below. The humidity was so bad you sweated just sitting there outside, and in the cabins the sweat just poured off in rivers. Because of this, I had been planning to sleep out on deck on one of the cockpit seat cushions until the no-see-ums and mosquitoes found us.

If you think no-see-ums are no big deal, you haven't ever been to someplace like the Everglades. They call them no-see-ums because they are so tiny you almost can't see them. They look like gnats, but they bite like fire and they came at us by the thousands. They get up under your clothes and in your hair and even try to get in your eyelids, ears and nose. We jumped around slapping and cussing and trying to get rid of them, but nothing worked. Terry said jumping in the water would get rid of them, but after seeing that shark I wasn't going to. But then, when the salt-marsh mosquitoes joined the no-see-ums in their relentless attack, I wondered if it would be better to be swallowed up by a shark in one big bite than to be eaten alive by all those blood-sucking bugs.

The mosquitoes swarmed over the boat in clouds of whirring wings that sounded like a million tiny motors buzzing, and they landed on every exposed part of our skin so thick it looked like we were wearing sleeves of bugs. I swept them off my arms with frantic brushing motions, smearing their guts and my own blood as I did. Mom and Janie were screaming and Janie started crying. Terry was scooping up buckets of water and pouring them over his head to get temporary relief and we all tried it but it didn't last but seconds before the swarms regrouped and covered us again. No matter how many we smashed or drowned, it seemed like there were a million more to replace them. We sprayed the insect repellent all over us too, but it just slowed them down a little and didn't do much good. With the wind completely gone and night closing in, there was no hope of things getting any better. When we tried going down below, it was so hot you couldn't breathe with the hatches closed up, and if we cracked them just a little, thousands of mosquitoes came in the gaps. We didn't have screens for the hatch openings because making them was just another item on Terry's long to-do list that didn't get done before we left. With no way to protect ourselves from the swarms, it was clear that it didn't matter how tired we were or how dark it was out on the Gulf, we had to pull up the anchor and leave Shark River immediately!

Twelve

MOM AND JANIE WERE furious at Terry for not making those hatch screens, but Terry said he never intended to stop someplace like the Everglades anyway and that he was going to finish them when we got to the islands. He blamed the weather and stupid anchoring restrictions in Florida for our predicament, but he wanted to get out of that river and away from those mosquitoes as bad as the rest of us did. He yanked and yanked on the outboard starter cord, unleashing the worst string of profanity I'd ever heard in my scant twelve years when it refused to crank. He was pulling on the starter cord so hard I was afraid he might break it, while at the same time wiping big clumps of buzzing and biting mosquitoes away from his face with his other hand.

He yelled at me to hand him his tools and keep pouring more water over his head while he pulled the spark plug out to clean it. When the motor finally cranked, we both hauled in the stern anchor rode hand over hand, because it was faster than fooling with the sheet winch. We finally got out into the channel of the main river and managed to get the ship moving in the right direction. But it was so dark out there you couldn't see much of anything, and Terry was in such a hurry to get away from the mosquitoes that he missed a turn marked by one of the floating buoys and ran us aground on a sandbar.

The mosquitoes seemed delighted at our misfortune and apparently called for reinforcements. Janie was sobbing like a baby and Mom was crying too as she tried to comfort her. My whole body was turning into a welt from all those bites, but I got a bit of relief when Terry and I jumped into the waist-deep water to push the bow off. I didn't care about sharks at this point, even if it *was* dark and this *was* their main feeding time. I just wanted to get out of that place and away from those mosquitoes or die trying. We were lucky this time that just one of the hulls had grounded out in the sand, and the bottom was firm enough that working together, Terry and I were able to push the *Apocalypse* back into the channel. This time I made sure I helped him look for the channel markers so we wouldn't get stuck again. I stood on the forward deck with the spotlight, pointing them out and yelling at him to turn to port or starboard when needed.

Once we got out of the Shark River and into the Gulf, I thought we'd be free of the mosquitoes, but most of them followed us, able to keep up because that stupid little eight-horse outboard couldn't push us fast enough to outrun them. The only thing that seemed to work was getting more than a mile offshore. I don't know if the mosquitoes knew they were getting too far from land to get back if they didn't go then or what, but we finally shook them once we got out there. I was so exhausted from lack of sleep at this point that I wanted to just drop, but I couldn't because I had to help Terry navigate. He said we needed to keep going south because this wasn't a good place to anchor this far out because we might get hit by a boat or a ship, and besides, if we couldn't sleep, we might as well be making headway towards the Keys.

The moon was up and nearly full by then, so we could see pretty well, and the land off to our port side had changed from mangroves to a long, sandy beach that stretched as far as you could see in the moonlight. Terry said it was Cape Sable, the longest uninhabited stretch of beach left in south Florida. He said it was still part of the Everglades but it was also the southernmost point of the Florida peninsula, at least on the Gulf side. The beach seemed to go on and on forever as we motored past it, staying about a mile out just to make sure we didn't attract any more mosquitoes. I thought all the beaches in Florida had condos and hotels on them, but there were no lights or other signs of human life to be seen on that shore at all. Terry said people camped there sometimes, but they had to have permits from the stupid national park service to do it. After our experience with those mosquitoes,

SAILING THE APOCALYPSE

I couldn't see why they'd want to.

We finally dropped the anchor when we got to the waters off the southern end of the cape. Terry said it was too risky to go any farther in the dark, because the next step was to cross Florida Bay to the Keys. His charts showed all kinds of shoal water in that bay and there were only a few ways you could go without running aground. Besides that, we had to get some sleep anyway or we would be completely worn out, so once the boat was secure we all hit our bunks and didn't get up until the morning sun the next day made the cabins too hot to stay in.

There was a light breeze out of the east that day, and it was a good thing too, because we were almost out of gas for the outboard after losing some of our jerry cans overboard and then all that motoring along the shore of Cape Sable the night before. Terry said that it was only about thirty more miles to the Keys, and that down there we'd be able to buy more gas before we struck out into the Straits of Florida on our way to the islands.

When I saw the water in Florida Bay, I couldn't imagine how it could be any better in the islands anywhere else. It was so clear that you could see every single thing on the bottom as we sailed over it, even though it was probably twenty feet deep in some places. Hanging my head over the forward beam and looking down, I saw stingrays, small sharks and all kinds of other weird fish I had never seen before. Most of the bottom was covered in some kind of dark green grass that grew about a foot or two up from the sand and swayed back and forth in the motion of the current and waves. Looking down there was amazing and I couldn't stop doing it. Even Janie was excited when she finally woke up and crawled out of her bunk.

Terry insisted that it still was nothing compared to where we were going, and said this wasn't a healthy ecosystem anymore anyway. He said there used to be a lot more coral in the Keys but now most of the reefs were dead. He said the whole island chain was over-fished, over-populated, over-developed, over-priced and of course, over-regulated. He said that even when he was here twenty years ago it was already ruined, and that the old-timers he knew back then talked about the good old days when Key West was still like a real island village and the whole chain was full of salty characters that were the real deal. Now it was overrun with tourons and the people who made their living off of them. The real sailors and fishermen were either dead or had moved on. What used to resemble a separate country of islands from Key Largo to the Dry Tortugas was now just like the rest of Florida.

I didn't care what he said though; this water was pretty awesome as far as I was concerned. And even if he did say most of the Keys weren't "real" islands because they were connected to the mainland by a bridge, I still wanted to see them. This was a whole other world to me and every time I looked down into the water, I saw something new.

SAILING THE APOCALYPSE

Although there was enough wind for us to sail without using the motor, it was only blowing about five to seven knots, and consequently we were sailing pretty slow. It took us most of the day to cross Florida Bay and finally get within sight of the Keys. From several miles out, you could see the long line of islands and between them, the bridge spans that connected them, most of these too low for a sailing ship like ours to pass under. Terry said we could have gone under the bridge called the Seven-Mile Bridge west of the town of Marathon, but he said if we did the only place to anchor around there was a place called Boot Key Harbor. He didn't want to go to Boot Key Harbor because he said it was popular stopover for cruising boats and as a result they had put in moorings where they charged some ridiculous price like twenty dollars a night for something that was no better than anchoring out for free on our own hook. He said it would cost a fortune to dock there and that if we bought gas or groceries there we would end up paying an inflated price because the people that sold everything around there were used to taking advantage of the yachties. Terry said we'd go to Islamorada instead, and that he knew a place there where we could anchor out for free and take the dinghy in to shore to buy what we needed. He said it was a little out of the way, but it would be worth it because we wouldn't have to deal with all the idiots at Boot Key Harbor.

To get to the place he wanted to anchor off Islamorada, we had to use the rest of our gas to motor east along the

SCOTT B. WILLIAMS

marked channel that went along the Gulf side of the Keys. We were able to sail some of it, but most of the channel was too twisty and surrounded by shoals, leaving little room to tack since the wind was coming from pretty much the way we had to go. It was a little farther to the anchorage than Terry remembered, and by the time we got there, the engine began sputtering and burned up the last drop of gas in the tank before we could drop the anchor. Terry said it didn't matter because we were close enough. But what sucked now was that we didn't have any gas to use the outboard on the dinghy, and we were still about a mile from the shore. We would have to row at least that far and then walk somewhere to get some gas before we could even start making trips back and forth for the other supplies we needed.

By this time, the wind had completely stopped blowing, so we went ahead and dropped the anchor. This was the first place we'd anchored where you could actually see the anchor lying on the bottom, as well as every bit of the rode. The water was so clear it was like looking into an aquarium, and I couldn't wait to go swimming. Terry said we needed to go get gas first though in case a storm or something came and we needed to move the ship. We got the dinghy inflated and when it was ready, Mom and Janie wanted to go with us because they were tired of being on the boat so long and never getting to go ashore. Four people could barely fit in the dinghy, but we finally managed to get ourselves arranged so that Terry could still row and then we were off, leaving the

SAILING THE APOCALYPSE

Apocalypse alone on her anchor.

There were a bunch of tables on a small beach with palm-thatched roofs shading them, and a building with the same kind of roof and more tables all around it nearby. Terry said it was some kind of tiki bar and restaurant, and that they were everywhere down here in the Keys. He said they tried to make their customers think they were in paradise or something, but most of them were poor imitations of anything you'd find in the *real* islands. It didn't look fake to me though, the closer we got. There were tall, curving coconut palms with the biggest leaves I'd ever seen on a tree in my life, and off to one side of the beach, at the water's edge, huge mangrove trees even bigger than the ones we'd seen in the Everglades. Skimming over the clear green water, watching all kinds of brightly colored fish scoot out of the way in front of us, it all seemed pretty exotic to me. I didn't see what wasn't real about it, but I didn't want to argue with Terry.

There was a little dock next to the tiki bar with a few old wooden fishing boats and a canoe tied up to it, so that's where we left the dinghy to set out with our gas cans to find a filling station. No one seemed to mind us tying up there and Terry said it was because people in Islamorada were more laid back than they were in the rest of the Keys and especially the rest of Florida. Most of the people sitting around the open-air bar near the dock didn't even seem to notice our arrival. Either that, or they were too busy drinking and talking to their friends to care. Terry asked a guy cleaning off tables where the nearest gas station was and he said we could buy it "right over there," pointing to the marina next door to the bar. Terry said he wasn't going to pay marina prices for gas when there were four of us who could carry it in jerry cans from a real gas station. It was pretty obvious the guy thought he was nuts, but he told us where to find one anyway, and we walked across the parking lot to the main road that would take us there.

Terry wanted to get the gas and come straight back, but we all pitched a fit to eat somewhere in a restaurant because there were a lot of them here and we hadn't eaten anywhere except on board since that first day we launched. He said we couldn't afford to eat in most of the places here but finally agreed to go to a little run-down-looking place with a sign saying they served shrimp and oyster po'boys, hamburgers and salads. It was one of those kinds of places that took forever to make the food, but that was fine with me and Janie and Mom, because we were all tired of being confined on the *Apocalypse*.

Terry was anxious the whole time though, saying a true sailor was never at ease away from his ship and that anything could happen. As it turned out, he was right about that, and by the time we left the restaurant, the wind had picked back up and was blowing pretty hard. Terry said he wasn't sure how well our anchor would hold on the bottom where it was, because there was a lot of rock and seaweed instead of soft sand and mud. He was torn between hurrying back to check on it and going ahead and getting the gas. Mom said we ought to get the gas while we were here because we were going to need it anyway.

It was a pretty long walk to the gas station, especially on the way back, each of us carrying a two-gallon jerry can in each hand. Janie started bitching and complaining as soon as we set out, saying how it was stupid to go that far to get gas when we could have bought it at the marina like that guy said. Terry told her every dollar we saved added up, and that if she didn't want to carry gas, she shouldn't have asked to eat a ten-dollar salad at a restaurant. That shut her up, but she was still mad about it.

When we walked back through the parking lot and onto the beach with the tiki bar, we were greeted by a sight that caused Terry to take off at a sprint. The *Apocalypse* was a whole lot closer to shore than she had been when we left her some two hours ago. In fact, she was practically *on* the shore, the wind and waves pushing her up against the edge of the mangrove trees just past the beach with the tables and tiki huts. A few people who had been drinking in the bar came outside to see what was going on, some of them following Terry but at a less hurried pace.

"What happened?" Janie asked.

"The anchor dragged! What do you think, dummy?"

"Shut up, Robbie! You're the one who dropped it, how should I know?"

236

"COME ON ROBBIE! WE'VE GOT TO MOVE FAST!" Terry yelled.

He had ignored the dinghy and instead headed straight for the catamaran. It was close enough to the beach that he only had to wade through waist-deep water to reach the starboard stern and climb aboard. I followed him as fast as I could, handing up my gas cans before I climbed aboard. Some guy who had the longest beard I'd ever seen and a thick gray ponytail that hung all the way down his back waded in after us, still holding a bottle of beer in one hand.

"Whoa! Is that a big Wharram cat? That's bitchin', man!"

I told him it was but I was too busy trying to do what Terry said to answer the questions he started asking next.

Terry was frantically measuring the two-stroke oil that had to be mixed with the gas in the running tank for the outboard. He was cussing because he had to do this extra step before the engine could be started, while the *Apocalypse* was still getting relentlessly pushed against the mangroves by the wind. I grabbed the boat hook and ran to the bow to try and fend off the branches, and by this time the hippy guy had climbed aboard too and made his way forward to help me.

"The holding off of this beach sucks, man! There's only a couple of spots where you can get a good set and where you guys dropped your hook is not one of them."

I don't know how he thought we were supposed to know that, since none of us had ever been here before, except for Terry. I was glad to have help holding it off though, because at least Terry couldn't blame everything on me if the trees tore up something. I heard the outboard finally start, and when Terry put it in reverse, the pressure against the mangroves relaxed and the bows eased away gradually. I knew he wouldn't be able to steer it straight in reverse though; he had already proven that so many times even when there was no wind blowing.

"Hey man, you got another anchor?" the stranger asked.

"We've got *two* more," I told him, thinking that would impress him with our seamanship and preparedness for dealing with situations like this.

"You should have set another one before you left the boat then! That's why this happened. Let's get one of them ready. But first, we need to haul in some rode on the one that dragged. I'll show the dude steering where to go so we can reset it where it'll hold. Is he your dad?"

"Stepdad."

"Cool. Where'd you guys come from?"

"Mississippi," I said. "We built the *Apocalypse* ourselves," I said proudly, knowing he liked it because he already knew it was a Wharram catamaran.

"Right on, man. That's far out! Welcome to paradise!"

He told me his name was Dean and that he'd been living in the Keys since he came down here from Delaware in 1975. He said he'd first gone to Key West, but he said the same thing Terry did about how it had changed so much there that he couldn't stand it, so he'd moved to Islamorada. I could tell

238

Dean was a real talker and I figured I was going to hear his whole life story even before we got the boat re-anchored. It took us almost an hour, even with Dean's help, by the time we got the main rode untangled and the anchor properly set, as well as the second anchor placed at about a forty-five degree angle to the first one, as Dean suggested.

Mom and Janie were stranded on the shore watching all this the whole time, because neither one of them could row well enough to make the dinghy go in a straight line and besides, Mom probably figured they'd just be in our way. Somebody had to go get them though, and we couldn't take the *Apocalypse* any closer, but in the new spot where Dean had us anchored, it was only about a hundred yards from the Tiki bar. Terry said it was close enough to swim and asked me if I wanted to do it but I didn't, because then I would have to row Mom and Janie back. Terry said that he would do it if I stayed on the boat with Dean. He didn't seem to trust him, even though Dean had done nothing but help us when he sure didn't have to.

While Terry was gone I told Dean the rest of our story, about how we'd built the *Apocalypse* and why we were sailing away on it to the South Pacific before the whole country fell apart. Dean said it already had, except for the Keys, but he said we didn't have to go any farther because we were already in the Conch Republic now and far enough from all that mess up north not to have to worry about it. He said all we really had to worry about here was the occasional hurricane, and then he asked me if we'd been keeping an eye on Leona.

"Who's Leona?" I asked, wondering who in the world he was talking about and how we could have been keeping an eye on her out there living on a boat.

"Hurricane Leona," Dean said.

"*Hurricane* Leona? Where is there a hurricane? Terry said it was too late in the year for most hurricanes. That's why we waited and left when we did, so we wouldn't have to worry about them."

"Well, it's not too late for Leona. We don't usually get hurricanes in November, but Leona just formed out of nowhere in the northern Caribbean, just off the eastern tip of Cuba. She's got everybody around here tripping out. She's a Category Three right now, but they're saying she could get stronger. They're also saying as she moves west along the south coast of the island, she's going to turn north and go across Cuba because of some kind of upper-level steering forces and head straight for the Keys."

I was flabbergasted at this. I knew Cuba was close because Terry said it was only ninety miles away from Key West. I knew he didn't know anything about the hurricane, because there was no mention of it on the last weather report we got before that night in the Shark River. The sky was sunny and the wind light when we left Cape Sable, so he didn't bother to turn on the radio then. He was going to flip out when he came back aboard and Dean and I filled him in. I wondered what we were going to do if the hurricane actually *did* come this way. Dean said the forecasters could be wrong and they usually were. He said the same thing happened in 2001 when Hurricane Michelle was headed right at Islamorada after crossing Cuba. They evacuated the Keys because it was a Category Four that was on track to wipe out the island and there was nowhere on Islamorada with high enough ground to survive the storm surge. But once it got in the open waters of the Florida Straits, Hurricane Michelle turned and went east to the Bahamas instead. Hearing this, I could only hope that Leona would follow Michelle's path, but I'd never been anywhere near a hurricane before and didn't know what to expect if it didn't.

Terry asked Dean what he'd been smoking when he came back with Mom and Janie and I told him about Leona. Janie was all happy to meet him because she knew somebody that looked like Dean really *would* have something to smoke. But Dean insisted he wasn't smoking or joking about the hurricane and told Terry to turn on the VHF right now and he would see. Terry did and we all stood quietly around the radio in the cockpit, waiting on the computer-generated voice to go through all the local condition reports until it got to the section on "tropical weather outlook." I saw Terry's jaw drop the first time the voice mentioned Hurricane Leona, and we all tensed up as we listened to the details. Like Dean had said, the storm was a Category Three hurricane right now, and it was moving west along the south coast of Cuba at about fourteen knots. Maximum sustained winds were estimated at one hundred and ten knots. I couldn't imagine how strong a one hundred and ten-knot wind would be. Terry said all that wind we had in Mobile Bay that tore up our jib and made it so hard to get the main down was about twenty-five to thirty knots. If that was true, I knew a wind like that hurricane was packing would probably blow our two masts straight down and tear up no telling what else.

We listened to the hurricane advisory until the report went back to current local conditions. Terry turned the radio off abruptly and began looking around in all directions. You could tell the gears were spinning in his head as he processed this new information.

"We've got to get this ship ready to sail, right now!" he said.

"Sail where?" Mom asked. "Shouldn't we get off of it and go ashore if there's a hurricane coming?"

"Yeah, you'd better stay put man," Dean said. "They're wrong about the track and the timing on those things over half the time. They always say one's gonna wipe out the Keys one day, but it never does. I think it's karma, man. We've got something righteous happening here in the islands that keeps them away." He went on to tell Terry and Mom and Janie what he'd already told me about Hurricane Michelle in 2001.

"Karma my ass! The Florida Keys are right in the middle of hurricane alley and you can bet there's gonna be a big one some day with your name on it if you stay here. People always say crap like that until they get nailed. They said the same thing up in Mississippi until Katrina leveled everything from Pascagoula to New Orleans; said that since Camille was so bad in 1969 they'd never get hit like that again. Idiots! I'm not leaving my ship in the path of a hurricane, no sir! A ship is safer at sea anyway, why do you think Navy vessels sail when a hurricane is coming?"

"I need something to chill out," Janie said, looking at Dean. "This is way too much stress to deal with."

I could tell Dean knew what she meant and I knew he would probably sneak her a joint when Mom wasn't looking, besides, Mom was so upset about the hurricane she didn't even hear what Janie said. Terry was working himself up into a major rant and Dean was trying to calm him down. I liked what Dean was saying about how it was better to stay put in one place than to go trying to run from a storm like that when it was changing directions and moving too. It seemed like it would be our luck it would move to wherever we tried to hide from it. Dean said nothing would be worse than being caught out at sea in a hurricane, and he said if it really did come across Cuba, there was nowhere we could go fast enough in a sailboat to avoid it.

"You should see it on the radar, man. Come on, we can walk over to the bar and watch it on The Weather Channel. That thing is huge! There'll be tropical storm-force winds five hundred miles out from the center. It doesn't matter if you sail north, east or west, you can't outrun it. You'll get hammered out there man, think about it! Stay here and relax man. There are worse places to hang out for a few days until it passes."

Terry kept saying that was crazy and that our ship was our life and we couldn't risk losing it. Mom told him no, that our *lives* were our lives and we didn't have but one each to lose. She said we could always build another ship but she wasn't sailing anywhere with a hurricane coming and wasn't going to let Janie or me do it either. She said she would get a divorce first, and I knew she wasn't joking because she got divorces more often than most people got new cars. I didn't want to get caught out in the ocean in a storm like that either, but I wasn't sure staying here was a better idea. Mom said if the storm really *did* cross Cuba and was still heading this way, we were going to rent a car or take a bus or something to get somewhere else besides this little island. That sounded like good thinking to me. Terry said it was ridiculous, but he reluctantly agreed that he wouldn't sail, because he knew the only way he could do it was if he went alone. He said he was staying on the *Apocalypse* no matter what though, and that if she went down, she was his ship and he would go with her like a real captain should.

"Good decision!" Dean said, when it became clear that we weren't sailing and that we'd weather the storm here, no matter what came. "I know a good place in the mangroves on the next key over that'll be perfect for your cat, man. That's what's so bitchin' about these Wharram cats! They don't draw anything, so you can slip up in the good hidey-holes where most boats can't. I'll help you get ready man. Just chill out, it's all gonna be groovy!"

Thirteen

THE PLACE WHERE DEAN said we should anchor the boat was a mangrove-surrounded lagoon on the next key east of Islamorada. Before we left the anchorage in front of the tiki bar to go there, we made several trips ashore in the dinghy to replenish our supplies.

"If you wait until the forecasters say for sure that it's coming our way, it'll be too late to get what you need," Dean said. "People will freak out and strip the shelves in every store on the island. Happens every time! What makes it worse is that all the tourists will be stranded too. There's no telling how many hundreds there are at any given time just on Islamorada alone, and most of them don't know what to do because they've never had to deal with a hurricane before."

"Like us," Janie said.

"No, because *we* are not tourists," Terry said. "We've got

our own ship. We'll have shelter and we won't drown in a storm surge because our shelter *floats*! All we need to do is buy some more food and fill the water tanks and we'll be better off than any of them."

Restocking the boat at anchor was way harder than it was when we started out, where we could just carry things up a ladder and put them in the hulls while they were still on dry land in Calloway City. We had to make several trips ashore in the dinghy, walk to the nearest store, and then walk back carrying the groceries. Dean couldn't really help us because he didn't have a car. He rode an old beat-up bicycle everywhere because he said you didn't need anything else in the Keys, and besides, he'd lost his license for good after getting one too many DUIs.

He said he would guide us to the place he recommended that we should take the *Apocalypse* to ride out the storm, and that he would help us set anchors and make all the necessary preparations because he was retired and didn't have much else to do anyway. It was too late to leave that day to go there though, especially by the time we shuttled enough water out to the boat in the dinghy to refill our tanks, so we stayed put where we were anchored. Terry wanted to keep track of the storm a bit longer anyway before we moved to Dean's hidey-hole. He said once you committed to a place like that and put out all those lines and anchors, if something changed it would be too late to do anything about it.

I was glad we were staying where we were the first night,

because it gave us a chance to get off the boat for a while and look around. I wanted to take my bicycle ashore and ride around with Dean to see everything, but Terry said it was too much trouble and that we didn't have time to be untying and retying stuff like bikes because we needed to keep the boat ready to move at a moment's notice. He didn't care if I walked somewhere though, so I wandered around the marina next door, looking at all the expensive yachts tied up alongside old shrimp boats that looked even rougher than the *Apocalypse*. Janie followed Dean off somewhere in the parking lot and I figured they were probably smoking a joint because Dean's clothes reeked of it and I knew he was bound to have one. Mom was too worried about the hurricane to notice, and she made Terry go sit with her in the tiki bar so they could watch the live reports on the big TV on the wall.

We were thinking about that storm all night, and I don't think anyone on board slept well except for Janie. She admitted to me she smoked some ganja with Dean, and she was pretty chilled out. I sure wasn't. I might have gotten two hours of sleep at the most before I saw daylight coming through the hatch and climbed up on deck. Terry was sitting there drinking his coffee and listening to the automated voice on the VHF as it gave out the latest information on the hurricane.

"It looks like it's coming our way, Robbie. We might as well get ready to move. But we'd better hope they're wrong."

"I thought you said we'd be better off than all the tourists because we've got everything we need and we're on a ship, instead of on land."

"We will be, but that doesn't mean it'll be a good thing, riding out a hurricane. The *Apocalypse* could still sustain damage. If we don't get our anchors and moorings right, she could be swept loose in the storm surge. Some other idiot's boat could come loose and hit us. A lot can happen in a hurricane, Robbie, that's why I wanted to sail away from here as fast as possible. If we had left yesterday, like I wanted to when we first heard about it, we would have had plenty of time to get out of its path before it gets here. Now we don't have a choice. All we can do is tie up where Dean said and hope for the best."

Dean had pointed out on Terry's chart the day before the approximate location of the hideaway he was talking about, but he said the channel into the good spot wasn't marked. He also said there were a bunch of old derelict boats in the lagoon there, some of them floating and some not, and that he knew where the sunken ones were. So we waited on him to get there, but even after we were all awake and had eaten breakfast, he still didn't show up. Mom made Terry take her back to the bar so she could see the weather report on the TV, because she said listening to that monotone computer voice repeating itself on the VHF every fifteen minutes was driving her bonkers. When they came back a half hour later, it was nearly oh-nine-hundred and Terry said we couldn't wait for Dean any longer.

"He's probably passed out drunk. A guy like that probably sleeps 'til noon every day. If we don't get going, we won't have time to make all our preparations."

Mom didn't like the idea of going somewhere like that without local knowledge. She said we might get in the wrong spot or hit one of those submerged boats going in there. But Terry said there was no way we could ride out a storm where we were now, and he reminded her that the bottom was so poor for anchoring here that even a light breeze had nearly blown the *Apocalypse* ashore. So we left without Dean, using the chart to find our way along the Gulf side of Islamorada until we came to the pass separating it from the next Key. Just as we came in sight of the bridge that connected them, Janie said there was somebody on top of it waving at us. I grabbed Terry's binoculars, and sure enough, it was Dean, standing there on the highest point of the bridge, straddling his bicycle. He waved and pointed to a little dock near the east end of the bridge and Terry steered us that way. By the time we got there, Dean was on the dock, waiting to be picked up. He locked his bike to a light pole and leapt aboard when Terry managed to bring the *Apocalypse* within three feet of the dock without hitting it. I was glad Dean could jump that far, because Terry would have smacked that dock for sure if he tried to get any closer.

"I'm sure glad you're here," Mom said to Dean.

"Yeah, sorry I'm late. I usually sleep 'til noon most days, but with this storm coming, I had things to do. Man, I wouldn't want to see anything happen to a bitchin' Wharram like yours. I had to come and do what I can to help out. They're saying Leona might be a Category Four once it gets across Cuba and hits the warm waters of the Gulf Stream. I still think it's gonna turn before it gets here, but it's better to be ready, just in case."

Following Dean's directions, Terry steered us along the edge of a dense wall of mangroves until we rounded a bend and came to an opening in the trees that led into an enclosed body of water that looked like a small lake to me. Dean called it a lagoon though, I guess because it was seawater and we were (almost) in the tropics. The water was clear and you could easily see the way the only deep channel went, because on either side of it the color was bright green from the light reflecting off the sand and grass on the bottom. On the way in, I saw a couple of sunken powerboats and one sailboat, it's stern railing close enough to the surface that someone not looking where they were going would hit it. There were some other old boats floating around in the lagoon, most of them tied up with one or two frayed-looking anchor rodes of inadequate size. Every one of these boats looked abandoned. Most of them were sailboats that didn't even have a mast still standing, and some of them had the portlights smashed out and other parts missing. All of them had thick crusts of barnacles and mats of weed growing at their waterlines too.

"I don't like this," Terry said. "All these damned junkers will come loose in any kind of a blow, much less a hurricane!"

"Nah, they've been here for years. Some of them for decades! This place is *sheltered*, man. See how thick these mangroves are? But out here in the lagoon with all these boats is not where I'm talking about. The real hole is farther in, just keep going, but stay in the darker water. There's just enough to get in with your draft. That's what's so great about it. You don't have to worry about a bunch of yacht club idiots coming in here at the last minute before the storm and blocking you in."

"This place is creepy, if you ask me," Janie said. "There're probably dead bodies inside some of those old boats."

"If there are any, they're just old skeletons by now," I told her. "Maybe we can go in the dinghy and look for some after we get anchored."

Janie just made a face at me like she always did when I aggravated her on purpose. Dean said they did find dead people on old boats around here sometimes, but usually they were homeless people or drunks living on some derelict long since abandoned by its owner.

"Why would anybody that owned a boat ever abandon it?" I asked. "Even an old boat costs money."

"Entropy, Robbie. Remember what I told you about boat maintenance? Most people who buy boats don't have a clue what they're in for, especially if they buy an old wooden boat like most of these. Some slick yacht broker sells it to them, knowing all along it's already too far-gone to be good for anything but firewood. They pour money into it until they're

253

broke, and then when they can't find another sucker to buy it, they just tie it to a mooring somewhere and walk away."

"Happens all the time," Dean agreed. "Dreamers! Sailboats always attract dreamers. Most of 'em dreaming about sailing to the islands. Me, I don't need a boat to get to the islands, because I'm like, already here, man! But this Wharram cat's really bitchin'. If I *did* want a boat, it'd be a Wharram cat for sure!"

We finally saw the spot Dean kept talking about when we reached the back end of the lagoon, in a far corner invisible from the entrance outside. It looked like a creek or channel or something, but Dean said it wasn't. He said it was just a dead end, a hole in the mangroves with just enough water to float a boat like ours and just enough width for us to fit in there. It looked tight to me, and Terry said the same thing. Dean said it was wide enough though and what did it matter if we brushed a few branches with our rigging? It wouldn't hurt anything, and being in a snug hole like this was way better than being somewhere there was more room for the boat to get blown around. He said that in a place like this, we could tie all kinds of extra lines to the tree trunks and roots.

"We'll put out so many warps your cat will look like a spider in the middle of its web," he said. "If you're worried about the branches scratching your paint, we'll just cut some back."

"He's already gotten a citation for cutting off a mangrove branch in the Everglades," Mom said.

Dean whistled. "Cutting mangroves in the Everglades! Man, do you know how much that's gonna cost you?"

"No, and I don't care, because I'm not paying any fines to Florida *or* the national park service. Just as soon as this hurricane business is over, we're outta here! But even if we cut some of this jungle back, there's no way I can back this wide cat into a tight spot like that."

"So put your bow in man, no big deal!"

"I don't like the idea of running up in a hole facing the wrong way so that I can't get out in a hurry. Backing out will be almost as hard as backing in. We ran into that in the Everglades, trying to get out of a place like this when the mosquitoes swarmed us at dusk."

"Nah, man. We'll set an anchor way out off the stern. When it's time to leave you can just haul in on it and pull the *Apocalypse* right back out. No big deal."

That was pretty much what we'd done before, in that place in Shark River, and I didn't see what the problem was. Terry was fretting about it, I could tell, but with the rest of us urging him on to do something so we could get started tying her up, he drove the *Apocalypse* forward into the hole. I think he just didn't like the idea of committing to one spot where he couldn't move quickly if the hurricane actually came.

The mangroves did brush against the shrouds and the plumber's pipe deck rails, sending leaves and small branches falling all over the deck. Terry cut a few of the longest ones with the machete after Dean assured him the marine patrol would have better things to do with a hurricane coming than ride around looking for people doing stuff like that. Even with some of them cut back, the branches still closed in around us and I wondered if there were snakes in those trees that would find their way aboard. I told Janie there probably were and that they would be slithering down the dorades to get inside our cabin tonight.

"If I even *see* a snake, I'm getting off the boat and walking to a hotel!" Mom said she would too and then she said maybe that's what we all ought to do anyway after we tied up the boat.

"What, and just abandon the *Apocalypse*? Are you out of your mind? A sailor doesn't leave his ship to fend for herself. This vessel is our home now! There's nowhere else to go!"

Mom didn't say anything else, but I could tell she didn't agree with Terry and she was getting more nervous about that hurricane with every hour that went by. Dean said everything was going to be cool and that there weren't many snakes around here to worry about. He did say we probably ought not to swim around the mangroves in a place like this though, because there were sharks and American crocodiles. He said the crocodiles hadn't ever attacked anybody that he knew of, but they were increasing in number and spreading out into this part of the Keys from the southern end of the Everglades, where they were a protected species. Before he said that, I was looking forward to jumping into that clear water with my mask and snorkel I hadn't even gotten to try yet; but not now. Alligators and sharks were scary enough; I sure wasn't about to go swimming somewhere there might be a crocodile too!

We tied off to the nearest mangrove branches just to hold our position while we sorted out the anchors and rodes, and Dean and Terry argued about the best angles to set the anchors and where to tie off the main lines. Dean said we didn't have enough when Terry pulled out our entire inventory of line, and he said we ought to get in the dinghy and go see what we could find on the derelicts.

"No, it's not stealing," he said, when Mom objected to the idea of doing this. "Nobody cares about those old boats; that's why they're here. Most of the good stuff's been stripped off of them a long time ago, but there's bound to be some rope on some of them."

I wanted to see the boats, so I went with Dean in the dinghy to see what we could find. He was a lot better at rowing than Terry, and it didn't take us long to cruise around the lagoon, stopping at each boat and climbing aboard to look for what we needed. I kept expecting to find some skeletons in one of them, but we never did. We gathered a few assorted lengths of tattered and frayed rope, most of it too small to secure a ship the size of the *Apocalypse*, but Dean said anything was better than nothing. The best thing we found was when we followed a long anchor rode attached to the bow of a rotten old plywood houseboat and discovered a big anchor on the other end, buried in the mud bottom. It was so heavy it was hard to pull up, but when we did, Dean said it was better than anything Terry had on board.

"That's a forty-five-pound Manson Supreme, dude! We need to set that off your stern out into the lagoon on the longest rode you've got."

"You think we should just take it?" I asked.

"Sure, why not. What good is it doing tied to this piece of shit? Besides, whoever put it here probably stole it. That thing's worth several hundred dollars. You can bet they didn't buy it!"

"Well, without an anchor, won't their boat get tore up in the hurricane?"

"Yeah, so what? Screw it! If who ever left it here cared, they'd be here now getting it ready for the storm."

Terry was ecstatic to see the big Manson. He knew it was a good anchor, but when he was buying stuff for the boat on EBay and Craigslist, he hadn't been able to find one at a price he wanted to pay. Like everything he put on the boat, he always got the cheapest he could find unless there was no alternative.

It took us half a day to get all the anchors and lines situated in a way that satisfied Terry and Dean. Then we had to take all the sails off the masts and fold them to stow below. We took down our blue tarp awnings too, and Mom said we ought to just throw them away because they were ugly enough when they were new and now they were faded by the sun and ripped by the wind. Terry wouldn't throw them away though, because he said we might need them. He said that because none of us would agree to sail with him to try and outrun the hurricane in time, we might be living on the beach under the tarps when all this was over.

I was so sick of hearing the stupid computer-generated voice on the VHF weather report that I felt like smashing the radio. Mom was sick of it too but she wouldn't turn it off because she didn't want to miss a thing. She was scared to death of this hurricane and was on pins and needles whenever it was almost time for a new update from the National Hurricane Center every three hours. The latest report that we got that afternoon didn't sound good. Hurricane Leona had turned north just like they predicted it would, and it was now about to make landfall on the south coast of Cuba. When it did, the experts said it would weaken some as it crossed over the island because of the mountains, but they still expected it to stay on the same track and strengthen when it got back over water. That water was the narrow Florida Straits, and it wouldn't be far from where we were at all when that happened. They had now put the entire Florida Keys under a hurricane watch and said it extended up to Marco Island on the west coast and Fort Lauderdale on the east. Dean said the watch would probably turn into a warning soon, and when it did, all hell would break loose on the island.

"They'll turn A1-A into a parking lot! Every gas station in the Keys will be pumped dry by dark and flights in and out of Key West will be cancelled. The motels will start closing and all the tourists caught here will double the problem of getting everybody off the island."

"Where will all those people go?" Mom asked.

"Miami, most likely. They'll open shelters there and bus out as many as they can, but there's only one road off the Keys. It's impossible to evacuate everybody without a lot more time, and all these stupid warnings will compound the problem. Most of us that live here know better than to leave, because nothing would suck worse that being stuck on one of the long bridges when a hurricane hits."

"We need to leave immediately then!" Mom said, in a panic herself now.

"Wait just a damned minute!" Terry said. "Don't forget it's not even a warning yet, just a watch! It could still turn and probably will. The talking heads always make a big story out of these things just so they'll have something to yammer on about. They thrive on panic and fear, and they know people want to hear it. The TV watchers and radio listeners want to believe there's a disaster coming because otherwise, their lives would be so boring they couldn't stand it.

"*A hurricane is coming!* Yippee! Hot freakin' damn! Now *that's* exciting! Let's all go apeshit crazy and run around like a bunch of ants that just had their hill kicked in! Let's buy everything in sight and then sit in the car in a gridlock until we run the tank dry to go five miles! It's a Category Four for Christ's sake! Maybe it'll be a Five when it makes landfall!

Death and destruction—a catastrophic disaster for sure—oh holy hell, now isn't that something?"

Terry was waving his arms in the air and practically dancing around the deck by now. He was so enthusiastic he had Dean laughing first and then me and Janie. Mom didn't think it was one bit funny though and stormed off below, slamming the hatch to their cabin shut behind her. Dean shrugged his shoulders and said everybody got all bent out of shape when these things were in the forecast.

"Jimmy Buffett wrote a song about all that, something about trying to reason with hurricane season. It's just part of the price of living in paradise man. We never feel the winter here, but sometimes, there's a storm or two. But like I said, we've got some pretty good karma happening in Islamorada. I think we're gonna be all right, and you're all set with the *Apocalypse* tied up in here like this. You couldn't have done better anywhere. So just relax, man. Chill out and enjoy the chance to rest. The threat will be over soon and then you can go or stay."

Dean said he needed a ride back to shore so he could take care of some stuff at the garage apartment where he lived beneath an elevated house in Islamorada. He said he would come back and check on us before dark, and give us the latest from the weather reports on TV. He knew of a path through the mangroves from the lagoon to the main road and said he would walk down there and yell at us to come pick him up when he got back. Terry took off with him in the dinghy, and

SAILING THE APOCALYPSE

Janie convinced Mom to come back out of the cabin while he was gone.

"Sometimes I think Terry Bailey is insane!" Mom said. "All this talk about getting out of Calloway City before the country collapses, and here we are in the path of a hurricane!"

I couldn't help but remember what that trucker, Hal Jenkins, said about Hurricane Katrina tearing up every boat on the Gulf Coast. He warned Terry that we were leaving at the wrong time of year, but Terry always thought he was right and everybody else was full of crap. After seeing all the problems we had along the way, I wondered how much sailing Terry had really done. But despite hitting things, tearing up sails and running aground, he *had* managed to get us all the way here, and Islamorada was a long way away from Calloway City.

"You're the one that listened to all his bullshit," Janie said to Mom. "I told you I didn't want to live on a stupid sailboat. Now we're all gonna die!"

"We're not gonna die," I said, trying to balance things out and look at both sides. "You heard what Dean said. They haven't been hit by a real hurricane here since 1935. He said they always turn and go somewhere else. I doubt Leona is going to be any different. Besides, if we had stayed in Calloway City, we would still be bored to death. At least if we die down here we got to see stuff like dolphins and sharks and coconut palms first. And look at that water," I pointed

262

down into the impossibly clear water upon which the *Apocalypse* seemed to be suspended over the bottom as if on a cushion of air. "Have you ever seen water like that before? Would you ever have if not for Terry?"

"Here he comes," Mom said. "I'm not going to argue with him about it right now, but I'll tell you this. If that hurricane doesn't turn and it really *is* coming our way, we're getting off this boat and evacuating to Miami like everybody else with any sense is doing!"

* * *

We spent the rest of the afternoon doing pretty much nothing but listening to the radio reports, Terry pacing back and forth on the deck and getting more agitated by the hour. Dean came back like he said he would to check on us and when Terry brought him back to the boat in the dinghy, he told us what he'd seen on The Weather Channel. Hurricane Leona was wreaking havoc in Cuba even now and was still tracking due north over the island after killing more than a hundred people there.

"They're saying it's not gonna turn, man. They said that about Michelle too, back in 2001, and they were wrong. But we're under an official hurricane warning now and they're saying that when it makes landfall here in Florida, they expect it to be a strong Category Four, maybe even a Five!"

"Dammit!" Terry swore. "I knew we should have left!"

SAILING THE APOCALYPSE

"We *are* leaving!" Mom said, in a voice that left no doubt that she had made up her mind and Terry or no one else was going to change it.

"I don't know," Dean said. "It's pretty crazy everywhere on the island right now. I don't know how you're going to go anywhere. But even if you do, you can't do it tonight. They're moving so many of the tourists up to the mainland that there's no point even trying. The best thing to do is hang tight until first thing in the morning. The hurricane won't be back over open water until sometime after daylight, and they're not going to know if it's going to turn or not until it hits the Gulf Stream."

Mom still wanted to go right then, but we all talked her out of it. We would have to take all the stuff we needed with us in the dinghy and that would be a real pain in the butt in the dark. Aside from that, if we couldn't find a bus or some other way to get to Miami, we wouldn't have anywhere to sleep on the island. Dean said no motels or hotels were renting rooms now after they had already turned out all their guests. And he said his garage apartment was really just one room and he only had one single bed, and besides, he had four cats living there with him.

Once we finally got her settled down, Mom was okay with staying aboard one more night, but the agreement was that if the hurricane was still heading north when we woke at first light, we were leaving Islamorada and Terry could do whatever he wanted. He took Dean back to the path ashore and when he returned to the boat, we sat up until way past midnight, talking about what we were going to do and hoping that we would get good news about the hurricane when we woke up in the morning.

We didn't.

Fourteen

THE AIR FELT DIFFERENT the next morning when we woke up
and went outside on deck. Terry said it was because huge
hurricanes like Leona brought with them the tropical warm
air and moisture from the Caribbean Sea. Racing across the
swath of sky that we could see overhead between the
mangroves were patches of wind-driven clouds, all streaming
from the east-southeast in the direction of the hurricane's
rotation. Terry said these were the outer feeder bands of the
storm and that even if it turned at the last minute, it was still
close enough that we were going to feel tropical storm force
winds soon. He tried to talk Mom out of the idea of leaving
the boat, saying it was too late now and far too dangerous to
be going anywhere.

"We'd be better off hunkering down on board like I said
before. The worst that could happen back here in this hole is

the storm surge will cause the water to rise a few feet, but if we're on board to adjust the lines it won't be a problem. These mangroves will protect us from the brunt of the wind, just like Dean said. You see how many lines we have tied to them. Even if some of them fail these springy branches will act like cushions and protect the ship from hitting something hard. Mangroves are about the only trees that can stand up to a hurricane. That's why they have those laws against cutting them. I can see a fine for cutting the whole damned tree down, but trimming a branch? Ridiculous!"

Despite Terry's argument for staying put, Mom wasn't having it and demanded he take us ashore immediately. She'd already packed her bags and made Janie and me pack ours. She said we were going to Miami and that was that! Dean was supposed to be here first thing to give us an update from the TV report, but he hadn't shown up and Mom wasn't going to wait.

"That's the dumbest idea you've ever had, Linda! You're leaving the safety of a perfectly seaworthy ship; well stocked with all the water and food we'll need for weeks, to go join a mob of refugees. You'll be packed into some stadium or school with the drunks and homeless bums, sleeping on the floor; waiting for government handouts that'll take days to get there, if they come at all!"

"You said yourself before we left that we had to avoid hurricanes at all costs! And when you first found out about this one, you wanted to set sail immediately to miss it, but

268

Dean said it was too big and the path was too uncertain. Now that we know it's coming for sure, you've changed your mind and want to stay on the boat. You're not making any sense, Terry!"

"I didn't change my mind, I wanted to stay on the boat all along, but out at sea rather than waiting someplace that could be ground zero for a disaster! But you refused to sail with me. I had no choice but to stay here because my whole crew threatened mutiny! So with Dean's help, the ship is in the best place it could be to ride out the hurricane if it indeed makes landfall in the Keys. But now after I agree to stay put on the island like you wanted, you're all planning to abandon me—and abandon our ship and our home—the *Apocalypse*!"

"Maybe you shouldn't have named her that," Janie said. "Maybe it's bad karma! It can't be a lucky name."

I had thought the same thing a couple of times, but still, I liked the name, "Apocalypse." It sounded cool and it sounded like something big—something *important*—which it was considering we traded everything in our previous lives to build and sail it. I hoped Janie was wrong about the luck thing though. Terry said sailors were superstitious by nature, and that they had always had been, but even though he liked the old seafaring traditions and sayings, he wasn't superstitious at all. In fact, I don't think he believed in luck—bad or good. He had talked about it a few times before, saying:

"Bad luck is an excuse people use when things go wrong that are really the result of bad planning or bad decisions.

SAILING THE APOCALYPSE

Things don't just happen by chance, Robbie. It's up to us to make them happen."

He dismissed Janie's comment about creating bad karma in the same way:

"The name of a ship isn't going to steer a hurricane this way or that, Janie, anymore than Dean's wishful thinking that his little island is somehow charmed and protected from the wrath of Mother Nature. Hurricanes are guided by air and water temperatures and currents, and the closer they get the more accurate those who study the forces involved can predict where they'll go. We made our decision yesterday, when we moved our ship in here, and it's a decision I thought we would live with. It's too late to run from Leona now. That should be clear to every one of you, but apparently it isn't. So fine, we'll go ashore and you can do as you like, but as for me, I'm coming back to my ship. This is where I'll make my stand, come hell… high water… hurricane… or all three at once!"

Mom didn't argue with him because it was clear that Terry wasn't changing his mind. I didn't know who was right when it came to what we ought to do, but I didn't really like just sitting there in those mangroves where we couldn't see what was going on. I figured it would be a good idea to go ashore and see what everybody else was doing. If they were all leaving the island, it seemed to me that would be a good sign that we ought to leave too.

With our bags packed to stay somewhere else for a few days or however long we had to, there wasn't enough room for all of us to fit in the dinghy at once. Terry rowed me and Janie ashore first and then went back for Mom and the rest of our stuff. We could hear Terry arguing with her the whole time while we waited at the beginning of the path through the mangroves. I knew it wouldn't do him any good, and I hoped Terry would shut up before he really made her mad. Terry didn't know Mom as well as Janie and I did, and I don't think he realized how quickly she would divorce him if he pushed her too far. I hoped that didn't happen and hoped this stupid hurricane didn't tear up our ship, because now that I'd seen the Keys, I really wanted to keep sailing and see more islands. Going back to Calloway City and back to school again would suck after coming this far.

"I wondered when you guys were going to get off the boat."

I turned around, startled by Dean's voice. We had been talking while we waited and didn't hear him coming down the path.

"We figured you had left the island by now."

"Nah, man. Where am I going to go? I'll ride it out here, but I wouldn't stay on that boat if I were you. They're saying it will be a Category Four when it hits, and they're saying the storm surge will be twelve to fifteen feet! That's more than enough to flood the highest spot on Islamorada."

"Why are you staying then?" Janie asked. "Your apartment is under a house. It's going to get flooded!"

Before he could answer, we heard Mom and Terry

271

approaching the landing spot in the dinghy. When Dean saw them and all the bags, he told Terry we were doing the right thing to get off the boat.

"I'm not going anywhere," Terry said. "My crew wants to leave, so I'll help them carry their stuff to the bus, but I'm coming back."

"They're not running any more buses," Dean said. "The last one left sometime last night and the state troopers have stopped all traffic coming back to the Keys from the mainland. Both lanes are now one way from here to there, so there won't be anymore buses coming."

Mom became almost hysterical at this news. "What about a cab? You've got to call us a cab, Terry. There's got to be a cab that can take us to the shelter!"

Dean just laughed at this. "Yeah, there were a bunch of them, but with all the tourists packed in hotels, they've all gone too. They would come back for more if not for the roadblock though, believe me. I heard the shameless bastards were charging as much as twelve hundred dollars for the one-way fare from Islamorada to Miami!"

"That's the kind of thing that always happens when these storms come," Terry said, launching into a rant about the depravity and indecency of most of society. They'll jack up the price on everything essential, and all the idiots who go through life unprepared and oblivious of what they need to survive are at their mercy. See what I told you, Linda? It's too late to leave! Now we need to just go back to the *Apocalypse*

272

and wait it out."

"Dean said that would be crazy!" Janie said.

"Like he's got a better plan!" Terry shouted back.

"Where *are* you going to go?" Mom asked him.

"That's what I came here to tell you," Dean said. "They didn't want to announce anything sooner, because they wanted as many people as possible to leave, but they are opening a shelter here for the last few who couldn't get a ride out. It's not supposed to be available for tourists, but I talked to a dude I know in the fire department and told him you guys were a special case, you know, a family stranded here on your boat and all, and he said they would let you in. It's a private school, and when they built it, they designed it to withstand up to a Category Four hurricane. The main classrooms are on the second floor, high enough to be safe even with the storm surge they're predicting. It's the best place on the island to go that I know of. So if you're ready, just follow me and I'll make sure they know who you are so they'll let you in."

Terry said if we wanted to go huddle inside some school building with a bunch of people we didn't know instead of staying home on our ship that was fine with him. He said he would walk with us to see where the shelter was so he would know where to look for us when it was over and we were sick and tired of the rations they would dole out. Mom told him he was being ridiculous and that he ought to just stay with us so we would all be together. She said if that hurricane was as

273

bad as they said it was, we would probably never find the *Apocalypse* or his body either when it was over. I tried to tell him too, and I reminded him that Hal Jenkins said they still hadn't found all the bodies from Katrina yet. Terry just laughed and said we were all being gullible to media hype. He said he would be fine and the *Apocalypse* would be too, just as long as her captain was on board to look after her.

It was a long walk to Islamorada because we had to cross the bridge from the little key where the lagoon was, and we were carrying our bags with the clothes and other things we needed. It was strange how the highway was deserted now after most everyone who had a car or truck had left and no one else was permitted to come this way from the mainland. From up on that bridge, we got a good look at the sky all around and the angry waves on the Atlantic side. It was starting to look like a storm was coming for sure. There were whitecaps everywhere out there on the steel-gray water and the passing clouds overhead were bigger, more ominous and more numerous, all of them moving in the same east-west direction like they had been all morning. The wind was blowing at a steady twenty-five to thirty-five knots but a couple of times we felt gusts that Dean said were nearly fifty. They were strong enough that I had to lean into them to keep my balance, but they only lasted a few seconds. Terry said that back in the hole where the *Apocalypse* was tied up, we wouldn't have even felt them. I wondered if he was right as I turned to look back one last time before we left the crest of

274

the bridge. From up there, you could see the tops of the two white-painted spars of our ship's schooner rig poking out in stark contrast from the green canopy of mangroves. Before I turned away, it occurred to me this might be the last time I ever saw them, but I was keeping my fingers crossed that it wouldn't be.

When we got to the school, the building *did* look pretty substantial. It was made of concrete and brick, with steel columns and steel staircases going up the second floor, where a balcony wrapped around the entire upper level. There was a small crowd of people standing around outside talking, all of them discussing one thing—Hurricane Leona. Dean said there were probably a lot more people on the island who chose to ride out the hurricane in their own homes, despite all the warnings that it was not a good idea. He said the ones who came here to the school were mostly the homeless and a few people like him who lived somewhere that clearly wouldn't be safe in a hurricane. I was glad Dean was staying there with us, because that way at least we knew somebody there and he could tell everybody else that we weren't homeless too. Janie said it wouldn't matter because to most people, living on a boat was the same thing, just look what that park ranger in the Everglades had said.

Terry wouldn't go inside with us because he was afraid the cops that were there to keep things organized wouldn't let him leave again "for his own safety." He said they did things like that in shelters and that's why he wouldn't stay in one even if he didn't have a perfectly good ship to take refuge aboard. He waited around awhile, staying outside talking to Dean, while we went in and got our things situated after learning where our assigned space on the floor was. Then we all went outside to give him the latest update on the storm and try one last time to talk him into staying there with us.

"They're saying it's going to hit sometime before dawn tomorrow," Mom told him. "They're still saying the storm surge could be as high as fifteen feet and they're warning people that nowhere in the Keys is safe from a storm surge like that. They said they're expecting extreme property damage and destruction, and that loss of life will be likely for those who ignore their recommendations to seek safe shelter immediately. Please, Terry! Just be sensible and stay here with us until this is all over!"

"Even if I wanted to I couldn't, Linda. After all that damage, if it happens, it'll be nearly impossible to get back to the lagoon to the ship. Power lines will be down, debris will be ten feet deep on the roads, and the bridge to the other island may not even be there. Katrina knocked down two major bridges on Highway 90 in Mississippi and it took years to build them back! I'd be stuck here for days at best, but you know who would get to the boat first? Looters! The scum of the Earth who crawl out of their holes like a colony of cockroaches to pillage and plunder everything left in the aftermath of disaster. They'll find our ship and strip it to two bare hulls in a matter of hours! They'll take everything we own and worked so hard for and leave us with nothing. Then, we really *will* be homeless! Do you want that Linda? I didn't think so! So you just stay put with Robbie and Janie and I'll go do what I have to do as captain of my ship. I'll be fine through the storm, and when it's over, I'll be there waiting with the SKS and that Colt .45 that I told you we were probably going to need sooner than later. I intend to break them out of hiding as soon as I'm back on board, and you can believe me when I say any looters thinking they're going to plunder the *Apocalypse* will be in for a nasty surprise when they try!"

I didn't know anything about looters because I had never been around the aftermath of a disaster before, but Dean said Terry was right and that even when there wasn't a storm, theft was a real problem here in the Keys. He said you couldn't leave anything of value unlocked or out in the open because there was always somebody on the lookout for what they could steal next. He said it was even worse in Key West, but after a hurricane looting would be a problem all over the Keys and on the Florida mainland too.

"I just can't imagine people being so evil they would take advantage of someone else's misfortune like that," Mom said.

"Believe it! It's going to be a whole lot worse when the entire country collapses! What have I been telling you for more than two years now? Why do you think we're here in the first place? We couldn't survive the onslaught if we stayed in America, especially way up there on the mainland and as far inland as Calloway City. Looting is nothing compared to the rape, murder and arson that will take place when the crap really hits the fan! Think of this storm as just a small taste of it—a drill. We'll get through this and then get the hell out of here, and maybe after you see how things really are, you'll understand what I've been trying to say all along and why we're never coming back!"

"This dude's a trip, isn't he?" Dean said, giving me a jab. "He's pretty serious when he says he's done with the whole American way, isn't he?"

"Yeah, it's all he ever talks about, at least to anyone who will listen. Nobody else seems to be worried about it though. Why is that? What about you? What do you think about all that stuff?"

"Man, I don't know. I'm just living on island time, you know. One day at a time is about as much as I can stand. Some days like today living in the moment is not so cool, but what can you do? You just gotta keep believing the storm will turn or fizzle out. You gotta believe the Universe will keep it in check. The rest of the country? Who cares what happens up there? I haven't been back in twenty-five years. I don't plan to ever go north of Key Largo again for any reason I can think of right now. They can do what they want up north!"

Terry gave us all hugs and kissed Mom goodbye, setting out alone on foot to go back to the lagoon before it got dark. The wind was already blowing near gale-force and the people in charge of the shelter told us it was time to go inside and stay there. A few of the other people standing around outside who heard that Terry was planning to ride out the hurricane on a boat said he was insane and that what he was doing was the same thing as suicide. I wondered if they were right but hoped they weren't. Like everything else Terry believed, it seemed like he was the only one on the island who thought going back to the ship was a good idea. It was no different than when we first built it and told the people in Calloway City we were going to sail away across the ocean. They thought Terry was crazy, and he thought they were all idiots. Some things just never changed.

Everyone inside the school crowded around two big TV screens in the main hall, watching the National Hurricane Center's updates on Leona. The hurricane had left a swath of devastation across the island of Cuba and was once again over open water in the Straits of Florida. It had diminished to a Category Three while over land, but they were saying for sure now that it would regain strength and become a Category Four before its next landfall. That landfall was predicted to be somewhere between Key West and Key Largo. Islamorada was smack dab in the middle between those two edges of the cone of probability.

"We're all going to die," Janie said.

"No, we'll be fine. They wouldn't let all these people stay here if they didn't think the school building could withstand it," Mom said.

"Terry's going to die for sure, being outside like that."

SAILING THE APOCALYPSE

"I think he'll be okay," Dean said. "He's going to be in for the ride of his life though. I'll bet he won't ever ride out another hurricane on a boat after this."

"You don't know Terry like I do. He's about as hardheaded as they come. I thought Janie's father was bad, but Terry beats them all in that department. I hope you're right though. I'm *really* worried about him out there in this."

The first bands of near hurricane-force gusts were already pelting the building, and looking outside you could see the rain going sideways in the wind and palm trees bent so far over they just had to break in two if it didn't stop. I thought it was bad when this first started happening, but Dean said we hadn't seen anything yet. He said when the hurricane got here you'd see trees flying by in the air along with pieces of houses and appliances and cars and all kinds of stuff like that. He said the ocean would come all the way over the island and that the tops of the waves might even reach the balcony on the second floor if the storm surge predictions were right. I knew I wouldn't be sleeping a wink that night for sure, because not only was I too scared to sleep, I didn't want to miss seeing all that stuff because most people never got to.

What I hadn't counted on though was how dark it was going to be in a hurricane that hit during nighttime. The wind got strong enough by midnight that it tore down most of the power lines on the island and put us in the pitch black. They had battery-powered lanterns and flashlights in the shelter, and Dean said they had generators they would run later when it was over, but that didn't do any good for seeing what was going on outside. Everybody inside kept going to the windows to look until they made us stay away from the glass because it was bound to break. When the wind got stronger, it turned out they were right because glass started shattering everywhere, letting in the rain that was blowing sideways so hard it stung like BB's when it hit your skin.

Every time I thought it was as bad as it could possibly get, things just got worse outside, at least from the sound of it. You could hear metal clanging and banging against stuff and wood tearing and breaking. Things kept hitting the building too, some of them really big from the sound of it and the way the concrete walls shook on impact. On top of all that was the roar of the wind and crashing of waves that were now breaking against the first-story walls beneath us. I thought for sure the building was going to fall in or be blown down at any minute, and Janie and Mom did too. Dean wasn't worried about it too much though because he had fallen asleep before it got really bad. I don't know how he did it, but he had been pretty chilled out anyway from all the dope he'd been smoking all day and Janie said he probably took something stronger to knock himself out. Some of the other people in the shelter were passed out drunk and not too worried either, but others were screaming and freaking out. It was hard not to scream with them the way everything sounded outside.

Even though we had lost the TV reports along with the

power, the firemen and policemen at the shelter had radios and they were keeping up with the storm. They did their best to keep everyone calm as they passed along the updates on the position of the storm's center. It seemed to take forever, but finally sometime just before daylight, they said the eye of it had already passed over Key West. Now it was headed north towards Marco Island. We were still in for a few hours of storm-force winds, but they said the worst was over and that the building had come through fine.

When it was light enough outside to see, I got as close to a broken window as I could without getting soaked by the rain and looked outside onto a scene of utter destruction. Nothing within view looked the same as it had the afternoon before. The stores, houses, signs, power line poles and most of the trees that had been there were gone or reduced to piles of rubble. Cars were stacked up in crumpled heaps on top of each other or turned sideways or upside down, sitting on what was left of houses and buildings. Boats that had been anchored or docked somewhere were on their sides in the highway or in people's yards, some of them smashed-in and broken up beyond recognition. I could only imagine what had become of the *Apocalypse*. Was she thrown onto the island somewhere in scattered pieces with all the rest of the debris, or had she been swept out to sea on the storm surge and torn apart in deep water, only to sink? What had Terry's final moments been like when it happened? Did he go quickly, bashed in the head by a flying tree trunk or chunk of metal?

282

Or did he end up treading water somewhere in the dark, trying to stay up for air a little longer before he drowned with no hope of reaching the shore? Whatever had happened to him, I was sure it must have been fatal, but looking out there I didn't know how we would be able to find him to find out. Hal Jenkins' words about bodies never being found kept replaying in my head. I felt an arm around me and realized it was Mom. She'd finally worked up the courage to come to the window and look outside herself.

"Oh. My. God!" she whispered. "My poor husband, Terry! How could anyone caught outside have survived this?"

Fifteen

IT TOOK A LOT longer than I expected for the storm to completely die down enough for us to go outside. Even though the center had long since moved off to the north, the Keys continued to be hammered by wind and rain until well after noon. Most of the storm surge had receded, but pools of seawater still covered the ground in many places hours later. The hardest part about waiting was not knowing what we would find of our ship or Terry, if anything. We wouldn't know until we made our way back to the lagoon, and it was obvious that getting there would not be easy. From what we could see from the school, the devastation on the island was unbelievable. The school itself was the only building around still standing intact. Without electricity, television or any kind of phone service, we couldn't know how bad the damage was everywhere else, other than what the officials at the shelter

285

were gathering from radio broadcasts.

But listening to a voice on the radio wasn't the same as seeing actual footage on TV, the kind I had watched on the news at home of other disasters that happened to other people. Those had never seemed real, since they were far removed and involved people and places I didn't know. But now, *we* were those victims you see on the evening news after something like this happens. *We* were the shattered, the dazed and the confused, left with nothing but the clothes we were wearing and what few extras we'd packed in our bags. Like so many others left in a disaster's wake, we were unsure where to go or what to do next.

Mom was crying most of the time during the waiting, saying she wished she'd never let Terry talk us into such a crazy adventure and that if we'd just kept the boat on the coast and sailed on weekends or something, none of this would have happened. She said she shouldn't have listened to all his nonsense about having to leave right away, and that she should have put her foot down and said we weren't going.

"Terry was always talking about how there was so little time left and that if we didn't go now, we weren't going to get out in time before it was too late. I believed him because he was so convincing and because he had been so many more places than I had, and was so much more educated. We should have just taken the boat down to Mobile or Biloxi and kept it there while we waited to see. One time I asked him why we couldn't do that and he said that when the poop *did* hit the fan, it was going to happen so fast that we'd never make it all the way to the coast from Calloway City. He said that even if we did, we'd get there to find our ship already gone, stolen by someone else just as desperate to get away. Terry was just *so* convincing. He had an argument for everything and he always won."

Dean told her that we could have lost the boat to a hurricane just as easily if we had left it on the Mississippi or Alabama coast and never sailed anywhere. He said owning a boat in hurricane-prone areas always brought with it the risk of damage or loss and that over the years several of his friends had lost theirs in marinas and in boatyards. But he also said that just because everything looked so bad here, that didn't mean that Terry and the *Apocalypse* could not have weathered the storm okay where they were.

"I think we can start heading that way now," he said; when we were at last able to go outside again.

Dean didn't even want to go look at the house beneath which he'd been living in the garage apartment. He said he didn't have to because where it was situated facing Hawk Channel on the Atlantic side of the island, he already knew it couldn't have survived getting swept off its foundation by the storm surge. The police were urging everyone at the shelter to stay put and wait for relief supplies to arrive, but when Dean explained to them that our stepfather might be hurt and in need of help, they didn't try to stop us from going to see. They did warn us that we were on our own though and to be careful. They said there would be all kinds of hazards out there, from spilled chemicals and broken glass to displaced wildlife like snakes, alligators and crocodiles. They said that we should stay away from any structures still standing, because they could fall in at any minute, and that we should stay out of the water because there would be all kinds of debris in there that could cut or injure somebody. They also warned us that there would be a curfew after dark and that we'd better be back at the shelter by then and not caught out walking around on the island. They said there would be looters and that many of the local residents were armed and might shoot on sight at anything that moved after dark.

Hearing all this, Janie said maybe we ought to just wait at the shelter and see if Terry showed up, because he *did* say he was coming back here to check on us after the storm was over. Mom said she couldn't stand to sit there and wait like that, knowing we were all fine but that almost anything could have happened to Terry. She said she just had to know, and not wanting to stay there with the other refugees by herself, Janie reluctantly agreed to come with us. We left our stuff in the shelter in our spaces on the floor where we'd been assigned to sleep, and set out walking, carrying only a few bottles of drinking water given to us by the officials, along with some snack foods we'd brought from the *Apocalypse* when we'd left her the day before.

I could tell that just getting back to the lagoon was going to be an adventure as soon as we left the school grounds.

There was no way to walk in a straight line or even follow the road because of all the piles of debris. We had to work our way around them, cutting through yards and climbing over fallen tree trunks and all kinds of other stuff. People yelled at us several times for getting too close to their personal rubble that was all that remained of their houses or businesses. They were bent over searching the grounds of their property, picking through what little was left to try and salvage anything of value they could find. It was sad to see so much of the island torn up like that. Even all the awesome coconut palms that had given it such a tropical feel were either blown down or had their fronds stripped away by the wind from still-standing bare trunks. Dean said the big heavy coconuts that were on them before the storm tended to fly loose in a hurricane and become cannonballs hitting houses and stuff. That must have been true, because we saw them everywhere, mixed in with the rubble.

When we got to the bridge that connected Islamorada to the next island over, where the lagoon was, we were relieved to see that span was still intact and passable. The storm surge had washed over the highway and swept away big chunks of pavement, but the bridge itself was elevated so tall boats could pass under it, and as a result it was safe from the rising water. I was still a little nervous when we walked out on it, thinking maybe it could still fall in, but Dean said it probably wouldn't. He said as soon as they inspected it, they would probably open it to traffic again once they cleared all the debris off the road and repaired the pavement.

From up on the bridge, you could see a lot more of just how bad the damage from the hurricane really was. We stopped and looked back at Islamorada before we got to the highest part and Dean said he would have never believed this could happen. He said it might be as bad as the Labor Day Hurricane of 1935, except there wouldn't be near as many people killed because of the warnings and evacuations that got most people out of the Keys before it hit. Looking down in the water, we could see all kinds of stuff floating: everything from furniture to toys to dead birds. I hoped I wouldn't see any, but I figured there were dead bodies bobbing around out there too.

We all held our breath as we neared the crest of the bridge, knowing that from up there we would be able to see out over the green mangroves surrounding the lagoon where the *Apocalypse* was anchored. We were afraid of what that view would reveal, and our fears came true when we reached the top. The mangroves were still there, and for the most part didn't look much different than they had before, except for all the bits of paper, plastic, clothing and other flotsam littering their branches. But nowhere in sight were the tall masts of the *Apocalypse*. Where yesterday they had been clearly visible from this vantage point, today they were simply *gone*!

"TERRY! Oh my poor Terry!"

"It's okay, Mom. Maybe the masts just blew down, that's all."

"True enough," Dean said. "His rigging may not have been able to stand those hundred and fifty mile-an-hour gusts, with the masts sticking up above the trees like they were. Just because we can't see his sticks doesn't mean the boat's not there."

I hoped he was right as we picked up the pace and rushed to the other end of the bridge. As soon as we came to the place where the path through the mangroves began, it became clear that getting through there was not going to be easy. The trail was choked with rubble and debris and the mangrove roots had caught so much of the floating junk that it was almost an impenetrable barrier. There was no way to traverse it without a lot of climbing and crawling, and Dean warned us to watch where we put our hands and feet to avoid getting cut on broken glass or torn metal.

Mom began calling out to Terry as soon as we left the road, but there was no answer from the lagoon. With no traffic noise to drown out the sound, I knew that if Terry was just sitting there on the ship waiting and unhurt, he should be able to hear her shouts. As we pushed through all the junk, we came across several of the old derelict boats that had been shoved into the mangroves by the storm surge, one of them a thirty-something-foot monohull sailboat that had been broken completely in half. When we finally came within sight of the main part of the lagoon, none of the vessels that had been floating at their moorings were still there, but you could see the top of the mast of one sailboat that had sank. I looked for the plywood houseboat Dean and I had taken the anchor from, but it was nowhere in sight. From this vantage point at the end of the path, you couldn't see the spot where we'd secured the *Apocalypse* anyway, so we all shouted louder, hoping Terry would hear us and that he would be able to come pick us up in the dinghy. When he didn't answer, we knew we were going to have to wade along the edge of the mangroves roots to try and reach the hideaway hole on foot.

Dean led the way, reminding us about the crocodiles and saying to watch out for snakes too. Mom and Janie were freaked about that but they followed us anyway, not being able to stand just waiting to see what Dean and I would find. It took twenty minutes to reach the entrance to the hole, and when we did, we saw that the *Apocalypse* was definitely not as we'd left her. It was hard to get a good view of her, because the old plywood houseboat and a couple of the other derelicts had washed into the hole practically on top of her, but it was clear that although our ship was still afloat, she was *upside down*! There was still no sign of Terry or anyone or anything moving in the tangled mess. Mom and Janie were crying and Dean and I were already wading and swimming, trying to get through all the boat parts to reach the overturned hulls and try and find Terry.

Somehow the whole catamaran had flipped end over end, so that it was now upside down and pushed to the far end of the hole, the bows facing out, opposite the way we had moored it. I noticed that stupid houseboat had broken about

292

five feet of the port hull's bow completely off when it hit, and I immediately regretted taking that big Manson anchor that had secured it before we came along. Dean said it didn't make any difference and that if we hadn't taken it, the hurricane would have broken the houseboat's rotten anchor rode anyway. When we finally reached the side of the starboard hull where the nav station was located, we both yelled for Terry again and banged on the side. There was a moaning sound from somewhere inside and then a faint return knock in answer to ours.

"HE'S ALIVE!" I shouted to Mom and Janie. At that, they were both in the water and swimming over to join us.

* * *

Terry told us everything he'd experienced in the height of the storm and how the *Apocalypse* had seemed to be doing fine until the surge pushed up into the lagoon, causing the water to rise so high that the tops of the mangroves were barely above it. As a result, the once-sheltered lagoon was now exposed to the full brunt of the huge breaking seas created by the hurricane-force winds. He said they were rolling in like an angry surf break of churning water and that the wind was so strong it was tearing things like hatch covers right off the decks. He went below and tried to secure the main hatch so he wouldn't lose it, but by that time the derelict boats in the lagoon began piling up against the *Apocalypse*, smashing her wood and fiberglass and threatening to break her to pieces. He said that damned plywood houseboat was the worst and that it was what broke the port bow off, and he cussed the idiot who left it out there on an inadequate anchor. Dean and I exchanged a quick glance but didn't say anything about "borrowing" that Manson anchor.

Terry said he never dreamed the *Apocalypse* could be capsized because of her length and her twenty-four-foot beam, but that's exactly what happened next. He wasn't sure if it was an exceptionally big wave that did it or if it was a micro-burst of super-intense wind, powerful enough to simply lift her out of the water and flip her on her back. Whatever it was, all he remembered was a brief sensation of weightlessness inside the cabin and then he said he must have hit his head on the impact when she landed. He had barely regained consciousness when he heard us calling his name and knocking on the hull, and he had no idea how much time had passed since the storm.

He told us all this once we were all gathered on a small patch of muddy ground amidst the mangrove roots. Getting back aboard the *Apocalypse* was impossible, as there was no place to sit on the inverted V-hulls and the bridge deck between them was submerged under two feet of water. Dean had to swim underwater to enter the main hatch and drag Terry out when we first realized he was trapped inside. Dean said Terry was lucky he hadn't drowned in the water that was in the cabin when he was knocked out. He said the only thing

294

that saved him from that was that his head was resting on the bottom of a shelf that was high enough to remain dry when the hulls flooded.

Mom was fussing over his cuts and bruises and making sure nothing was broken while Terry told his story.

"I'm just glad you're okay," she said. "I was so worried that you couldn't have survived this when we looked outside this morning and saw how bad it was."

"I did though," Terry said. "I told you I would be okay."

"Too bad about your boat, though man," Dean said. "I hate to see a cool Wharram like that just totally destroyed."

"What do you mean, destroyed?" Terry asked, looking at him as if he had lost his mind. "The *Apocalypse* is hardly destroyed! We'll have her out of here and sailing again in no time!"

I glanced over at the wreck of our ship when he said this and thought he must have hit his head hard enough to knock the sense out of his brain. This wasn't minor damage or entropy. This was *catastrophic*! I figured fixing it would be harder than building a whole new boat.

"Terry, you know that's unreasonable. The ship is upside down in the water! The masts and rigging are gone, and no telling what else. We're on an island that's been devastated by a hurricane, and who knows how long it will be until the power is restored and you can even buy something to eat here? We have no place to stay and nothing left but the things the kids and I took with us. We have to leave this place and go home to Calloway City. You know that as well as I do."

Hearing this, Terry just looked at Mom like she was the biggest idiot he had ever met in his life. Then he looked at me and Janie to see if we had anything to say; to see if we were in agreement with Mom. He even looked at Dean before he spoke again, but Dean said nothing and neither did we. I didn't know about Janie or Mom, but I was afraid to, because I knew what was coming next, and I was right:

"You mean you're ready to just *give up*? You want to just give up and walk away from everything we've been working at for more than two years because of an *inconvenience*? A *minor setback*? I thought when I married into this family I was getting a crew that would stick with me through thick and thin! I thought we were in this together and that we would do whatever it took to accomplish our goals. We built our ship with our own hands. We sailed her this far, almost to the edge of the tropics already. But then, at the first threat of bad weather, the three of you bailed on me. You would have left the islands all together if you could have found a ride. And if you had, no one would have found me until I was dead and even then you wouldn't have known about it for days— maybe weeks! Now, after all I did to try to protect our ship, you want to give up on her and on me too and run back to that stupid house in Calloway City! After all this, you want to go back to living on dirt with the rest of the shore bastards just like you were before. Well, you can do what you like, but I'm staying right here! I will rebuild the *Apocalypse* and I will

296

resume this voyage as planned, with or without you—any of you—or all of you!"

Terry might have hit his head too hard, but if he did, it didn't change his mind one bit or make him forget anything he had been talking and ranting about since we first met him. I knew after hearing him lay it out that there would be no talking him into walking away from the wreckage. He was determined to resurrect the *Apocalypse*, and even though I didn't see how anybody could do it, I knew he would find a way if it could be done. If there was one thing Terry Bailey didn't understand, it was when to quit.

Mom said she wasn't staying here though and from the tone of her voice I could tell she was as adamant about that as Terry was about not leaving. Janie was pretty much on Mom's side as usual and that left me wondering who was right. I could sure see Mom's point in wanting to leave all this mess behind and go back home. I couldn't imagine how much hard work it would be to get the *Apocalypse* turned back over and repaired. It would be a tremendous job even with a crane to flip it and a big workshop like the barn we had in Calloway City in which to do the repairs. But here in the middle of a mangrove lagoon, there would be no crane or other machinery to move it. And I didn't know where we would find a workshop when there were barely any houses still standing, let alone any with a roof still on them. But Dean, hearing the determination in Terry's voice, said that he would help, and that it might be possible to rebuild our ship if we didn't mind the hard work and didn't mind spending a few months here to do it.

"If we can get her turned over again, man, we can get her towed back over to Islamorada. I know just the place you can do the work. It's a little waterfront lot a friend of mine owns. He won't be using it because I know the bungalow he had there must have been wiped out in the storm. You can set up camp there and eventually get a generator to run your power tools."

* * *

A week after the hurricane, we were still in Islamorada, even though Mom was ready to leave immediately after we found Terry in our upside-down ship. She didn't let anything Terry or Dean said change her mind about going back to Calloway City; what kept her here this long was the reality that there simply was no way to get to the mainland and beyond. The hurricane had done so much damage throughout the Keys that the road remained closed except for emergency and relief vehicles bringing supplies in, and electrical and phone service would not be restored for weeks.

Terry retrieved the blue tarp awnings he stashed inside one of the cabins while preparing for the storm, and with Dean's help we rigged them as a big open-sided tent on the little piece of waterfront property that belonged to his friend. The food and most of the other supplies we had on the boat before the hurricane were still inside, and over the course of several days we salvaged what we could and carried it all on foot across the bridge to our makeshift camp. We were as well off or better off than anyone else on the island, as all the survivors were living like us in tents or out in the open, most of them depending on relief supplies just to have something to eat.

The wheels never stopped turning in Terry's mind the entire time. When we were at the wreck, swimming into the cabins and carrying stuff off, he would stop and sit there thinking, tossing around ideas for getting the *Apocalypse* right side up again.

"What we've got to do, Robbie, is disassemble her completely. First we need to get the bridge deck and crossbeams off so we can separate the hulls. That's the beauty of a Wharram. Just like when we built her, each component is lighter and easier to manipulate separately than when assembled into the whole ship. If we can get that port hull pulled over to the water's edge by the mangroves, we can temporarily patch up the hole where the bow broke off so it won't fill with water. Then, if we can find a skiff with an outboard that we can rent or borrow, we can drag the hulls out of the lagoon one at and time and tow them to our camp. Once we get them to the beach, we can pull them out of the water with a come-along and then we can do the rest of the repairs right there under tarps."

It sure sounded like a lot of work to me, but I still didn't know if I was going to be helping him or not. Every day that went by though, it looked more likely that I would. Terry and Mom argued almost the whole time, but as usual, Terry was wearing her down with his persistence. If Mom could have found a way out of there that first day or two after the hurricane, I have no doubt that she and Janie and I would have been right back in Calloway City by now. Going back would have meant the end of her marriage to Terry though, because it wasn't even an option in his mind. He kept telling her she needed to stick with him and do what she'd promised him she would do. He said when they got married she'd committed to his plan to build the *Apocalypse* and sail away, and that if she broke that commitment now it would be her fault they got divorced, not his. He reminded her that he was husband number four for her, and that if she didn't do what it took to make this marriage last, she might as well give up at her age.

"We're in the perfect place to build or rebuild a sailing ship! It never gets cold here and the sun shines most of the time. The epoxy will cure fast and working outside on the beach, we won't have to waste money on heat, lighting or rent! There are probably thousands of boats here that'll get written off by the insurance companies, leaving us a treasure trove of salvageable parts and equipment. When we sail out of here in a few months, the *Apocalypse* will be better equipped than she was when we launched!

"It'll be like a new beginning. Our voyage is hardly over,

in fact, it's just getting started! Do you think real sailors quit just because they hit a little bad weather? Do you think they abandon and walk away from a ship just because she sustained some damage? Look at the great Bernard Moitessier —he lost not one, but no less than three of his vessels to shipwreck during his famous voyages around the world. Did he just give up and quit? Hell no! He started over from scratch right on the beach. Homeless and penniless each time, he set right to work designing and building his next vessel and soon put to sea again. If he could achieve so much working alone, we'd be total losers if the four of us couldn't manage to fix up a little hurricane damage working together!"

Every day that went by, it looked more and more inevitable. I was going to be here living in a tent for no telling how long, and my life was going to be nothing but hard work, just like before when we were building the boat. But even though I knew I wouldn't have much time to swim or explore the island or do other fun stuff, it still sounded better than going back to Calloway City. At least I wouldn't have to go back to school and sit in a dumb classroom all day. No matter what happened next, it had to be better than that, and it was bound to be an adventure!

Author's Note and Acknowledgements

I want to point out that although this is a work of fiction, James Wharram catamarans are very real indeed and the Tiki 46 depicted in this story is a design that can be built in your own backyard. The Tiki 46 is a bigger project than most would care to undertake, but plans for Wharram Catamarans are available both larger and smaller. The trailerable Tiki 21 still holds the record for the smallest catamaran of any design to circumnavigate the globe. I have personally owned a Tiki 21 and have built a Tiki 26 and the Hitia 17 beachcruiser. All Wharram Catamarans are seaworthy, shallow draft, and capable of taking you most anywhere you care to go by boat. Find out more at www.wharram.com

I want to thank Scott Finazzo and Bill Barker for reading and giving me initial feedback in the early stages of drafting the manuscript. I am indebted to Betsy Barker for an outstanding and quick turnaround on copyediting the final draft. I want to thank Sam H. Barker for a great job of creating the interior images of a Tiki 46 under sail just the way I envisioned it for this book. I am especially grateful to Jasmine Calvert for proofreading the finished manuscript and offering her helpful suggestions. And of course, I owe it all to my dearest Michelle for always believing in what I do.

Scott B. Williams has been writing about his adventures for more than twenty-five years. His published work includes dozens of magazine articles and twelve books, with more projects currently underway. His interest in backpacking, sea kayaking and sailing small boats to remote places led him to pursue the wilderness survival skills that he has written about in his popular survival nonfiction books such as *Bug Out: The Complete Plan for Escaping a Catastrophic Disaster Before It's Too Late*. He has also authored travel narratives such as *On Island Time: Kayaking the Caribbean*, an account of his two-year solo kayaking journey through the islands. With the release of *The Pulse* (2012), *The Darkness After* (2013) and *Refuge* (2014), Scott moved into writing fiction and has many more novels in the works. To learn more about his upcoming books or to contact Scott, visit his website: www.scottbwilliams.com

40391047R00183

Made in the USA
Charleston, SC
01 April 2015